D1066021

RICHMOND NOIR

WITHDRAWN

RICHMOND NOIR

EDITED BY ANDREW BLOSSOM, BRIAN CASTLEBERRY & TOM DE HAVEN

AKASHIC BOOKS
NEW YORK

This collection is comprised of works of fiction. All names, characters, places, and incidents are the product of the authors' imaginations. Any resemblance to real events or persons, living or dead, is entirely coincidental.

Published by Akashic Books
©2010 Akashic Books

Series concept by Tim McLoughlin and Johnny Temple
Richmond map by Sohrab Habibion

ISBN-13: 978-1-933354-98-9
Library of Congress Control Number: 2009922934
All rights reserved

First printing
Printed in Canada

Akashic Books
PO Box 1456
New York, NY 10009
info@akashicbooks.com
www.akashicbooks.com

ALSO IN THE AKASHIC NOIR SERIES:

Baltimore Noir, edited by Laura Lippman
Bronx Noir, edited by S.J. Rozan
Brooklyn Noir, edited by Tim McLoughlin
Brooklyn Noir 2: The Classics, edited by Tim McLoughlin
Brooklyn Noir 3: Nothing but the Truth
edited by Tim McLoughlin & Thomas Adcock
Chicago Noir, edited by Neal Pollack
D.C. Noir, edited by George Pelecanos
D.C. Noir 2: The Classics, edited by George Pelecanos
Delhi Noir (India), edited by Hirsh Sawhney
Detroit Noir, edited by E.J. Olsen & John C. Hocking
Dublin Noir (Ireland), edited by Ken Bruen
Havana Noir (Cuba), edited by Achy Obejas
Istanbul Noir (Turkey), edited by Mustafa Ziyalan & Amy Spangler
Las Vegas Noir, edited by Jarret Keene & Todd James Pierce
London Noir (England), edited by Cathi Unsworth
Los Angeles Noir, edited by Denise Hamilton
Manhattan Noir, edited by Lawrence Block
Manhattan Noir 2: The Classics, edited by Lawrence Block
Mexico City Noir (Mexico), edited by Paco I. Taibo II
Miami Noir, edited by Les Standiford
New Orleans Noir, edited by Julie Smith
Paris Noir (France), edited by Aurélien Masson
Phoenix Noir, edited by Patrick Millikin
Portland Noir, edited by Kevin Sampsell
Queens Noir, edited by Robert Knightly
Rome Noir (Italy), edited by Chiara Stangalino & Maxim Jakubowski
San Francisco Noir, edited by Peter Maravelis
San Francisco Noir 2: The Classics, edited by Peter Maravelis
Seattle Noir, edited by Curt Colbert
Toronto Noir (Canada), edited by Janine Armin & Nathaniel G. Moore
Trinidad Noir, Lisa Allen-Agostini & Jeanne Mason
Twin Cities Noir, edited by Julie Schaper & Steven Horwitz
Wall Street Noir, edited by Peter Spiegelman

FORTHCOMING:

Barcelona Noir (Spain), edited by Adriana Lopez & Carmen Ospina
Boston Noir, edited by Dennis Lehane
Copenhagen Noir (Denmark), edited by Bo Tao Michaelis
Haiti Noir, edited by Edwidge Danticat
Indian Country Noir, edited by Liz Martínez & Sarah Cortez
Lagos Noir (Nigeria), edited by Chris Abani
Lone Star Noir, edited by Bobby Byrd & John Byrd
Los Angeles Noir 2: The Classics, edited by Denise Hamilton
Moscow Noir (Russia), edited by Natalia Smirnova & Julia Goumen
Mumbai Noir (India), edited by Altaf Tyrewala
Orange County Noir, edited by Gary Phillips
Philadelphia Noir, edited by Carlin Romano

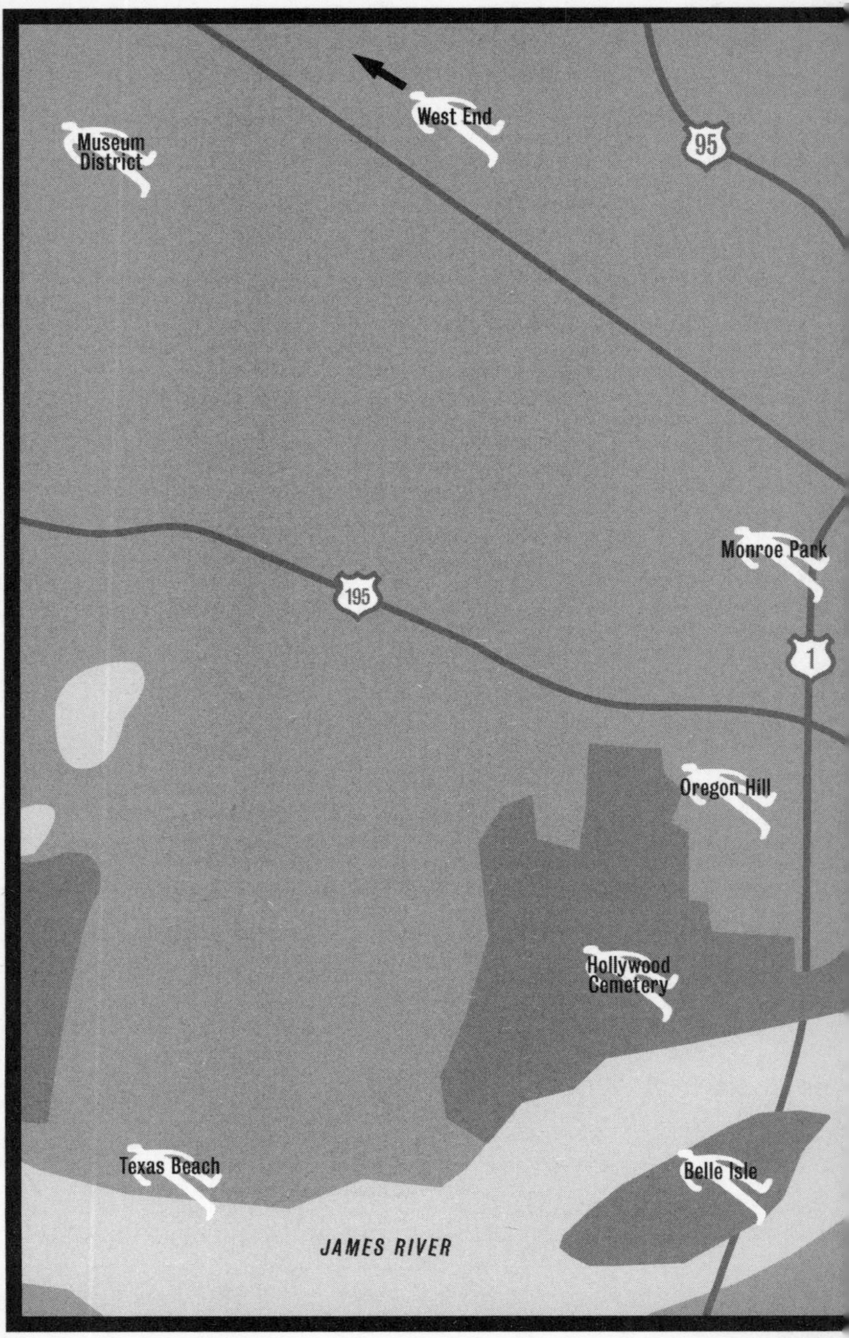
West End
Museum District
95
Monroe Park
195
1
Oregon Hill
Hollywood Cemetery
Texas Beach
Belle Isle
JAMES RIVER

RICHMOND

Providence
Park

64

Jackson Ward

250

Devil's
Half Acre

East End

Jefferson Davis
Highway

Shockoe Slip

Manchester

Church Hill

TABLE OF CONTENTS

PART III: NEUROSIS

PART IV: NONSUCH

Just think of all the people not fortunate enough
to be born in Richmond, Va.
—Tom Wolfe

FOREWORD

BY TOM ROBBINS

I t may sound odd, but when I think of Richmond, Virginia—
or, at least, when I look back on my years in that charming,
antebellum, ostensibly conservative town—my thoughts
turn frequently to alleys. And considering the images and
moods that most people associate with those narrow, secluded,
generally unlit and gritty little passageways, it should not then
be totally unexpected that my memories of Richmond's alleys
tend to be colored with shades of *noir*. Which is to say, colored with seamy urban romance and suave big-city vice, the
twin elements most responsible for the seductive throb at the
murky heart of *noir*.

Presumably, alleys in other parts of Richmond are quite
different in character, but the bohemian/bourgeois/badass Fan
District, where I lived, boasts to this day alleyways that are
simultaneously inviting and forbidding, elegant and squalid,
ominous and suffused with grace. Old, cobblestoned (Stone
Age marshmallows in the silver moonshine), lined with wisteria, rose bushes, and carriage houses (servant quarters become
artist studios, stables become garages); perfumed by honeysuckle, motor oil, invisible kitchens, brown-bagged beverages,
garbage cans, and history; resonant with dog-bark, woo-pitch,
bottle-shatter, domestic squabbling, financial plotting (legiti-
mate and otherwise), fervent intellectual discourse, and stray
fragments of Southern rock and jazz; they become all the
more interesting after nightfall, when secrets—some merely

naughty, others more darkly hued—seep increasingly into them from shadowed crannies or the backrooms and walled gardens of abodes along the way.

On scores of hot, sticky, summer nights, with a restless city feeling like the interior of a napalmed watermelon, I walked the alleys of the Fan, sometimes until dawn; and having thus been privy to certain of the secrets they protected, having trusted them with a secret of my own (I was desperately in love with a married woman at the time and fully expecting her armed husband to leap out at me from every spooky nook), it doesn't exactly surprise me that there is sufficient *noir* in Richmond—enough hidden larceny, lunacy, and lust—to fuel the fiction of the fine writers who enliven these pages.

INTRODUCTION
NEGOTIATING THE JAMES

In *The Air-Conditioned Nightmare*, Henry Miller tosses off a hard-bitten assessment of the City on the James: "I would rather die in Richmond somehow," he writes, "though God knows Richmond has little enough to offer." As editors, we like the dying part, and might point out that in its long history, Richmond, Virginia has offered up many of the disparate elements crucial to meaty *noir*. The city was born amid deception, conspiracy, and violence.

In 1607, after Christopher Newport paddled up the river that would one day be the city's lifeblood, he installed a wooden cross at the future site of Richmond, claiming the area for England. The local Powhatan rightly perceived the symbolism in his act, but Newport, with the aid of flattery and gifts, convinced them that the cross indicated friendship, not conquest. His lie, soon revealed for what it was, led to conflict—not only between settlers and Native Americans, but also among the settlers themselves. Within two years, a second English expedition, excited by skirmishes with the Powhatan, attacked an exploratory party led by John Smith (yes, *that* John Smith). When Smith retreated, the Powhatan besieged the unruly colonists once more and killed some number of them. Smith returned, calmed the natives, arrested the English ringleaders, and put them in the stocks. He then forced the remaining men to take up residence in a Native encampment at the site of Newport's cross. The men revolted, freeing the conspirators and abandoning the site. At that point, Smith gave up, but famously noted in his journal that he'd found no place so pleasant in all of Virginia as that site of consternation and bloodshed. (Oh, and then he was horribly burned in an accident.)

Four centuries later, as Clay McLeod Chapman makes clear in his Belle Isle story, you can't wander far in Richmond without being reminded by some cast-iron marker that this is where *history happened*—here's the church where Patrick Henry declared, "Give me liberty or give me death," here's the factory that forged cannonballs and shot during the Civil War, here's the row of warehouses that churned out America's tobacco (lately they've gone condo), here's the site of the Negro (read: slave) cemetery, now paved over into a desolate parking lot. Richmond is a city of statues and monuments to the past—Confederate generals mostly. Occasionally you'll come across something odd, but never anomalous—a statue of tennis player Arthur Ashe, a statue of dancer Bojangles Robinson. Yes, history happened in Richmond, and so did crime, malfeasance, and cruelty. That's because it's hard to have the former without the latter. Richmond may be steeped in history, but its residents can seem as ambivalent about that fact—or even ashamed of it—as they are proud.

Sure, Edgar Allan Poe spent a good part of his life in Richmond, and even went so far as to credit it with shaping his identity, as Pir Rothenberg's story in this volume might remind us. ("I am a Virginian," Poe wrote, "at least I call myself one, for I have resided all my life, until within the last few years in Richmond.") Sure, two U.S. presidents lie buried in the hallowed ground of the city's Hollywood Cemetery. (It's also home to the grave of Jefferson Davis, President of the Confederacy, as Clint McCown's tale playfully and darkly points out.) Sure, Thomas Jefferson spent a lot of time in Richmond as governor of the Commonwealth; he was even the architect of its beautiful Capitol building. But Jefferson had to run for his life from Richmond when the British came rolling through during the Revolutionary War; later he found himself put on trial for treason and cowardice by none other than Patrick Henry (yes, *that* Patrick Henry.)

During the nineteenth century, the city was a-crawl with slingshot- and shotgun-toting gangs—the 4th Street Horribles, the Bumtowners, the Butchertown Cats, and so on—who preyed on shopkeepers and pedestrians and warred with each other. These groups were forebears of the drug gangs that are very much active in Richmond today, and whose presence here in the 1990s earned the River City the distinction of Murder Capital of the United States—a reputation further buoyed by the presence of the Southside Strangler, the first serial killer ever to be executed following a conviction based on DNA evidence. In Richmond, as in many of America's great cities, history is a mixed bag.

Greater Richmond—which means not only the city itself but also the surrounding suburbanized counties (white flight havens that began to grow in the mid-1950s)—has a population of roughly one million. In other words, Los Angeles it ain't, and the Philip Marlowes and Jake Gitteses of the world might find its palette a little limited. However, Richmond's size hasn't precluded the city from falling victim to its own versions of *Chinatown*-style political chicanery—like the boardroom schemes and bamboozlements that led to entire sections of Jackson Ward (at the time a poor black neighborhood) and Oregon Hill (at the time a poor white neighborhood) being emptied out and cleaved in two to make way for, respectively, an interstate highway and a commuter bypass.

Richmond is well versed in the political buffoonery of the public figure—as Howard Owen reminds us, the city is home not only to a municipal government, but also to the Virginia State Legislature and the governor's office. It's a place where a junkie councilman can get pinched buying heroin in a housing project and state legislators can spend whole sessions attempting to define what kind of underwear shall be illegal to wear, where a historic American figure can torpedo his political legacy simply by signing on as mayor and deciding to pick a fight with the school system.

For all the dark marks on Richmond's past, the darkest and most permanent is its role as hub of the Atlantic slave trade. Richmond was the spot on the James River where traders unloaded their captives to market, and where white Virginians sold enslaved peoples "downriver" to the deeper South. It was the gateway through which the cruel institution was spread into Virginia and much of the country. In present-day Richmond, the monuments to this part of its history are few (the recently erected Reconciliation Triangle statue is a notable exception)—so few that absence, in a way, becomes its own monument. The auction houses of Shockoe Bottom have vanished to time. The extensive slave prison, holding pen, and marketplace in the northwest corner of the Bottom—a site of so much suffering, pain, and heartbreak that captives called it the "Devil's Half Acre"—lies beneath the empty expanse of that aforementioned parking lot. Also buried beneath that asphalt is Gabriel Prosser, the blacksmith who, as Hermine Pinson's story stunningly recalls, was leader of one of the few large-scale slave revolts in American history.

Meanwhile, Richmond has benefited immeasurably from 400 years of African American culture, never more so than in the 1920s and '30s, when the neighborhood of Jackson Ward was home to a cultural zeitgeist that saw it labeled "the Harlem of the South." Jackson Ward was the place where Maggie L. Walker chartered the first African American–owned bank. It was a place where jazz-era legends came to perform—Billie Holiday, Ella Fitzgerald, Duke Ellington, Cab Calloway, and of course Bojangles Robinson, to name but a few. Like any good scene, it was also home to con men, gamblers, and hustlers, a legacy that is celebrated in Robert Deane Pharr's *The Book of Numbers*—the first and to date best noir treatment of Richmond, and a scathing indictment of the racial boundaries of the 1930s.

These days, Richmond is a city of winter balls and garden parties on soft summer evenings, a city of private clubs where white-haired old gentlemen, with their martinis or mint juleps in hand, still genuflect in front of portraits of Robert E. Lee. It's also a city of brutal crime scenes and drug corners and okay-everybody-go-on-home-there's-nothing-more-to-see. It's a city of world-class ad agencies and law firms, a city of the FFV (First Families of Virginia) and a city of immigrants—everywhere from India, Vietnam, and Africa to Massachusetts, New York, and New Jersey. It's a city of finicky manners (you mustn't ever sneeze publicly in Richmond) and old-time neighborliness, and it's a city where you think twice about giving somebody the finger if they cut you off on the Powhite Parkway (that's pronounced *Pow*-hite, not *Po*-white, thank you very much) because you might get your head blown off by the shotgun on the rack. Richmond has a world-renowned art school, a ballet, a symphony orchestra, and galleries galore; it also has semi-annual NASCAR meets that clog the city's arteries for days. Even in its best moments, it's full of stark and sometimes vast contrasts, a dynamic captured poignantly here in the wonderful story by Dennis Danvers.

Richmond, in its long, complex history, has seen everything America has to offer, and has at times stood for its worst, darkest bits. It is the oldest of those churning urban centers whose simple existence gave birth to America's particular art form of violence, desolation, and hard knocks. It's also a hell of a place to live. We, the editors and authors, love this city. Try standing on a rock in the middle of the James River as the evening sun lights up the tinny but somehow magnificent buildings of downtown. You'll see. It's quite a sight. When you accept a city not only for its strengths but also for its weaknesses, when you realize that the combination of the two is what gives the place true beauty—when, indeed, you recognize that the combination might also make for some very good storytelling—well, that's love. We love Richmond, Virginia. We hope you like it too.

Andrew Blossom, Brian Castleberry & Tom De Haven
Richmond, Virginia
December 2009

PART I

Nevermore

*Then—in my childhood—in the dawn
Of a most stormy life—was drawn
From ev'ry depth of good and ill
The mystery which binds me still . . .*
—Edgar Allan Poe, from his poem "Alone,"
on childhood in Richmond

THE ROSE RED VIAL

BY PIR ROTHENBERG

Museum District

When I got inside I called her name. My house was dark and quiet, and although nothing appeared altered I felt that something had happened since I'd left for the museum's summer gala. There was a note on the kitchen table. I scanned it and it made no sense. I stuffed it into my pocket, took back a shot of whiskey, and walked the narrow hallway into the living room. I thought of the note; the words were going to make sense in a moment. I was sure of it, and felt so much like a balloon steadily expanding that I held my breath and winced at the inevitable explosion.

One month prior, in a storage room below the Virginia Historical Society, I sat before an empty glass cabinet preparing the lamps I would mount on the shelves. There were to be six items of Edgar Allan Poe memorabilia here, among them a lock of dark hair taken off the poet's head after his death; the key to the trunk that accompanied Poe to Baltimore, where he spent the final few days of his life; and a walking stick, which Poe left here in Richmond ten days before his death. The items were on loan from the Poe Museum across town for the city's celebration of the poet's bicentennial, as yet seven months away.

I took a pull from the small metal flask I kept in my utility belt. When I noticed I wasn't alone, it was too late to hide it. It was the new intern, a dark-haired girl with a small scar across her lower lip.

"Sorry," she said. "Didn't mean to scare you."

"You didn't," I said, and took another swig before recapping the flask.

She'd started at the museum on Monday, but I'd seen her the weekend before in my neighbors' backyard. The Hamlins had installed a six-foot privacy fence years ago, but by the unobstructed view from an upstairs window I'd watched the young woman standing like the very portrait of boredom, hand on the flare of her hip, as Barb Hamlin pointed out the trained wisteria and the touch-me-nots in her garden. She'd had one leg stretched into a band of sunlight when she glanced up and noticed me.

I went back to work on the lamps. "They give you something to do in here?"

"Rebecca," she said, strolling through the makeshift aisles of cases and boxes. Her dark hair fell in angles around her face and she wore a white summer dress unsuitable for an intern's duties. "And I wish they *would*. This room is why I'm here."

"Poe fan, huh?"

"You too," she said. "Or so Uncle Lou tells me."

I chuckled softly but did not look up. I was well acquainted with "Uncle Lou," former captain of the Third Precinct, famous for his supposed paternal brand of policing. Really, he'd never been more than a squat old tyrant. We'd been neighbors for a decade and the only thing that kept our peace was that six-foot fence. Now I was humbled to learn that "Uncle" was not a total misnomer; Lou, who'd sired no offspring, had a pretty young niece from Cincinnati.

"Maybe you could ask them to give me an assignment back here," Rebecca said.

I told her I was just a lighting technician, contracted, not even staff.

"But you know John," she said. John was the head curator. "You two are friends."

I thought she ought to ask Lou, a patron of the museum whose connections had likely procured her the internship in the first place. But I agreed to put in a word, if only to end the conversation: nothing good could come from associating with Hamlin kin—much less from upsetting one with a refusal. Yet it excited me too, the thought of Lou's scowling displeasure were he to discover Rebecca and I chumming around at the museum. *Displeasure* was a euphemism; he'd put his wife's garden shears through my skull.

Still, when she asked for a drink, I handed her the flask.

At sunset she was at my front door. I glanced toward Lou and Barb's house. Rebecca told me not to worry, they'd gone to play bridge with friends.

"So," she said, wandering into my living room, "do you have any first editions?"

"What?"

"Of Poe," she said.

"Did your uncle tell you that too?"

Glancing into corners, trailing her fingers along windowsills, she smiled. "I was hoping that a Poe aficionado—who works in a museum, no less—would have an artifact lying around."

"What," I said, "just lying around like junk mail?"

"Don't be nasty," she said, then picked up a green glass ashtray. "Like this," she said, holding it to the light. "It'd be great if you could say, 'And this is Poe's ashtray, recovered from his writing desk at his last residence at Fordham.'"

"That was my grandfather's."

She set it down. "Lou would like that. History buff."

Yeah, I thought. He had a hard time letting go of it.

"All sorts of Civil War memorabilia everywhere. Ever been inside?"

This was beginning to feel like a game. "What do you think?"

"How should I know where you've been?"

I told her she'd better not let Lou see us together.

"Together?" she said, hiding a smile.

"You know what I mean."

"Why, doesn't he like you?"

Now I just sat back and looked at her.

"Oh, I *know*," she said, grinning. "He told me to stay away from you."

Then she asked for a drink, even though, by the way she'd cringed earlier, I could tell she'd hated it. I was disappointed. She was only there with me for a little rebellion against the stuffy uncle and aunt.

So be it. I went to get the whiskey.

I spoke with John. I owed my job at the VHS—my very livelihood in this city—solely to him. By the end of the week Rebecca was putting in shifts assisting me in preparing the illumination of over 1,500 objects for the bicentennial exhibits. John and the staff unpacked items every day and created layout plans. It was my job to determine how best to light those books, paintings, and curios they wanted in cases, mounted upon walls, or perched on podiums. Rebecca was happy the hour or two a day she worked with me—rather, with the objects, to which her full attention was devoted. She was ecstatic watching the items emerge from their boxes, or gazing into the cases once the lighting was complete, all the pieces illuminated perfectly before they went back into their boxes for safekeeping. The lights from the displays would strike her face full on, or under her chin like a flashlight beam, or sidelong as in a Rembrandt painting. I wanted to pose her and arrange the light so as to expose every molecule of her simple beauty.

On my back, my head inside a case, I heard Rebecca gasp. "Wow," she called, "have you seen this?"

When I stood up Rebecca was crouched by a case that John and I'd worked on that morning and had yet to finalize. She moved aside and looked at me, leaving one finger pressed to the glass.

"The perfume?" I said.

It was a small red vial, chipped along the lip—like Rebecca, with that nick running the width of her own. The original cork stopper, disintegrated long ago, had been replaced by a plastic facsimile.

Rebecca read from the placard: "*The essence of rose, believed given by Poe to Virginia the year of their marriage, 1836.*" She looked to me again, this time with a lusty sort of gaze. "Can you open the case?"

Although I was technically disallowed, as I was not a member of staff, I did have a key. John gave it to me for the sake of convenience—and because he trusted me. But I couldn't shake her eyes and thought, What the hell, the museum had better let her touch anything she wanted if they liked her uncle's money. I opened the case, then cradled the vial in my palms.

"If this breaks," I told her solemnly, "that's it. The end of us both."

I felt her warm fingers coax the vial free from my hold,

and noted the light that shone from the case upon her thin nose and lean cheeks, a cool, sterile light that was all wrong. Then, with a move of her thumb, off came the stopper and my heart kicked like a horse.

"Rose," she said ecstatically, the vial beneath her nose.

I took a whiff. "Yup—now be care—"

She flipped the vial over upon her finger, then dragged the scent across her neck desperately, back and forth. I paled, took the bottle as forcefully as I dared, replaced the stopper, and put it away. She was grinning, her fingers down her dress top.

"Jesus, Rebecca!"

"Emery," she said softly, almost pityingly, "you knew I was going to do that."

I heard her call me in the parking lot behind the Historical Society. I didn't stop, but slowed. We walked together into a long, thin park of magnolia trees that bordered Sheppard Street. The humidity was palpable and a damp wind was gathering strength. I turned into an alley and Rebecca followed, eyeing the flask when I took it from my belt.

"You don't even like it," I snapped.

The evening light on her face reminded me of the light that shines upon generals or angels in classic paintings: the exultant yellows and oranges bleeding through churning clouds. I reminded her how quickly I'd be fired if anyone discovered what had happened, then plopped the flask into her hand.

To avoid being seen together, we stuck to the alleys, hopping over streets—Stuart, Patterson, Park—and cutting through the neighborhood diagonally. Below our feet the cobblestones were mashed together like crooked teeth, and on either side crowded slim garages, wooden fences, bushes and woody shrubs, and walls of ancient brick. Green plumes of foliage, heavy with flowers and fruit, alive with the frenetic song of mockingbirds, spilled over everything like lush curtains; and the ivy-draped limbs of mammoth tulip trees wound intricately overhead like the soft arms of giants. It awed me how wild and vivacious the wilderness could be on these nameless roads. It was hard to imagine that a city existed beyond the houses we walked behind.

"Here once, through an alley Titanic," intoned Rebecca, "Of cypress, I roamed with my Soul—Of cypress, with Psyche, my Soul."

She watched me for a reaction.

"That's Poe," she said, as if to a very slow child.

The trees were loud in the wind and I caught the distinct scent of rose.

"You've got to wash it off as soon as you get home."

"No one's going to know, Emery."

I glowered at her. A large, bulbous rain began to fall and rattle the magnolia leaves.

"I'm sorry," she said. "I didn't think it was that big a deal. I'll wash it off tonight." Then she threw her arm around my neck and pulled me down to her. "But just smell. Isn't it nice?"

I tensed, restrained for a moment, then drew in the scents—the deep rose, the sticky warm skin of her neck, the rain—and shivered. She leapt away and screamed with delight at the storm, and ran the length of the alley for her house. I didn't hurry. When I reached my back gate, I saw the blurry shape of Lou in his kitchen window, looking out.

That night I dreamed Rebecca was breaking into my house through a loose window. It was dark but there was a spotlight on her and she was naked. I spent the following morning distracted, preparing for work and wanting to see Rebecca. Wanting to see her in a particular light.

On my way to the museum, I found Lou in the alley breaking fallen tree branches for the trash. He was a stout, wiry man, white-haired and mustachioed, with a thick, soggy cigar between his teeth and sweet blue smoke clinging to his face. He cracked a limb under his knee and I imagined my bones making a similar sound. I felt sure that he'd seen me in the alley the previous night, that he already suspected something. But he said nothing, and did nothing more than nod curtly.

At the museum Rebecca and another intern were sanding walls in an empty exhibit room. When our paths crossed—Rebecca sweaty, covered in white dust, looking unhappy—I smelled the rose perfume. I eyed her, but said nothing. Lou's lack of reaction had me on guard, probably more so than if he'd clocked me. That, at least, would've been in character.

Once alone, I asked if she'd showered, and caught the image of her slick body in steam.

She played indignant, then laughed. "Maybe it's my natural scent."

I smelled rose the next day too. It lingered in the replica wood cabin where she'd worked. I followed it through the Story of Virginia exhibit, down thousands of years of history, from the Early Hunters of 14,000 BC to the Powhatan Indians to the Belmont Street Car. Was it a game? Had she bought some cheap spray from the drugstore to irk me? But the odor of an imitation would be like a candy apple compared to the earthy fruit I'd smelled upon her in the rain. I went into the storage room. I found the box where the perfume had been repacked, but it wasn't inside. Even its placard had vanished. I took a swig from my flask and found that I wasn't much surprised.

On Saturday evening Rebecca knocked on my door. She'd told her uncle she would be at Trina's, an intern she ate lunch with sometimes.

"What will you and Trina do?"

"I don't know," she said, shrugging. "Paint our nails. Talk about boys."

"Try on perfume?"

She spun around, swore the stuff simply hadn't washed off, that she had on a different perfume, that I was imagining things. I hadn't alerted John about the theft because I needed to get the perfume back myself. As much as I wanted to know how she'd done it, I'd already decided confronting her would get me nowhere. But now she was blinking. Big-eyed, disarming blinks. It infuriated me, this show of innocence while the scent of rose was so potent my eyes were practically watering.

"Perfumed from an unseen censer," she said, raising a brow.

"Poe," I said. "I know." Then I took her arm and pulled her up the stairs. She played nonchalant but I could feel her legs resisting. I moved her into the bathroom and sat her on the edge of the bathtub.

"What the *hell* are you doing?" she said.

I turned on the hot water in the sink and lathered a washcloth with soap. If she was having so much trouble ridding her neck of the scent, I told her, I was going to help. Rebecca's angry eyes grew challenging, playful. I kneeled, brought the cloth to her skin, and started scrubbing.

"That's hot," she said, but she acquiesced, tilting her head.

I wrung the washcloth, soaped it again, and resumed on the other side, taking hold of the back of her neck to steady her. This was a task, this was work—or so I told myself as I watched the soapy rivulets streak her skin. I felt her gaze on me, cool and calm now, and I didn't look up before kissing her. I tasted rose and chalky soap, and saw red behind my eyelids, pulsing in time with my chest.

Rebecca was curled on one end of the couch and asleep. The whiskey had knocked her out. I put a blanket over her and sat on the opposite end, staring into shadows. A breeze moved my hair and disturbed Rebecca's purse. I saw her keys in the purse. I took them, went barefoot into the Hamlins' yard, and let myself in.

I did this all as though in one unthinking movement, and only when I heard snoring did I note my own thrashing heart. For Lou, shooting intruders was dinner conversation. I found Rebecca's bedroom. Clothing was scattered in piles, and the tangled covers upon her bed made a fossilized impression of her body. On a dresser I fingered through a few trinkets, some cash and letters, then opened the top drawer. Here I found the girl's undergarments, which, perhaps for posterity, were the only items she'd stowed out of sight. I ran my hands through the silky contents, inhaled the scent of fabric soap and rose. Feeling into the corners I came upon a small, smooth object: the red vial with the chipped lip. I crept out of the house, flooded with excitement and pleasure.

That was Saturday; I didn't see Rebecca again until Monday afternoon, when I came in for a half-day shift. She was reading a magazine in the break room, a mug of tea below her chin.

"Rose hips?" I said, a sparkle in my voice.

"Chamomile."

"Yeah," I said. "It doesn't smell like rose."

She gave a small smile but didn't look up. I left and headed toward the storage room. The glass vial bulged in my pocket. When I arrived, the door was already open and John was inside with several other staff members. They were unpacking boxes. The room was a disaster.

"Ah," John said. "Just the fellow I was waiting for."

My stomach dropped. John explained: he'd been working in storage with Rebecca that morning when she noticed a loose placard; when they tried to return it to the item it described—a red perfume bottle, of course—they discovered it missing. Did I remember it? Did I know anything about it? I made a series of noncommittal noises, difficult as it was to think straight, much less be clever. Rebecca's little smile danced vividly to mind.

"We're ass-deep in here the rest of the day making sure it's really missing, not just misplaced." I offered to help; I could produce the vial from the first box I unpacked and *voila!* Case closed. But John refused. Staff only for now. "You know," he said, "to avoid any confusion."

"Why would you *do* that?" I said, nearly shouting.

"Why would *you* creep into my room and steal it?"

I scoffed. "You're accusing *me* of stealing!"

We stood facing each other under the magnolias. Rebecca stared off petulantly.

I took a few long breaths. "Do you want to know why 'Uncle Lou' doesn't like me?"

Rebecca's lips parted as if to speak, but she said nothing. She wanted to see what I'd say first, the crafty girl. I didn't care at that point, so I told her.

"He thinks I stole a painting." I laughed. "From a museum, no less."

"*Francis Keeling Valentine Allan,*" Rebecca replied. "The

portrait by Thomas Sully. Stolen in 2000 from the Valentine Museum. I know."

I watched her fixedly. By the end of this revelation, her eyes had drifted down the row of magnolias, her gaze light and airy.

She continued: "Poe said she loved him like her own child. It's a beautiful painting too, not that I've seen it in person."

"Did Lou also happen to tell you he and a squadron of police burst through my door and tore apart my house eight years ago? That if it wasn't for John choosing to trust me I'd have been blacklisted from working in any museum in this city again?"

Rebecca returned my stare; she looked ready to play rough. "He told me he saw you with a painting—covered by a sheet. He saw it in your hands the night of the burglary. You were trying to get it from your car to your back door. He *saw* you, Emery."

I shook my head and laughed. "So, you're Lou's little spy? Looking for lost treasure?"

"Lou is a horse's ass," she said. "Anyway, would I find it?"

"It was a storm window, for Christ's sake. Kid put a baseball through the old one a few days before. Once the cops were done demolishing my house, they were kind enough to look into it. Your uncle hates me because he made a fool of himself at the end of his career. He went out a laughing-stock."

Rebecca shrugged. "He thinks you have it. Still."

"Do *you* think I have it?"

"You have my perfume," she said. "And I want it back."

Rebecca avoided me the next few days, which was fine, as the restrictions placed upon the non-staff made my job difficult enough. Gone was my key to the storage rooms and cases; gone the days I could work without staff watching over my shoulder. Rebecca had sealed her own fate too; she was back sanding walls all day. John hadn't ruled it theft, but neither did he believe the missing perfume an inventory list blunder. He simply called it "Missing." I could feel the growing weight in his eyes when he looked at me.

Lou found out about the perfume through his museum connections. That's what Rebecca told me a week later, when she appeared at my door again. She'd heard Lou speaking of it on the phone, invoking my name more than once to John and others she didn't know. I listened to her, weighing the veracity of what she said. I doubted Rebecca would tell Lou or John about my having the perfume; she wanted it for herself, and ratting me out wouldn't accomplish that. No, given the opportunity, she would steal back the perfume. Probably it was the only reason she was here now. I told her as much.

"I won't have to resort to that," she said, stepping close. "I think you'll give it back."

"Why, because John and your uncle are hot on my heels?" I said, cockily.

She considered it. "Maybe because you like me?"

I watched her eyes for sarcasm, but she closed them and burrowed her face into my neck, running me through with chills.

"And because I like you," she added.

One thing nagged me: if Lou had spoken with John and learned of the perfume, wasn't it likely he'd also heard of Rebecca working with me in the storage room? Uncle Lou knew plenty of the staff—hadn't *anyone* put his niece with me? We were careful, but there's only so much one can do. It's a small city. By Rebecca's account, though, Lou was clueless about us.

In bed we made love. She pressed herself close and said, "Smell. Not as nice, is it?"

I smelled rose, but it was sugary and cheap. She wanted the real stuff, just a drop—a molecule.

When I took the perfume from my dresser drawer, she said, "Not much of a hiding spot."

"That's what I thought of yours."

Then she grabbed for it. I held tight and we crashed back onto the bed. She was giving me a good fight, biting my ribs, pulling my hair. When exhaustion wore us down, I tipped the vial onto my finger and applied it to her neck. We lay in bed deep into the night, the perfume high upon the dresser. She was in my arms, and I knew I had to hide the vial before I fell asleep. Then I heard her voice, low and hypnotic.

"I'm going to turn you in."

I roused, tightened my embrace as though it was lovers' talk.

"You can't. I didn't steal it."

"But you have it."

"Darling," I said, "if you turn me in, I'll tell them the real story. Then John knows you're a thief, and your kindly uncle knows you've been cavorting with the likes of me. You lose both ways—and you don't get the perfume."

"If I turn you in, your life becomes a living hell."

I pinned her, gripped her neck with my hands. "I could kill you now," I said. "And that would be the end of this nonsense."

There was a flash of real fear in her eyes, but only a flash—something had come to her. "I'm at Trina's tonight," she said. "When I don't come home, Lou calls Trina."

"And?"

"And then Trina tells him about you."

I was suddenly so pleased with her, with her cunning and forethought, her tenacity. I lowered my head to kiss her, all the while feeling that I was losing myself to her, about to give her something she hadn't even asked for. I snatched the perfume and took her to the basement, where I pulled boxes away from the wall. When I removed a section of the fake wood paneling with a screwdriver, she laughed and said, "So, you're going to brick me up back there. I should have figured."

Then she saw the vault. She stood wide-eyed, the sheets in which she'd wrapped herself slinking down her shoulders. The dial spun swiftly under my fingers, right-left, left-right, and then there was the clean, cold click of the lock giving way. The massive door opened noiselessly. I reached into the darkness and drew out what was inside.

"I knew it!" she screamed. "You sneaky bastard!" She hurled a string of delightful profanity at me, then reached out to touch the painting. She held it while I flicked on a series of mounted spotlights that came together on the opposite wall. I hung the portrait in that pool of radiance—it was alive now, the woman who raised Edgar Allan Poe. She was depicted young, and had a small nose and mouth, large dark eyes and roseate cheeks; her black hair was pulled up, and long strands of it curled past the edges of her eyes down to her jaw. There was a ghostly light about her long neck and her gauzy white dress.

I lost track of how long we stared into it.

Eventually, Rebecca asked, "What's the point? I mean, it just sits in there. In the dark."

"What should I do," I said, "put it up in the living room? Rebecca, having this painting in the vault is dangerous enough. But it's worth it. It does something to me. Every morning I wake up and remember what's here, in my house. I'm sitting upon a great secret, and it makes everything . . . vibrate. But it's a *crime*." I brought my fingers to her neck. "And you don't wear your crime."

I put the painting back and the perfume in with it—now she couldn't rat me out without exposing herself as an accomplice who knew where the secret vault was. I swung the door shut and met Rebecca's contemptuous gaze. She apparently got the point.

"I want to trust you, Rebecca. And you to trust me. This assures that trust."

"That's not trust," she said. "That's mutually assured destruction."

The longer the perfume stayed missing, the more my hours diminished. The museum's auxiliary technicians were increasingly around, assigned to projects that ordinarily would have gone to me. I was not outright expelled, but more like a child faced into the corner. The cloud of suspicion that had loomed over me eight years before was above me again, and it was dark.

When I confronted John, he said, "Emery, there's just a lot of talk."

"Since when do you believe talk?"

"Let's give it some time," he said, "let it blow over."

"Is it Hamlin? Are you listening to Lou Hamlin now?"

"Emery," he said sharply, "you were the last one with the . . . People are suspicious."

Christ, I thought, he defends me when I'm guilty, and condemns me when I'm not—not completely, anyway.

The only bright thing in my life was the source of my troubles. I found it strange that Rebecca's uncle didn't try leashing her. Was he duped so easily, believing she spent all her nights at Trina's? In the basement I'd retrieve the perfume from the safe and trace the oil along her curves. We'd sleep upon the daybed with rose and sweat in the air. Rebecca was surprisingly agreeable to the situation, washing off the perfume dutifully before she left my house each morning, not arguing when I put it back in the safe. If we didn't make love, or study the painting, Rebecca would pose and I'd manipulate the lights so that I'd swear she floated in them, my treasure.

Rebecca's internship was nearly complete; she'd be leaving for Cincinnati in a matter of days. It struck me hard, and maybe her too, but neither of us spoke about it. Following my first day of work in four days, Rebecca, walking home beside me in the alleys, presented me with an idea.

"Would things be better for you if they found the perfume?"

I supposed they would, but the small red vial had been so long in our possession, and become so important to us, that I couldn't imagine being without it.

"I want you to give me the perfume," she said evenly. "I'll plant it in a box in one of the storage rooms."

Her face was confident and serene, and I wanted to kiss the little notch upon her lip for her offer. But it was too dangerous—besides, neither of us had access to the rooms. Then she handed me an envelope. Inside was a key she'd stolen, copied, and returned the day before.

I held onto the key. "It's too dangerous, Rebecca. If they catch you . . ."

"Then what? They send me home?"

"Or prison."

There was the Summer Celebration gala the next night, a fund-raising party for members, staff, and interns. I could do it then, slip in and out amidst the crowd.

"Why do you suddenly want to get rid of it?"

"For you."

I looked all around at the alley we were in, one of a thousand veins through which coursed the blood of our city to its heart, where a great and mysterious history seemed preserved for us.

"Poe should have died here," I said, "in these alleys. Not on some bench in Baltimore."

That night was our last with the perfume.

We took my car. At the museum, Memorial Hall was bustling with ritzy summer gowns and tuxedoed bartenders, colorful spreads of hors d'oeuvres, live jazz. Rebecca and I spent only a few minutes together—the Hamlins were expected shortly—and gulped down our wine in a corner. She was especially striking, having spent so long with her compact mirror as we dressed in the basement, painting on her dark eyes, making her face radiant.

"Rebecca . . ."

"You have to," she said. "You can't lose everything because of me."

"No, I mean, will you still . . ."

I was conflicted, afraid that returning the perfume was tossing away the only card I had, tossing away Rebecca herself. I couldn't finish, but she seemed to know what I meant, because she pulled me to her by my waist and gave me a slow, full-hearted kiss.

"Do it soon," she said. "I'll meet you later. Goodbye." And she disappeared into the crowd.

I waited, put crackers into my dry mouth, said quick hellos, then made my move. I was fueled with wine, sliding through back hallways, full of love for Rebecca. It wasn't fair that we couldn't keep it—I hadn't been fair, keeping it from her.

Wouldn't it all blow over sooner or later? The old case of the missing perfume, just like the painting, which was by now a tired page on an FBI website. In the storage room I stood still, feeling the weight of the vial in my jacket pocket, and Rebecca's hands still around my waist. I had *my* treasure—not the painting anymore, but Rebecca. And *she*, such the devoted student of Poe, deserved to have the perfume. If it was time to return anything, it was the painting. With a wild surge of clarity and elation I rejoined the throngs of people, who had begun dancing as if to emulate my joy. I couldn't wait to tell Rebecca, to see her face; I'd have liked to see her uncle's too, just to show him my pleasure and confidence. But I found neither. Someone tugged at my elbow. It was Trina.

"You looking for Rebecca, Mr. Vance? She left a little while ago."

I stared at her, baffled, then said, "No, Trina. I'm not looking for Rebecca."

The row of magnolias was empty so I circled back to the parking ramp. She'd be waiting for me, my getaway driver. At my parking spot I discovered three things almost simultaneously: Rebecca wasn't there, my car was gone, and my keys were no longer in my jacket pocket. I ran home through the alleys trying to keep my mind blank, trying not to remember that last embrace with Rebecca, her hands snaking around my waist. Lou's house was dark, as was mine. My door was unlocked. Inside I called her name.

Then I read the note:

Please forgive me. But you must see the bright side. The cloud of suspicion above you is lifted—evermore.
R.

I had my shot of whiskey, felt my body shudder, and then it came, the mean bang of fists against my door and the wave of blue uniforms through the halls. I heard my name from the lips of one officer, a young sergeant, who explained his warrant for search and seizure. I saw John in his suit, straight from the gala, and Lou Hamlin dressed in black like some prowler.

The young sergeant said solemnly, "Mr. Vance, is there a safe in your basement?"

I managed to ask if that was illegal.

"What you've got in it *is*," said Lou, sneering.

They ushered me into my basement and Lou coughed with laughter when he saw the safe in plain view. The sergeant tried the handle.

"Open it up, shitbird," said Lou.

The sergeant raised a finger to quiet Lou—this pleased me—and said, "You'll have to open the safe, Mr. Vance. That, or it'll be opened in the lab."

I felt my cold body rise and fall with my breath; I waited, but nothing came to me: no idea, no plan of escape. I was done.

"No need for that," I said, and went to open it.

"No," said the sergeant, blocking me. "Just recite the combination."

It was an unoriginal set of numbers, the poet's birthday: 01-19-18-09. As I recited them I remembered spinning the dial earlier in the evening to retrieve the perfume, Rebecca behind me on the bed doing her makeup, mirror in hand. The click of the lock woke me. The flashlights came out like swords and the beams ferreted through the dark, but where the light should have by now found the black hair, the thin nose, the quiet eyes, there was nothing but more dark, and more light chasing in until the beams struck the rear wall of the safe.

All eyes—and the beams of flashlights—turned upon me.

"Where is the painting, Mr. Vance?" asked the sergeant.

I looked at Lou's face, white and fishy, and kept my eyes on him when I said, "What painting?" It came out weak, unconvincing, but what did it matter? The empty safe was proof—the empty safe would hide my crime. Only John was touching the brackets on the opposite wall, and looking at the spotlights.

Lou erupted, snatching me by the collar and heaving me into the wall for some of his paternal policing. He got in one blow to my face before he was restrained by the officers. He fought at them too, and when he was finally subdued and handcuffed on the floor he was nearly foaming at his white mustache.

"She *said*!" Lou spat. "She said the painting was here! She saw it!"

Rebecca. His spy all along. I let this sit on my thoughts for a moment, as if seeing how long I could hold an ember.

The sergeant looked beat. He shook his head at Lou. Then his face brightened. "Mr. Hamlin, where *is* your niece?"

"She doesn't have it," he said. "She made this *happen*!"

Oh, treacherous Rebecca! But her note was coming into focus. She'd duped me good, but she'd gone to great lengths to dupe her uncle too, and leave me protected.

The sergeant peered at me. "Where is Rebecca? Does she have the painting?"

I said nothing.

That's when I heard John: "Rose. I smell rose."

Suddenly, I could smell it too, as if it had exploded in my pocket; it was all over me, all over the bed and the walls and the safe. I looked away from John.

"Mr. Vance," the sergeant continued, "if you can help us, it'll be good for you."

John leveled his gaze at me. "The perfume is here. I smell it. I smell the rose perfume!"

The sergeant patted me down and found the vial. He took a disinterested sniff, handed it to John, and turned back to me.

"Now there's this," he said, like a tired parent. "We could forget *this* altogether if you cooperate."

I looked at the sergeant and at Lou and I savored it, my chance to turn the tables on her, to beat her at her own game. And then I let it go. "Sergeant," I said, "Mr. Hamlin. Respectfully, I don't know where Rebecca is and I have no idea what painting you're talking about."

"Arrest him," Lou barked, sandwiched between officers. "Arrest him for the perfume!"

And they might have. But there was John again, the vial in his hand. "This isn't it."

"What?" I shouted, unable to stop myself.

John held up the vial and pointed to an unblemished lip. "No chip," he said. "Anyway, smell it. Putrid!" He placed the vial on a cabinet and made sure I saw the great disappointment in his eyes.

I was berated for another hour by the officers. What kind of game are you playing with us? Do you think you've gotten away with it? Don't you know it's just a matter of time? Do you really think this is going to end here, tonight? I just stared into a corner, hardly listening. I was thinking of Rebecca on westbound 64, driving fast with my car into the night. The questions weren't for me; they were for her. And when I found her, I would make sure she heard them.

When I was at last alone, I found the forged bottle where

John had set it. Rebecca must've made the switch during our final night together. The vial rolled around on my palm. I was so disappointed that she'd forgotten to add the chip, I didn't have the heart to remove the cork and smell the candy spray she'd put inside.

HOMEWORK

BY DAVID L. ROBBINS

East End

He waited until the game ended. He did not know the score.

He watched parents greet their sons leaving the playing field. Some fathers tousled their boys' heads, others made the choice to have a teaching moment about a missed fly ball, a swing at a bad pitch. By these reactions, he guessed which team won. Mothers ended chats with other women to fetch their kids to the cinder-block refreshment stand for snow cones. Very few kids were loaded into cars and driven off; most had walked here. This was a beauty of the place, close-knit and small, that had not changed in the ten years he'd been gone.

More things were unaltered. Airplanes still droned low overhead, approaching or departing the airport a mile west. For thirty years, his granddad had worked in the tower there, been among the first ex-soldiers in the 1940s to read the electric green sweep of a radar screen. His father labored at the airport too, but the radar-man's son was not so clever—these things are known to skip generations—and for twenty-five years he flung down people's luggage hard enough to give himself heart failure. For six decades the airport bore the name Byrd Field, after the Arctic aviator Richard Byrd. Now the complex was Richmond International, a jumped-up title long ignored by the folks of Sandston.

At his back, behind the bleachers, ran Union Street. Two blocks down, past the elementary school, stood the saltbox house where he grew up. He didn't need to look to know it was there. Everything in Sandston lasted, another genius of the place. While the airport had been updated enough to get a new address, the little burg itself was designed to be time-less. Sandston existed in baseball fields and playground, VFW, dentist and barber, tack shop, elementary school, and several hundred houses too simple and affordable to ever be without some humble resident or other. All stood along roads with monikers that centuries would surely not pry away, named after the generals blue and gray who in 1862 struggled for this land, wooded then, during the Seven Days Battle. Jackson, Sedgwick, Magruder, Pickett, Garland, Finley, Naglee, Mc-Clellan, every street sign a banner to everlasting honor. But he'd left Sandston.

He wore no hat. The sun made him wince. He sweated and bore the unstinted summer and hot metal bleachers, no money for a soda, no care for the families of Sandston.

The afternoon aged, pinking toward dusk without cooling. Someone on the sidewalk behind the stands spoke his name, in a question, recognizing him without certainty. "Carl?" He did not turn to look. The inquiry died.

He stayed in the bleachers past the time when the field emptied, the snow cone stand shuttered, and the game and crowd were echoes in his head. The midsummer sun vanished but took another hour to pull dusk down behind it. A block away, the last tennis players quit from the dark. Once the pulses of their game stilled and the streets were vacant, Carl came down.

He rummaged through a big trash can for bottles of water, soda cans with flat remnants in the bottom, cups with water from melted ice still in them. He drank what he could find, but would not eat thrown-away food. He did not parse himself for hypocrisy. Some things were beneath him, some were not.

He moved away from the trash can and the flies drawn to it, returning to the bleachers. He did not climb up but sat under them, cross-legged like a Buddha with candy wrappers and napkins. Overhead, the bleacher seats blocked the stars like drawn blinds.

Carl stared only at the home across the street.

He had nothing. This suited him, because he wanted nothing.

No, there was one thing he had. It, itself, was multifaceted. He had hunger, but he was accustomed to it so it felt separate from him, like an item in his pocket. He had pain; this was diffuse, also familiar, and would go away soon, tonight. He had returning memories of the little ball field, these hot stands, his name called not cautiously but loudly so he could hear it out on the field, running hard to catch a ball or score. Lots of people cheering. The memories had no shelf or cubby inside him where he could tuck them away to wait until he was better. The images continued to rise, going the opposite direction of the sun. Tiny desks inside the elementary school, the tennis courts behind the VFW, parents wearing caps of their sons' teams, lawn chairs, chain-link fences separating small backyards in the Sandston neighborhood behind him. He tried closing his eyes against the old scenes. Instead, the emptiness beneath his lids made a canvas for the hunger and pain, both patient, so he opened his eyes and submitted to the memories. They were the thing he had.

Then, to balance and return to zero, there was one thing he wanted. Tonight.

He'd been in that house once. He did some quick math to

figure out how long ago, nineteen years. Nothing had changed about it: the clipped hedge on both sides of the flagstone side-walk still led to concrete steps, the house was scaled with weathered gray siding, the window mullions painted white, the door scarlet, a plastic wreath hung around the pineapple brass knocker. Inside, he recalled doilies. Hook rugs, flow-ery fabrics, a cool checkerboard of black-and-white linoleum on the kitchen floor. When he was nine, it was an old lady's house.

He'd been inside because he'd hurt himself here, on the ball field. He'd tripped on the base path, rounding second, trying to be fast like a Yankee or a Cardinal. He'd skinned his knee and his palms, and ripped his uniform pants. The fall coated him with the red dirt of the infield and he was shamed at being tagged out, sitting between second and third, sucking his teeth, clutching a stinging knee to his chest. His coach yelled from the dugout, "What were you thinking?" The um-pire made a fist in the air to say, *You're out.*

He could get up but he wanted to sit and cry, to cover his mistake. No one offered him a hand from the other team, and his coach shouted, "Come over here!" The umpire walked away, back to first base, because there were two outs and no one left on base. Carl had hit a double and was stretching it into a triple when his feet tangled. Someone should give a guy a hand up when he does that, even when he doesn't make it.

The whole ball field went silent. Carl heard a crow, that's how quiet it was that day.

The metal bleachers sounded a slow drumbeat, hollow and dirgeful. Mrs. Wilcox stepped down them, resolute. She strode out of the bleachers, away from all the others who would not stand and who had shouted at him for making an out. She was a tall, pale, gaunt woman. He did not know her first name but believed it was Agnes, Mildred, or Virginia, something austere.

Mrs. Wilcox walked onto the field. She looked nowhere but at him. No one, not even his coach, shouted at her. When she reached him, she did not bend but sent down an open hand. He took it and was lifted to his feet. The torn knee smarted and dirt clung in the scrapes on his palms, but he walked with her hand-in-hand away from the game, across the street, into her house.

"You were showing off," she said, pulling out a kitchen chair.

"Yes, ma'am."

"And you see where that got you."

"Yes, ma'am."

She disappeared, to return with a bottle of iodine and a box of Band-Aids.

"Roll those pants up."

He did so gingerly, loosing dirt from his uniform onto her kitchen floor.

"I'll get that," she said. "Come on."

She soaked a washcloth, then took the chair beside him. She patted her lap, for him to lift his leg up. He did. Her leg under his did not feel so bony as he'd figured it might. She patted clean his scrape. When the blood and infield dirt were wiped off, the wound looked like claw marks, little trenches that filled with blood again. Mrs. Wilcox pressed the washcloth over his knee and watched his face for a reaction. He gritted his teeth and looked down.

When she pulled away the cloth, the gouges stayed white. "There, now."

She coated iodine over the cuts, blowing while she painted. Then she moved him to the sink, washed his hands, and dabbed the slices on both his palms with more iodine.

When she was done and the throbs in all his wounds eased, she stood back, hands on hips. She towered.

"Back to the field with you."

"You came to the game."

"It's right across the street from my house. Why wouldn't I?"

"I don't know."

"I've seen a few of your games, Carl. I like to keep up with my favorite students."

"I was your favorite?"

"One of my favorites."

She walked him to the front door. He went out first and held the screen door for her to follow. She stayed behind.

"You go ahead," she said. "Finish up. I'll see another game."

He looked into the white bottom of her chin. Her open hand floated to the top of his head to lift his ball cap. Mrs. Wilcox rubbed his crown.

"Mrs. Wilcox?"

"Yes?"

"Will I have you again in fourth grade?"

"No."

She handed him back his cap.

"Go on," she said. "And don't worry. You can come see me anytime."

He touched his own head now, beneath the bleachers, watching the dark windows of her house.

He crawled from under the stands, ducking the crossbars, and walked onto the diamond. The dimensions struck him, how small the field was. He sat in the red dirt between second and third, feeling gargantuan. He thought of his old coach and teammates, wondering where any of them were today. Did he get lost, to know nothing of them anymore? Were their lives so different from his, that they never crossed paths? Surely, he thought. He grew irritated, that he should be the one to consider himself lost. Why him? He was the one stretching a double into a triple. He fell, but he was the one. *They* were the lost boys. They never went for it.

An ache brought his hand to his gut. The last time he sat here, he hurt too. He rose, and like he did long ago, walked with his pain off the field, across the street.

He stopped in front of her home. He cased the house in a minute. One story, probably two bedrooms. No bars or electronic alarms. No lights inside, no car parked in front. He slid along a wall to the backyard. No doghouse or pet toys on the grass. He crept up the back steps to peer inside the kitchen door. No dishes in the sink or on the counter, nothing on the table, the same table where she'd painted him with iodine and blown on it. Curtains drawn against the summer sun.

He sucked one deep breath, considering another way to go. Walk off. Choose something else. That was the difference, he thought. Choice. He did not have it. In the end, that was what set him apart from everyone else. It made him innocent too. He took from his pocket a small flashlight. With the butt, he tapped the pane closest to the doorknob, just hard enough to break it.

The glass rived into fissures. He paused to see if any light or sound came from inside. He flung his eyes to the neighbors' yards, checking for lights flicked on, any attention paid to the suspicious noise he'd just made. Nothing. He returned to the broken pane. The house remained dark. He pushed in one crack; a lone shard grinded and gave way, to break on the kitchen floor with a tinkle. He pulled to him more swords of glass, until he had enough room to reach his hand inside to the locked bolt and doorknob.

He stepped on tiptoes into Mrs. Wilcox's house. The only glow came from a digital clock on the stove. He laid the sharp bits of broken glass in the trash can, and with the flashlight in his teeth chased down the busted pieces on the floor.

He quickly found the first thing he needed, a cloth grocery bag. Keeping the flashlight from straying across the curtains and Levolor blinds, he surveyed the kitchen. It matched his memory; a few new knickknacks had been added, but the layout, the tile floor, the feel, remained unaltered. He opened and closed a few drawers. There'd be nothing of value in this room, but he lingered until he caught himself running his hand over the kitchen chairs.

He moved into the den, careful with the flashlight beam. Just as on the ball field across the street, he felt huge against this room. The feeling swept not only out of his recollection, when he'd been so much smaller, but now, as a trespasser.

The shelves and tabletops in the den offered nothing he could sell. Mrs. Wilcox's own memories were on display, in pictures and bric-a-brac. He cursed under his breath before shining the light on one silver cup, engraved with an acknowledgment of forty-three years' teaching in Henrico County. There was her first name, *Julia*. He never would have guessed. He dropped the cup in the sack. Keeping his touch light, he slid open the drawer of a side table.

"I don't have any jewelry."

He whirled, shining the flashlight straight at her. She stood in pink nightclothes, barefoot, her long hand on the wall of the arch leading to the hall.

"I do have two gold fillings." She shuffled forward. He left Sandston Elementary sixteen years ago; he had not seen her again until now. She remained taller than him. She said, "But if you were a dentist, I doubt you'd be breaking into people's homes."

Mrs. Wilcox felt her way through the room, one arm outstretched. She dodged a table and lamp to deposit herself on an easy chair, which rocked back when she sat; a pad lifted under her feet. The chair was a recliner.

"Go ahead," she said, wagging the back of a hand at him across the little room. "I can't be expected to sleep while I'm being robbed."

He aimed the flashlight directly into her face. Crinkles creviced her eyes and the circumference of her mouth. Her face was spotty and white like a full moon. She didn't flinch.

"Did you call the police?" he asked.

"No."

"Why not?"

"Because I honestly do not possess one item that anyone could find a reason to steal. And I do not want the ruckus the police will bring with them. So, grab whatever you think will have value. I likely won't miss it."

He took steps toward her, not on tiptoes now, searching her with the flashlight beam. She held no phone, no weapon. Her nightdress exposed her contours, breasts sagging at her age; she concealed nothing. She wore no necklace or brace-let. Her arms and legs in the sallow light were paler than he recalled. Her hair, cut short, had gone snowy.

So had her eyes.

He strode to within a few steps of her. He wavered the light across her eyes. They did not blink or follow.

"You're blind."

"That's right."

"What happened?"

"The sugar diabetes."

"When?"

"Took awhile."

He waggled the light again, disbelieving. She did not register, but lifted her gaze to where she approximated his head must be. She missed, looking just to the left of his face, and this was disconcerting.

She said, "Go ahead and take what you need. Then please leave without breaking any more of my windows. You'll find the newest thing in the house is the stove."

He did not move away, or pull the flashlight from her eyes. She stared blankly and intently ahead, keen with her ears, he could tell. He examined her features for some modicum of fear, regret, even disgrace at being sightless, but saw none on Mrs. Wilcox.

"I'm going into the bedroom. You sit still."

"That is my intention."

He made quick work of her drawers and closets. True to her word, he found no valuables or loose jewels. She had no iPod, laptop, or cell phone. She'd pared her possessions down to only furniture and items of comfort. He found her purse on the dresser table and rooted inside. Her wallet surrendered one credit card and four twenty-dollar bills. He took the cash. Credit cards were a sucker steal, a fast way to get tracked and caught. He left it.

He didn't bother with the guest bedroom. He returned to the den where she had not moved, her feet still up. A pang struck, widespread in his body, in his veins.

"You've got to have something," he said.

"I don't."

He raised his right hand high across his chest, above his left shoulder, and brought the knuckles down hard across her cheek. The blow knocked Mrs. Wilcox sideways in the lounger; she almost rolled off it but the arm of the chair caught her. He stood in front of her, his hand followed through high, stinging.

"You do."

She righted herself in the chair. She worked her jaw and touched fingertips to the angry mark spreading on her face.

"What I find fascinating," she said evenly, "is that, somehow in your view, I deserved that."

"You weren't supposed to be blind."

Lowering his hand, he backed away to the sofa. He cut off the flashlight, to sit and join Mrs. Wilcox in the darkness. They sat silently for a minute. He began to feel at a disadvantage, that she could function like this better than he.

"Why on earth," she said into the inky room sizzling with the aftermath of the violence, "would that matter to you?" This was no plea or whine. Mrs. Wilcox was puzzled, and figuring. "Do you know me?"

"I know you."

"Were you one of my students?"

"Yes."

"Well, I had over a thousand. Stands to reason one of you would turn out a bad penny." She said this with her hand returned to her cheek. She nodded into the darkness that was only hers.

He sat rigid on the sofa, afraid of her fixed stare. She cocked her head. Across the street on the ball field, a few children whooped, playing night-blind baseball. Mrs. Wilcox listened to them for a few moments, perhaps trying to recognize voices.

She spoke, still with her head tilted, as if the man across the room from her and the misbehaving children outside were no different.

"Where did I fail you?"

Did she just call him a failure? The notion smacked him across his own cheek. He hadn't failed. Lousy luck, rotten economy, poor employees, greedy bankers, bad blows. These had failed *him*.

"What are you going to buy with my eighty dollars? Drugs, I assume, and what else?"

"Some food. A bus ride back downtown."

She shook her head at the hook rug between them. Then she seemed to understand, or unravel, something. She put clouded eyes on him.

"Are you homeless?"

"For now."

"How did that happen?"

He did not like the question; it seemed too complex a thing to ask about so simply. He was not sitting at a little desk anymore answering her.

"It took awhile."

Her cheek glared a harsh vermillion. He expected to strike her again.

"Son, listen to me. In every life, at some point, we can't predict when, a snapshot goes off, and there you stay. I'm seventy-seven years old now, but inside I'm just fourteen. You, I can tell, you're still nine. You still hurt."

He rose to take a step toward her.

She stopped him with an open hand. Her thin white fingers looked like pieces of chalk. "I don't know who you are."

"I think you do."

"I don't. Anyway, why would that be a concern? I'm blind. No court is ever going to let me be a witness."

He stood rooted, halfway to her in the room.

"I can't help you," she said.

These words condemned him.

"I can't help myself."

Mrs. Wilcox's hands flew from her sides, a familiar flapping gesture from long ago, for a wrong answer.

"Well, that's downright ignorant, and disappointing to hear. I clearly did let you down, if that's where your life has wound up on you. Can't help yourself. What kind of pitiful fool did you grow into?"

Mrs. Wilcox pushed forward, collapsing the lounger into a regular chair. She put her bare feet down and rose, steady and spiteful.

"Let me be plain about this. Smack me around, if it soothes you. But you, young man, have to take care of your problems yourself, instead of dragging them in your third grade teacher's back door. Aside from the obvious illegality, this is farcical and not worthy of you."

He followed her with the flashlight, illuminating her way without considering that she did not need it. She stepped with her gray head high, back to her bedroom. She did not close the door between them. The bed springs creaked when she lay down.

She announced, "I am going back to bed."

Carl cut off the flashlight. His need and his ache swelled.

He felt his way to the lounger. He sat on the warmed upholstery and leaned back, lifting his legs. In the blackness he sat like this, listening to her breathe in the next room. Little by little, his eyes adjusted to seeing nothing.

Across the street, children continued to laugh. A ball hit the chain-link backstop behind home plate. A boy called for it to be thrown again. Moments later, a wooden bat struck solidly. Carl used to do this with his buddies, thrilling to the peril of trying to hit and catch a baseball in the dark. He cringed in his memory, unable to see the ball out there in the night, falling somewhere.

"Tell them," Mrs. Wilcox called from the bedroom, "to go home. It's too late for that nonsense. Someone could get injured."

He rose from the recliner to do as she instructed. He walked out her door to the field. High above, a jet streaked home to the airport, lights at the extreme of each wing like falling stars. Sandston hummed to window units, cooling behind closed doors and windows. These kids on the ball field broke that pact which Sandston made with itself, to stay quiet, and, in that way, stay.

"Y'all need to go home," he announced to five boys.

The one batting answered: "Who says?"

"The lady across the street."

"Who's she?"

"A teacher."

This seemed enough, and they quit.

Carl mounted the bleachers to watch the boys shuffle off. He sat for another ten minutes to guard against their return. Years back, if he'd been one of those kids, he'd go directly home down Union Avenue after being told by an adult. He recalled his mother, who kept brownies in a tin on top of the refrigerator, or German chocolate cake slices in wax paper. His father, shutting the front door with a loud click after struggling all day with high blood pressure and passengers' bags. His grandfather, Lucky Strike on his lips, gazing like a green-faced gypsy into the sweeping screen. They all fought hard over this land, though not in blue or gray, and without streets named after them. Mrs. Wilcox will depart too, from this town out by the airport.

Carl considered staying.

He climbed down from the stands to cross the street before she locked him out and he had to go in again through the
back door.

GAIA

BY MINA BEVERLY

Providence Park

Long before she was a stripper, nicknamed *Blaxican* because of her mixed parentage, Gaia Esparza was a good student. As a schoolgirl, she'd learned that her street, Ladies Mile Road, had been a haven, a mile-long neutral zone in Providence Park. It was named for the white women who'd been tucked away there, safe to consider their fate and care for children while their men fought Union soldiers in Church Hill. That had been a long time ago. Now, it was probably difficult for most people to imagine that anyone had ever felt safe in Providence Park.

In a way, Gaia understood that feeling, but she didn't share it. The neighborhood was mostly board houses, a few small clusters of project apartments, a boarded-up group home, and an ancient brick church, all just a few miles away from an industrial district. It wasn't as dangerous as the evening news would have people believe, if you knew how to survive. And Gaia did. She'd had to learn the hard way, but she wasn't a child anymore. Now, she knew the secret: money, knowing how to get your own, so no one could ever say you owed them anything. Money meant freedom, power, and protection. It meant that Gaia's best friend, Charlene, could afford a real attorney. So, early on Saturday morning, when Felicia Doolittle came rattling her window screen, Gaia knew she would say yes before Doo even opened her mouth.

Gaia squinted against the morning sun and leaned into the doorframe. As usual, Doo's breasts were flattened, hidden underneath a crisp white shirt that looked oddly stark against her sepia-colored skin. The long shirt reached her knees and, in large black letters, it read, *Stop snitching.* A fitted camouflage cap, tilted to the side, covered her close haircut. Several layers of pants made her petite frame appear bulky. It was January and cold outside, and Doo wasn't wearing a coat, but Gaia didn't invite her in.

"You in?" Doo asked, her hand pressed against the screen, her dark, slanted eyes taking in Gaia's long legs stretched out beneath a short, silky robe.

Gaia shifted uncomfortably.

Doo licked her lips, blackened from years of smoking. "What's the problem? The guy is a sure thing. He has the perfect family. Two kids. Even a fucking dog that looks like Lassie."

Gaia nodded. "I know. I'm in."

Gaia had never met Mr. X, but Doo's description of him was probably dead on. He probably even had a little blond PTA wife. Gaia had met many men like him before, had enjoyed taking their money. This time was different, though. Charlene wouldn't be there and Gaia could feel her pulse pounding in her neck at the thought of being alone with just Mr. X and Doo.

Doo started to walk away, but turned around as Gaia was closing the door. "Hey, I could come by here earlier if you want to get fucked up before."

"Let's just keep this business, Doo."

Doo grinned, shaking her head. "All right. Midnight then."

Doo was unpredictable and working alone with her worried Gaia. The one person who could keep Doo in line, her lover and Gaia's best friend, Charlene, had been locked up the week before for boosting GPS consoles and assaulting the arresting officer. Charlene needed a lawyer, a real one, and Gaia knew that working with Doo was the only way to get the kind of money necessary. A court-appointed lawyer was the surest way to lose her only friend to the prison system. Even if, lately, Gaia had been wondering about their friendship.

Charlene had been Gaia's friend ever since Tenth House. Nine years ago, Gaia had been a shy ten-year-old who kept to herself when a fourteen-year-old girl with fuzzy braids, a bossy attitude, and a desperate need to mother something had hooked arms with her and declared that she would be Gaia's play mom. To Gaia, that was unwelcome news. Gaia had a real mom, whose face she could draw by heart, a mom who would get sober soon and who would never again forget to take Gaia to school for forty-five days straight. Besides, Gaia didn't want to be friends with Charlene Christmas of all people. The girl had these crazy, terrifying outbursts. One second she'd be calm, staring into space, and the next she'd be yelling at the top of her lungs. The counselors sometimes had to restrain her physically during these violent fits, when she would scream over and over again, "I want my baby!"

One day, when Charlene found Gaia balled up in a corner, weeping, she pried and prodded until, gingerly, Gaia handed her a small notebook. It was a diary and inside it was the truth about Mr. Gardener, the sixty-year-old man who oversaw the entire staff of Tenth House, and who had been molesting Gaia for a year. Three times a week, like clockwork, his bony fingers troubled her sleep. The jarring scent of his woodsy Outlaw cologne mixed with the smell of the old-people liniment he rubbed on his bad knees. He called those nighttime visits payment for putting a roof over her head when no one else would. Charlene shared the diary with another counselor and was punished for lying.

Still, it put a sudden stop to Mr. Gardener, at least up until Charlene left Tenth House for good two years later. To Gaia, Charlene was her savior, her protector, her god. She was only truly safe when Charlene was nearby. They kept in touch as Gaia went round and round the revolving doors of Tenth House, until she finally broke free from the confining walls of Mr. Gardener's punishment room in the attic, where he sent her when she was uncooperative. She moved in with Charlene, into the housing projects not more than three blocks from their now-abandoned group home, near enough to it so that a mother coming back for her long-lost child would still easily find her. The two women fell into a comfortable routine and were inseparable. Charlene had even convinced Slick, the manager of Club Pink Kitten, to hire sixteen-year-old Gaia, so that they could work together.

Now there was Doo. Doo, who in the last year had turned out not to be a phase at all but instead a permanent fixture. Doo, who stared at Gaia when Charlene wasn't looking, who bought new furniture, new tension, and new schemes. Charlene was so in love with Doo that she had threatened to evict Gaia if she told any more lies about Doo's flirtatious behavior. She was completely blind to Doo's faults. Slowly but surely, Gaia saw herself being pushed away to make room for another woman. Lately, she had done everything she could not to be alone with Doo, but tonight she didn't have a choice. Charlene, her defender, the only one who could keep the bad things at bay, needed help.

Around 6 o'clock, while Gaia was giving herself a pedicure, Charlene called collect from the Richmond City Jail.

"I'm in," Gaia said, after accepting the call.

"I know. Doo told me."

The sound of Charlene's voice came through clear, but she still seemed distant.

"Are you happy?" Gaia asked.

"Of course. I want the hell out of here."

"I'm nervous."

Charlene sighed. "Come on. You're a pro at this."

"Yeah. When *you're* there. When I can look at you."

"Just do it.

Gaia paused. Her lip trembled. She took a deep breath. "But what about Doo? You know how she gets when you're not around. Can you talk to her and—"

"Are we back on this? Listen, and this is the very last time I'm going to say this: Doo loves me. She thinks you're an immature little kid, Gaia. I had to beg her to do this with you because she doesn't trust you to keep your head straight. Was she right?"

"No. No, I can do it. I'm just a little nervous."

"Damnit, G. This is my life on the line. And you owe me. You better not back out. I swear to God, Gaia."

"I won't, Char! I swear."

"Okay. Good. You my girl."

Gaia tried to imagine what Charlene could be wearing. Probably an orange jumpsuit. She wondered if Charlene's hot pink nail polish was chipping away. Wondered if the phone was pressed between her shoulder and her ear or if she was clutching the receiver with both hands, like Gaia was.

"I love you," Gaia said.

"Aw, don't get mushy. Just do like Doo says and everything will be fine."

"Okay."

"Don't let me down."

"I won't."

A half hour before midnight, Gaia slipped into a curve-hugging black minidress and put on her favorite pair of red patent-leather stilettos. She painted her lips a fiery red and pulled her long braid free, letting her heavy brown curls fall around her shoulders and down her back. She found Charlene's loaded Glock underneath the mattress and hid it in a black handbag for protection. With her short leather trench belted at the waist, she walked outside onto the dark patio to wait for Doo. She thought about Charlene in handcuffs a week before, violently kicking Officer O'Rourke's cruiser.

Outside, the air was bitingly cold against Gaia's bare legs, but she had been claustrophobic inside the small apartment, battling the deafening silence, the persistent emptiness, and a constant stream of thoughts that told her to double check the door to make sure she wasn't locked in. She felt safer out in the open, where no matter how far up she stretched her hands she'd never touch a wall. On either side of her was yet another one-level apartment. These project apartments all looked alike on the inside: cold cement walls, two small bedrooms, few windows, and a clear view of the back door as soon as you walked in the front door. Outside, plastic chairs and card tables cluttered the tiny front patios, and one of Gaia's neighbors was sitting out smoking a cigarette. Gaia settled into a cold plastic chair and watched the neighborhood pulsing around her.

The wind blew, rushing like floodwaters between the small gaps that separated buildings, blowing litter around on balding lawns and into deep potholes in the street. The street came alive at night, bustling with activity. It was rush hour for the corner boys. They hopped in and out of cars like musical chairs. Gaia took deep breaths and listened as the one-woman Neighborhood Watch Association, Ms. Nora, shooed a group of the boys from under the big shade tree in the front yard of her shabby clapboard house across the street from the projects.

"Go stand under that street lamp and let Jesus and the rest of the world see what you doing, niggas. Go on, you little hooligans!"

The boys moved their operation a few feet down the block, joking around in front of the fenced-in playground behind the recreation center, where Gaia had played as a child. Tonight, she thought she saw the dim glow of a lit cigarette briefly penetrate the darkness of the basketball court, its smoker cloaked in nightfall. Gaia knew that the blood of gunshot victims had touched the blacktop almost as often as basketballs had. She sometimes wondered if other people saw the ghosts of those victims roaming at night, haunting the neighborhood, hiding in shadowy corners. It made her wonder if she'd ever leave Providence Park, even after she died.

Restless, Gaia's legs bounced up and down, the heels of her shoes rhythmically clicking the concrete. It was a unique feeling she got right before she, Charlene, and Doo set out on one of these kinds of nights. It had been three months since she'd felt it, the anticipation of being in complete control of a man's fate, his life, his livelihood. It was intoxicating. But tonight, most of what she felt was anxiety about Charlene's absence.

When Doo's shiny Cadillac pulled up to the curb, Gaia pinched the cold flesh of her right leg between two acrylic fingernails and squeezed her eyes shut. She felt for the piece of Charlene she had hidden in her handbag, and told her legs not to shake as she walked briskly over to Doo's car.

Doo jumped out from her side of the vehicle and ran

around to open the passenger-side door before Gaia reached it. Charlene usually rode shotgun and Doo had never made this kind of gesture for her.

In the car with the windows up, Gaia could smell the booze coming through Doo's pores and knew she was feeling no pain. That was no surprise. The most dangerous place in the world was between Doo and a bottle of Southern Comfort.

Doo took her hand off the steering wheel, turned toward Gaia, and rubbed her thumb back and forth against the rest of her fingers. She smiled, her eyebrows shooting up questioningly. "Feel me? Lot of money on the line with this one. You gotta be on point tonight. He's expecting two." She stopped talking and looked down at Gaia's bare legs, illuminated by the streetlight they sat parked under, then chuckled lightly. "But I'm sure he'll be more than happy when he sees you."

"It's Charlene that's on the line. Remember?"

"What?" Doo's head snapped up. "How the fuck could I forget that? She's my number one priority, and I'm hers. You remember that."

"Well, she's the only reason I'm doing this."

"Yeah, well, if you're serious, you need to hike that skirt up a little bit more." Doo grinned and pushed back Gaia's stretchy black mini until the hem rested on the upper thigh. Her finger grazed and lingered over the bare skin of Gaia's leg. Gaia used her foot to drag her handbag toward the seat. Her pulse quickened.

"Doo," she warned, hoping a firm tone would be enough.

Doo threw her head back and laughed. "Easy," she said, and pulled away from the curb.

Seeing both of Doo's hands occupied with steering, Gaia

leaned back against the headrest and tried to relax. Her neck felt tight, her muscles tense.

"Can I have the rest?" she asked Doo, pointing to the bottle of whiskey lying overturned on the floor mat.

Doo glanced at it quickly and nodded. Gaia put it to her lips and emptied in one gulp. It burned her throat, made her choke. Doo laughed.

They drove out of Providence Park and hit the interstate going west. They traveled past where the bus line ended; it was not more than twenty-five minutes away, but far beyond where many of Gaia's neighbors without cars had ever ventured. Eventually they arrived at a hotel in the West End called The Studio.

After she got the key from the desk clerk, Doo pulled the car into a parking space directly in front of their room. The world was resting in this part of town. Stepping out of the car, Gaia heard the click of her high heels echo in the air. She could feel the whiskey mixing with her blood. She shuddered, feeling the wind wrapping around her legs, blowing against her face, whispering her name. She stepped up onto the sidewalk and waited as Doo opened the door to the suite that she'd reserved and paid for earlier that day.

Inside, Doo sat on a chair and put her feet up on the sofa. She lit a blunt right away. Gaia didn't want to risk an incident with Doo, especially when Doo was high and tipsy. She went into the bedroom to get away from the smoke and sort her mind out.

Gaia hadn't grown up wanting to be this way. At eight years old, survival wasn't something that entered into daily decisions, like whether to play dress-up or hopscotch. And though, shortly after, she could no longer make sense of her upturned life, it had taken Charlene's words to make her realize that it wasn't beauty alone that determined her fate. There were plenty of beautiful girls in the home. She had been marked. It was an obvious fact and the only possible thing to do was embrace it—the same way she had embraced how her legs eventually grew like stems—and use it to her benefit.

Tonight, she would be as irresistible as ever and she would be paid because of it. She set her handbag on the nightstand and took out the Glock, which she slipped underneath a pillow. She sat down to lotion her penny-colored skin and thought about what Charlene had said a year ago, the first time she approached Gaia with Doo's big scheme. *Girl, look at you. You already know they gon' come after you, whether you like it or not. So why not make them pay for it? Make him forget his own name, his wife's name, shit, his kids' names. He'll think he's winning, until he gets the bill. Don't be scared, girl. I'll be right there.* She could almost hear Charlene's voice, almost feel her in the room.

Doo knocked on the door.

Gaia took a deep breath before she opened it. Doo was standing there with Mr. X. His cropped brown hair was slick with hair gel. His pale blue eyes set a sharp contrast against his all-black business attire. Towering a foot over Doo, his belly was the only part of his body that had already crossed the threshold. He looked to be in his late forties.

"Where's the other one?" Mr. X queried, scanning the room.

Doo had met Mr. X while she was bartending a party in one of those sprawling estates on Monument Avenue. She had been keeping him well-stocked in pills and cocaine ever since, and had been secretly following him, studying him for weeks.

Gaia reached for his hand. It was plump and sweaty. She

slowly rubbed the back of it with her thumb. "Char's not feeling well. It's just me tonight. Is that okay?"

He hesitated, looking thoughtfully at Gaia. She didn't doubt for a second that he would stay. She was a magnet, a stronger force than even she herself could control. She felt the tension go out of his hand.

"Are you just going to stand there and watch? Get the fuck out," he told Doo, never taking his eyes off Gaia.

The corners of Gaia's red lips turned up into a seductive smile. "Watch? I can make her go away like this." She snapped her fingers.

Mr. X laughed as Gaia pulled him forward over the threshold and kicked the door closed with her foot.

She led him to the bed, purposely swaying her ass, knowing his eyes were fixed there. He sat down and started taking off his shoes. "No," she said. He looked up at her. His lustful stare felt like a tongue licking her face. "Let me do that."

She undressed him, throwing his pants clear across the room toward the door, as he ran his hands up the inside of her leg, making low, guttural noises. He stood up and she was eye to eye with his coarse chest hair. He was impatient with her, almost tearing her dress.

"Slow," she whispered.

She had done this dozens of times by now. Each man desperately wanted to invade the space between her legs, not knowing that it did not belong to her. She could never feel any sensation down there because it wasn't a part of her real body, and any man who entered soon found he would have to pay a higher price than he had thought. That is why she welcomed them and laughed inside while they grunted and moaned. A soundproof wall separated her from them, kept her from hearing the compliments they choked out between heavy breaths. The only sound she would listen for tonight was Doo, tiptoeing back into the room to get their insurance.

Mr. X had Gaia pressed against a wall, between the bed and the nightstand. Her nose was crushed against his neck and she breathed in his woodsy cologne. The scent stung her nostrils and went sliding down her throat, into her mouth. It sat bitterly on the back of her tongue. She hadn't smelled it in three years, but the scent was unmistakable. Suddenly, his lips felt familiar against her skin. His hands were bony and wrinkled. She thought her knees might buckle as she squeezed her eyes shut tightly, her head growing light. She was losing it. The control was slipping from her hands and into his. She tried to take it back.

"Stop," she said.

He tore his lips away from her shoulders. "Why?" he asked breathlessly.

"Your cologne. Wash it off."

"What? No."

He pushed her against the wall again. Grabbing a fistful of her hair, he yanked her head back and smothered her protests with his lips. She looked up into his eyes, but they were closed. What color had Gardener's eyes been? Her breathing was so staccato that her chest started to ache. And the scent, his scent, was so thick she feared she might be suffocated. She gasped when he lifted her leg and forced himself inside of her. For the first time in years, she felt something. She tried to expand herself, to make herself wide enough for two ships to pass through.

She didn't know how long it lasted, but when it was over, she heard him say, "That was amazing." She heard his zipper going up, his expensive loafers sliding against the carpet, the door swinging closed. Lying naked on the bed, she wondered if it was her or the room that was spinning. She closed her eyes to try and regain her balance. When she opened them, she was not alone. Doo was leaning over her. Gaia tried to sit up, but she felt pinned to the bed. Her throat was dry and her tongue was like cotton.

Doo was smiling. "I got the pictures. You did good. See, we didn't even need Charlene. We're a great team." She brushed a stray hair away from Gaia's face.

Gaia watched Doo's lips come closer and closer and shut her eyes when she tasted whiskey and stale cigarettes on Doo's thick tongue.

Gaia shook her head, started to say no.

"Shh," Doo's mouth whispered. Her hands came up to grip one of Gaia's exposed breasts.

Trembling, Gaia's fingers searched for the cold steel underneath her pillow. Her arm felt like it weighed fifty pounds when she lifted the gun and swung it over and over against the back of Doo's head. The hard steel connected with bone and made a cracking sound. Doo shrieked in pain and covered her head with both hands. They fell to the ground with a thud, the lamp, the alarm clock, and the nightstand all clattering down with them.

Doo went limp, stopped moving or making any sounds, the back of her head against the carpet. Gaia dropped the gun and crawled to the corner behind the door, sitting with her red knees pulled up to her chest. She watched as the pool of blood coming from Doo's head turned the beige carpeting purple-red.

The muffled beeps of the fallen alarm clock sounded like they were coming from inside Doo's baggy jeans. Laughter bubbled in Gaia's stomach and rose up her throat like a gush of water. Her whole body shook with laughter as Doo beeped and beeped. Gaia crawled over to the body. She hovered above Doo and then lifted her shirt. Doo's breasts were strapped down in layers of ace bandages. "Shh," Gaia whispered, pulling the bandages down. She laughed as one soft breast tumbled out.

Gaia was about to touch it with the tip of her finger when a loud screeching of tires squealed just outside the window.

She shook her head and blinked rapidly. Her breathing hastened as a weight seemed to suddenly sit down on her chest. What had she done? *Oh God, Doo! And Charlene.* Charlene would hate Gaia, never speak to her again. Gaia's body collapsed and she dropped her head to the carpet. She felt like dying. She felt like disappearing, like hiding. She felt . . . cold. She spied her dress lying at the foot of the bed and crawled to get it. She pulled it over her head and felt the fabric wiping away the tears that rushed down her cheeks.

Turning her head slowly back toward the spot on the floor where Doo lay, she started to say, *I'm sorry, Charlene,* but the words caught in her throat. She stared at Doo's tar-stained lips until they were two brown blurs, and realized it wasn't true. She wasn't sorry. She stood up momentarily and then sat on the bed as she surveyed the room. Overturned tables, blood-soaked carpet. She was sitting on something hard. She got up, saw that it was Doo's small, silver camera, and squeezed it between her hands. She was holding one of the only pieces of real evidence that she had ever been here tonight. She studied Doo's small body. Doo couldn't be more than a hundred and twenty, a hundred and thirty pounds. Could she?

Gaia drove east toward Providence Park, by instinct, not choice. She knew exactly what was waiting for her back there. Zooming down the interstate, Gaia felt only relief when she thought about Doo's lifeless body wrapped in a sheet on the floor of the Cadillac. She had protected herself and taken control of what belonged to her. Doo had been right. She *didn't* need Charlene. Charlene didn't love her. And she could take care of herself. She didn't need a play mother. She didn't need any mother at all. She understood now how to keep away the bad things, the ghosts, the past, and it was not by fear. It was by force.

At 3 a.m., she stood in front of the abandoned group home. She waved at Doo, who was lying at peace in Gardener's attic. An empty fuel can dangled from Gaia's fingers.

Wrongs did not correct themselves. Someone had to make the decision to fix things. People could not live their lives the whole time expecting things to happen; people had to make things happen. Cold gasoline had to be spilled deliberately, dousing the ground, the walls. A match, struck in the dark, had to be dropped in a shallow puddle of fuel. And the girl, the one in the wrinkled black dress, would not run away yet. She had to watch as the scorching flames licked and devoured the home. Ladies Mile Road had been a haven, a place where women felt safest. This building had mocked that history and tainted the whole neighborhood.

TEXAS BEACH

BY DENNIS DANVERS

Texas Beach

He lies sprawled facedown in the water just short of the beach as if he tried to swim across the James and came up short. I turn him over, pull his upper body out of the water, then discover his lower torso hasn't quite turned with the rest of him. He couldn't have been swimming anywhere like this. His pelvis is crushed. He's dark, probably Mexican or Guatemalan. He has on one battered leather garden glove, on his right hand. His left hand is bent at an odd angle, and a bone protrudes from his left forearm.

I throw up in the river and call 911.

I'm at Texas Beach, I tell them, on the water. There's a dead man here. They tell me to stay with him. I say I will. That's what I need. To sit with a dead man. I've come down here to wallow in grief. My old dog whose favorite haunt this was when she was alive died a couple of days ago, and I've been pretty much useless ever since. I was almost on top of the dead man before I realized what I was looking at. It's early Thursday, the sun just coming up. I haven't slept much.

His feet are still in the water. He's wearing heavy, oil-stained work boots, almost cracked. His jeans have ridden up on his oddly pale shins. Something floats out of the top of one of the boots, and I grab it before it drifts off. A wood chip. I put it in my pocket. It could be evidence of something. I pull him the rest of the way out of the water. More chips spill out as the jeans catch on the sand and unfurl, covering his shins.

When I moved to Richmond from Texas twenty years ago, I missed seeing brown faces. Richmond was a town in black and white. That's changed since NAFTA, like the rest of the country. When I was a kid walking across the bridge into Juárez with my parents, there'd be kids my age standing in the tarnished water of the Rio Grande, their hands uplifted for pennies tossed from the bridge. This man, the dead man, has gray temples, crow's feet. He could be my age, sixty. He could've been one of those kids half a century ago.

I wonder how he ended up here—not in Richmond, I understand those economic realities well enough—but here, washed up on the shore of Texas Beach, almost broken in half. I wonder if he was the victim of a hit and run. I wonder if he was murdered. When the sun shines upon his face, I take pictures of him from several angles.

I sit with him another fifteen minutes, absorbing what I can. I've probably disturbed the body too much already. I want to look in his pockets, but I resist. They appear to be empty.

Pretty soon there's a crowd. I hear one of the guys tending to the body telling another to be careful because "his midsection's smashed up pretty bad." The cop who's going to question me keeps me waiting while he gives the relevant facts over the phone to some anxious superior somewhere: a presumed illegal, no identification, appears to have died elsewhere of undetermined causes. He ends with, "Yes sir, I will, sir," repeated several times like a ritual response.

Most everyone else has gone with the body back through the woods and over the bridge spanning the tracks and the canal, up a steep trail to the parking lot. Off in the distance you can hear someone shouting, "Watch it! Watch it! Watch it!" We're standing on the beach beside where I found the body.

The cop asks me what I know, and I tell him. I tell him about the wood chips. He doesn't seem particularly interested. "Do you think it's a homicide?" I ask.

"We haven't ruled it out. We plan an immediate autopsy to determine cause of death. We don't want any idle speculation in the press."

"What happens if it is homicide?"

"Since we don't know who the man was, the investigation would be difficult. We hope someone will come forth with information, of course. It's not likely in my experience, with cases like these, but you never know."

"Cases like these?"

"Victims from the illegal immigrant community. They fear bringing any scrutiny upon themselves. Understandable. Times like these. To tell you the truth, I doubt anything will come of it. We've got nothing to go on."

Times like these. I suppose that phrase means the strident debate over "illegals," as if that's the single quality that matters. I would share with him what I think of these times, but what point is there telling a cop what you think of the law? He's only entitled to one opinion. In the silence between us, I hear the river. It's never completely silent down by the river. Dog and I used to sit on the beach and listen, or maybe for her it was the smells. Whatever it was, it always made her smile.

I walk home across Byrd Park where dog used to retrieve Frisbee, ball, stick, anything, until she got too old. I imagine, if she were here, I'd talk it over with her. She'd agree, I imagine, that I can't just let this thing go. She had a highly developed sense of fair play and a good heart. Concern for the law, not so much: no dogs are allowed in Byrd Park. The signs are everywhere, right next to the ones fantasizing about the speed limits. A few blocks away is a drug-free zone, in case you're in the market.

By the time I get home, I'm pissed off. *Nothing to go on?* Why isn't a dead man enough to go on? Anger seems to take the edge off the grief.

I sit in front of my computer and try to write for a couple of hours with a negative word count of 325. I quit while I'm behind. I call a former crime reporter I'm friendly with. He was recently downsized in the local newspaper's successful attempt to make itself even more fluffy and irrelevant than before, while retaining its essential reactionary character, a task I would've thought impossible. I ask him if he can find out what the autopsy turns up. He calls the dead man "Juan Doe." Ha-ha. He's kind of a macho jerk, but a good reporter.

He calls back Friday evening. Usually dog and I would be out walking. I'm just sitting around thinking about that. My wife's upstairs in bed, crying or sleeping.

He tells me about the dead man: "Crushed by something big, probably a tree, causing massive trauma. He was dead before he went in the water. Accidental death. The tree did it. Case closed."

"You're shitting me."

"The wheels of justice, my friend."

"How did he get in the water, when he was pinned under a tree with massive trauma?"

"Undetermined. The river did it. But he died on dry land, and he died slow. Somewhere between forty-five minutes and ninety minutes between trauma and death. He bled out. Within twenty-four hours of when you found him, probably less."

"The river level hasn't changed in a week."

"Nobody wants this one. It's got a bad smell to it. This way it goes away. Another illegal dies in a work-related accident. Tough break. Adios."

Sunday morning I'm back at Texas Beach. Dog and I used to go upriver from here all the time. About a half-mile up, the outflow from the canal cuts off easy passage. The rocks are slippery as hell, so you can either trespass on the railroad tracks or wade in the shallows. It's chilly, so I illegally trespass. I'm not sure what I'm looking for, but I suspect the dead man was dumped in the water somewhere on the north bank and floated down to Texas Beach. I guess I'm looking for the killer tree. Then maybe I'll interrogate the beavers who chewed him out from under the killer tree and dragged him to the water after the muskrats emptied his pockets.

This is the wildest stretch of the park, spectacular towering pines, sycamores, oaks, and hickories. Woody Woodpecker and his girlfriend swoop through here often. It's just a narrow strip of land sandwiched between the James and the CSX tracks. The old Kanawha Canal runs on the other side of the tracks, cutting off easy access. Dog and I spent many a wilderness hour here. I reach the end of park property, just opposite the three-mile canal locks and the old pumphouse, which have their own park.

Unfortunately, the only way to proceed west is to continue trespassing across the tracks. There's a break in the fence, familiar to dog and me, a short jog away. She hadn't been able to make the dash in a while with her stiff hind legs, and it turns out the fence has been repaired. I jog a little farther and scramble up the embankment into Pumphouse Park. The always short-handed Richmond police used to have undercover cops working the park looking to entrap gay men back before the Supreme Court decided homosexuality isn't illegal after all. Amnesty for nature. What is the world coming to? Sunday morning, there's nobody around but dog walkers, and they won't care.

The canal continues west from the park all the way to the water treatment plant, the old towpath alongside it. It's not clear to me who owns the canal and the towpath. *They belong to history* would be a truly Richmond sentiment. CSX, however, seems to be the ones putting up the *No Trespassing* signs. There's a verse of "This Land Is Your Land" not sung much around the campfire that points out there's two sides to such signs, the side saying nothing being the one belonging to you and me. I wanted to quote that neglected verse as an epigraph in a novel of mine a few years back, but I was told I'd have to pay the owners a few hundred bucks or it would be illegal. Woody Guthrie was dead by then. I'm sure he would've been amused at the ironies.

Stretches are overgrown with greenbriers, but I've brought a folding handsaw and gloves. Dog hated greenbriers and slunk along reluctantly when I'd get one of these bushwhacking urges, but slink along she did, through damn near anything. Dogged, they call it.

By the time I pass under the spectacular railroad bridge Richmond likes well enough to use on its logo, the worst of the greenbriers have thinned out. I've reached the limits of any exploration dog and I ever made. Before 9/11 my wife and I paddled a canoe up the canal, right through the water treatment plant. With a couple of portages we made it the length of the canal. Land passage is trickier, especially with a dog, but I'm dogless now, so I persist. The way becomes increasingly obscure and likely even more illegal, but I'm determined to find the truth, if not necessarily eager to confess how I get there.

I smell it first, the scent of fresh cut wood. A dozen trees of various sizes are scattered about like jackstraws. It doesn't take long to figure out why. A house as grand as its view of the James stands on the bank above me. These trees were in the way. There've been a couple of cases in recent years like this: rich folks on either side of the river cutting down trees to get the view they paid for, willing to pay the fine and repent, claiming ignorance of the law. The rich don't read the paper apparently. You see, it's illegal to fuck with the watershed like that. Who better to do an illegal job than an illegal?

Every level of the house has a grand balcony of some sort. Windows gleam in the sun. All empty. No eyes at home. Maybe they're looking to heaven in some slate-roofed church. I climb among the fallen trees. There's sawdust everywhere. I approach a fallen sycamore trunk lying flat that comes up to my chest. About ten yards from the water, a hollow has been dug out of the sandy soil beneath it. I stare into the shallow recess, and I can hear the shovels hitting the dirt to make this hole with quick, frantic strokes. I buried dog in our tiny back-yard. It's probably illegal. I fought with my wife about it. She was probably right. I can't say it's actually delivered on the promised closure I've heard others say it gave them. Maybe I don't want closure.

I crawl into the hole to see the underside of the syca-more, like a beached white whale, and there's blood, has to be, soaked into the bark. The tree indeed did it. There are at least four distinct shoe tracks on the beach, not counting mine. There's a furrow through the sand to the water. A bea-ver maybe, or a man's heels. In the grass beside the furrow, I find an ordinary work glove like the dead man was wearing. A left. The river had an accomplice.

* * *

It doesn't take long to find out who owns the house. I even have a nice Google Map photo of the place from space taken back when there were trees along the river. Naturally, I've heard of the guy. If you're rich enough to have a big place on the river, chances are you've made a ripple. This guy's more like a deep current. Lately he's been riding that current right into the legislature. Illegals are his hot-button issue. His TV ad promising he'll get tough on illegals has him in front of St. John's Church where Patrick Henry made his treasonous speech.

I call up the cop who questioned me, leave several messages. I'm sitting in the backyard beside dog's grave, drinking a beer, when he finally calls me back Monday evening. I tell him what I've found out. He tries to talk me out of it meaning anything.

"What about the glove?"

"And what links the glove to the victim?"

"The matching glove on the victim?"

"There was no glove on the victim."

"What are you talking about? I saw it. There was a glove on his right hand."

"I'm telling you. I've got the file right here in front of me, and there's no glove."

"Maybe I shouldn't have told you whose house it was right off."

There's a silence I take to mean I'm supposed to think he's offended. "I assure you we will investigate as we deem appropriate. I suggest you leave this matter to the proper authorities. And I remind you that trespassing on private property is a serious offense and potentially dangerous to the trespasser."

He hangs up.

I check the photos I took of the dead man. I must've

thought I was doing a portrait study or a mug shot. None of them show his right hand.

Next morning I'm at the corner of the Lowe's parking lot where I've seen brown men gathering looking for work. A dozen or so guys cycle through, hired by circling SUVs and pickups with law-abiding citizens behind the wheel. I show the workers pictures of the dead man, talk to them in my awkward, rusty Spanish. They're nice to me, patient. They admire my white beard. *Señor Barbas* one of them calls me. Mr. Whiskers. I figure they think I'm a cop, INS, or a crazy street person, but I hang around anyway, boring them with stories about my travels in Mexico.

Another man, however, who's been in Richmond awhile, gives me the nickname that sticks. "General Lee," he says. "El hombre a caballo." The man on horseback. We're only blocks from the statue, and he isn't the first to note the resemblance, especially if I haven't been eating enough fiber or I've just watched what passes for the evening news. I was once mistaken for a Lee reenactor while walking past the Confederate Chapel on my way out of the Virginia Museum of Fine Arts. The city's full of memorials to the leaders of the armed rebellion against the legal authority of the United States—the same one nation under God indivisible that the devoted admirers of those memorials like to wax pious about with a mystifying lack of irony.

The conversation turns to politics. They have questions about the Civil War. Mexicans understand revolutions, revolutionaries. They're curious why the losers got the statues. It's complicated, I tell them. Fortunately, they understand class and race too.

I get a few odd glances from the people looking for workers.

A neighbor from a few blocks away whose name I can't recall spots me, and he seems genuinely alarmed to see me sitting on the fence with the Mexicans. I approach to reassure him or to offer to do light carpentry, I'm not sure which. He only knows me because dog and I used to walk by his house, but she hadn't been able to make it that far in over a year.

"How's your dog?" he asks me. Of course he's going to ask me. Everyone's going to ask me. He just happens to be the first.

"She died."

"I'm sorry to hear that."

"She lived a good life."

He tosses his head toward the workers. "You doing research for a story or something?"

"We were just talking about the Civil War. Can't become a true Richmonder, become assimilated as it were, without talking some Civil War trash, right?"

It's supposed to be a joke, but he doesn't crack a smile. "Do any of these guys do tile work?"

I get out of the way of commerce. Antonio, who's hung around for the whole General Lee gringo show and looked stunned when I first showed him the pictures of the dead man, asks how old my dog was. "Quince," I say. Fifteen.

"My oldest sister," he says in English. "She have a dog. In Kansas City. She crazy about that dog."

I give him the pictures of the dead man. I've written my phone number on the back. "I found him, okay? I pulled him out of the river. I have to do something. Maybe you know someone who knew him. Maybe someone else will know."

As I walk home through the Fan, the word sticks in my mind, a quick, stabbing chant, *quince, quince, quince.* When I get home there's a message from my ex-reporter friend who kay-aked over to see the site only to find there'd been a bonfire, still smoldering. Teens, they're saying, drinking, getting out of hand, or maybe homeless. Or illegals. Damn them all to hell!

I walk through the house with a garbage bag, gathering up every tennis ball, veterinary prescription bottle, squeaky toy, busted leash, food dish, rawhide, etc., getting down on hands and knees if necessary until I'm sure I've found them all, then I put the bag in the trash can in the alley.

My wife returns home from work desolate and exhausted from having to hold it together all day at some inane training about terrorism. We have a quick dinner, narrate the fragile bones of our days, and go to bed early. She wants to be more engaged by my story of trying to help the dead man, but nei-ther one of us has anything left. "Be careful," she says, and falls asleep. I lie awake awhile and finally get out of bed.

A little after midnight my phone rings, and I take it. I'm at my computer, staring at the screen, at the Google photo of a time when the dead man was still alive. It's Antonio with an address out Jeff Davis Highway, a trailer park. Can I come now? Some of the people I need to talk to just got off work. Others have to go in early. Two men are arguing in the back-ground in rapid-fire Spanish too faint and fast for me to track. Sure, I say.

It's a grim, tired place, but affordable. If it has a name, I don't see it. There's a certain coziness about the old trailers crammed in close together, the sounds of TVs and radios, cooking smells. I roll through slow, my General Lee beard must look like Casper floating by. A woman watches me pass through a tiny trailer window. She must be bent over her kitchen sink.

At number seventeen, several somber men are waiting

for me. We go inside where there are several more men and a single woman packed into what is likely the largest living room in the park. The men whose voices I recognize from the phone continue their argument. Not everybody thinks inviting me was such a great idea. Enough, several say. Let the man speak. So I tell my story. They're not taking any chances on my Spanish. A woman named Irayda translates.

Then they tell her their story, and Irayda tells it to me, though I get the gist in Spanish. They were working with Felix—Felix is the dead man—when the man who hired them—the man who lived in the big house up above—showed up to hurry them. People were coming to his house, and he didn't want anyone to see them working, but it was a big job and dangerous because there were some large trees and not much room to get out of the way if anything went wrong.

The big white tree came crashing down on Felix while the man from the house was there shouting at them. He told them not to call 911 or they'd all be arrested and deported, and they could dig Felix out and take him to the hospital just as fast themselves. They started digging. They didn't have enough shovels for everyone. One of the men went back to the truck to get some more, but they couldn't get Felix out before he died. The man said he'd call 911 after they took off, so they wouldn't be arrested. They had left the man alone with Felix's body Wednesday night. Then I showed up at Lowe's the following Tuesday with his picture. Antonio stayed with Felix's son when he first came to Richmond. His son was killed in a robbery last year.

Irayda says, "They appreciate what you've done for Felix, but they would like you to stop now. If it was only them, it would be different, but they must consider the welfare of others—their families, their neighbors, their children. They know whose house it is. Things are hard enough already, the way things have been lately. You understand?"

I wish I didn't, but I do, so I don't give her any argument. I shake hands all around. She leaves when I do, driving to a more affluent part of town. Probably here legally, well-educated, from a prosperous family back home in Mexico or Guatemala—maybe she knew Felix, or maybe she just wanted to help.

I miss my turn, or something inside me refuses to take it, and I head for the house of the man promising on the radio to keep America safe for Americans or some such gibberish. I twist and turn through streets all named with a bit of the lord-and-manor about them. Once you get anywhere close to the river-fronting properties, the roads are all private. If I hadn't pored over the Google photo, I don't think I would've known which one to take. I roll right up front. I'm surprised there's not a fence or something. Maybe there's a virtual fence, like the one in Arizona. The lights are on. Someone's home.

And quite a home it is, stretched to make room for windows on one side and plenty of pavement on the other. Several cars much nicer than my Civic are parked here. They're all wearing the host's bumper sticker on their ass. Sounds like a party going on, people talking and laughing over Cuban jazz. Campaigning must make for some late nights, or maybe he just can't sleep. The air is heavy with the smell of charred wood. Must put a damper on the festivities.

I button up my shirt and tuck it in, ring the bell, and smile into the camera. General Lee calling. The candidate himself opens the door, and I tell him I'm a constituent wanting to discuss the issues. He has to shake my offered hand, an old white man, and I hang on, pumping his hand, so honored don't you know, herding him inside. He can't stop me. It's not nice to body block the elderly. There are a dozen or so folks, still all dressed up for a fund-raiser, standing around having a nightcap with the candidate. He has to make nice with an audience present. Virginia politicians know all too well a cell phone can bring down a senator.

A couple of big-chested fellows are eyeing me. Security obviously. Can't have too much of that. Everyone else is watching to see if I'll be amusing. There's a black lab sitting at the end of a long empty sofa. It's porcelain. Behind it is a wall of windows. "Would you look at the view?" I say. It's a dark night. The room is lit up bright. All there is to see is a bunch of white people reflected in the glass against a black backdrop, like a painting on black velvet of white-faced dogs playing poker.

"You can't really see anything with all the lights on, I'm afraid," says my host, chuckling amiably, professionally.

"It's always something, isn't it? Trees. Lives. Bright lights. I just came by to tell you I'm not voting for you. I don't like your stand on the issues—immigrant labor and watershed management in particular."

The two security guys have been moving in until they're standing on either side of us like we're about to huddle. One reaches inside his jacket and keeps his hand there. His right.

The candidate turns off his bright smile, so I can see inside, where he's actually a good deal meaner than he might first appear to be. But I already knew that. "I'm afraid it's late Mr. . . . ?"

"Lee."

"Mr. Lee. Perhaps if you'd come by my office we could discuss the matter further."

I have to let it go. I have to consider the welfare of others. "I'd rather not." I give it one last look, and they all follow my gaze, all of us glancing back. Mr. Whiskers looks like a faux full moon in the foyer. "Killer view."

He's standing right beside me. He makes a little grunt like I hit him in the gut. Nothing like the sound he'd make if I actually hit him. Nothing like the sound Felix must've made when several tons of tree came crashing down on him. But something.

I show myself out. The security guys watch me drive away, back to the public roads on the other side of a virtual fence, keeping the borders secure.

When the key turns in the lock, I still expect to hear dog struggling to her feet. Before she died I thought this silence would be better than listening to her gradual decline. Not so. Not yet, a little over a week now.

My wife's up, watching a muted television. Wal-Mart is cutting prices.

"How you doing?" she asks.

"Better, I think. What about you?"

"Someone asked at work today how my dog was doing."

"What did you say?"

"I said she had a good life."

"That's what I said too."

"Did you find out anything about the dead man?"

"His name was Felix."

I sit down beside her, and we hold each other in the silence and manage not to cry.

PART II

NUMBERS

It was a town of the cavalier, not the cracker.
—Robert Deane Pharr, on Richmond

THE BATTLE OF BELLE ISLE

BY CLAY MCLEOD CHAPMAN

Belle Isle

They dumped Benny by the river, wearing nothing but a green paper gown. Ambulance must've pulled over, rear doors fanning open. Bet the driver didn't even step out to help her. Just kept the engine running when they left Benny by the side of the road, all disoriented, shivering from the cold. No clothes, no shoes, no idea where she was anymore. Started making her way toward the water, all sixty-three years of herself crawling down the craggy rocks, bare feet slipping over the algae. Rested just next to the James for lord knows how long. All numb now.

There'd been rain out west, so it wasn't long before the river swelled. Couple of hours and the surface probably rose right up to her, currents taking her away. Carrying her downstream for half a mile. Two miles. Maybe more—I don't know. Depends on where they ditched her in the first place, doesn't it? Can't shake this image of her floating over the rocks, half naked, whisked off into the whitewater. The rapids dragging her body along before bringing her back to Belle Isle.

This island had been our home.

After they shut down the Freedom House on Belvidere, you either had to migrate up to Monroe Park or toward the Lee Bridge, where the nearest mission was nestled into this neglected valley on the south side of Chesterfield County, about a mile's walk beyond the city limits. It had been home to some battlefield long forgotten by now. Perfect for a skirmish during the Civil War—not much else. Only neighbors now were a couple of dilapidated factories, the soil all soaked with arsenic. Just about the only thing you could build on top of that poisoned property was a homeless shelter. And this mission—their doors didn't open unless it was below thirty-five degrees. Come 6 a.m., you were woken up and tossed right back into the street no matter how cold it was. Locked their doors until the thermometer reached the right temperature again.

Me and Benny tried our hand at it for a couple nights, hefting everything we owned back and forth over the Lee Bridge, just looking for work. Got all of our belongings on our backs, like a couple of ragged privates marching with fifty pounds of provisions slung over our shoulders. Just praying for the mercury to sink below thirty-five. That one degree's the difference between you and your own cot—even a cup of watered-down coffee—or freezing to death on some park bench.

Can't call that home. Nobody should.

Richmond's labeling all this shifting around *revitalization*—but I'm not buying it. Pushing us out to the periphery. Forcing us to find a new home every night. Their Downtown Plan has nothing to do with me. Never had Benny's better interests in mind. When I first met her, couple years back, the boys-in-blue had just busted her lip for sleeping out in Monroe Park. She shuffled her way into Freedom House after curfew, an icicle of her own blood hanging off her chin. Weren't that many cots left at that hour, so she took the one next to mine. Dropped her plastic bags, all her junk spilling over the floor. I leaned over, thinking I'd lend a hand, getting a slap on the wrist for my troubles.

Don't touch my stuff.

Just trying to help.

Help yourself is more like it.

Asked her what her name was. Her jaw refused to move much because of the cold, just enough to keep her teeth chattering, so when she answered—*Bethany*—I didn't hear the *tha* part. Her tongue missed the middle syllable, like the needle on a record player skipping over a groove.

Sounded like she said *Benny.*

No funny stuff now, she warned, brandishing her wrinkled finger like it was a blade. *I'll have you know I'm a respectable lady.*

There have got to be thirty years between us! The hell are you expecting me to do?

Just better watch it, young man. I've got my eye on you.

Most folks made their way to Monroe Park after Freedom House closed its doors—but that was a trap, if you're asking me. Used to be a training camp for Confederate soldiers. Military hospital after that. Lot of cadets ended up dying on that patch of land. Too many homeless ghosts out there now. People who spend the night there end up disappearing. Some say this city gives you a bus ticket to any town you want, one-way, no questions asked—just hop on board and *bon voyage*—but I'm betting that's a rumor the boys-in-blue spread around town so you drop your guard and follow the brass right into the paddy wagon. Act like some mutt trusting the dogcatcher—transfixed by the biscuit in one hand, not even paying attention to the net in the other.

Benny's vote was Monroe. Mouthing off about the handouts down there. College kids managed a meal plan in the heart of the park, serving up soup on Sundays or something.

Step in there, Benny, I said, *and you won't be walking out ever again.*

You're just being paranoid.

Sure shut down Freedom House fast enough—didn't they? Sure don't see the Salvation Army marching into Monroe to save the day. I'm telling you, Benny—the police own that park!

Then where the hell are we gonna go?

That left Belle Isle. You got the Lee Bridge reaching right over the James River. Just another memorial to another dead Confederate general. Connects the south side of the city to the rest, shore to shore, like a stitch suturing a wound. Got the James bleeding up from that gash, no matter how many bridges there are sewing up this city. But nestled in between the concrete legs of Robert E. Lee, there are about fifty-four acres of public park, all wrapped in water. The river splits, rushing down either side of the isle, its converging currents forming a sharp point at the tip. A real diamond of an island. Only way to reach land is to hoof it. Got this footbridge slung under the interstate, a little baby-bridge suspended from its father. You can hear the hum of automobiles passing along the highway just above your head—but down there, once you've set foot onto the island, it's like the city doesn't exist anymore. Sound of cars just melts away.

We'd be like—like our own Swiss Family Robinson down here.

More like Robinson Crusoe, Benny said, shaking her head.

No one'll bother us, I promise. As long as we stay on the far side of the island, away from the footpaths, no one'll even know we're here.

You're crazy, you know that?

No more missions, no more shelters, I said. *We'll never have to set foot on the mainland again.*

Yeah, yeah—just lead the way, Friday.

There are ruins of an old hydroelectric plant tucked away on the far side of the island. Closed its doors in '63, the electric company gutting out all the iron, leaving the concrete behind. Nothing but a husk now, all empty. Good for a roof over your head when it gets raining. We set up camp in one of the old water turbine rooms. Have to crawl through this hatch just to get in. The air's damp down there. Soaks into your bones if you're not bundled up enough. But the walls keep the cold wind from nipping your nose. Made that room a hell of a lot better than sleeping in some refrigerator box. The generator was long gone, the rotors removed, leaving behind this empty shaft as big as any room in those mansions you see lined up along Plantation Row. We're talking ballroom here. Perfect fit for all of Benny's stuff. She hefted a whole landfill's worth of accumulated junk along with her. A dozen plastic bags busting open at the seams, full of photographs. Toys. Anything she could get her hands on.

Home sweet home, Benny said. Started decorating the place right away, slipping her pictures inside a rusted wicket gate like it was some sort of mantelpiece. All the shorn cylinders were now full of photographs, every severed duct a shelf for her past.

Who's that? I asked, pointing to this one black-and-white snapshot. Cute little brunette smiling for the camera. *She looks familiar to me.*

Who do you think?

You're telling me that's you?

Damn right I am.

Didn't recognize you under all that baby fat.

Yeah, well—they fed me better back then.

The island's supposed to be vacant once the sun sets. Every day, like clockwork, this ranger comes to lock up the footbridge. Not like that ever keeps the kids away. Teenagers always sneak in after dark, building bonfires. Spray-painting the walls.

We had a whole novel's worth of graffiti wrapped around the place. Couldn't really read what it said. The words were barely there anymore, losing their shape. Tattoos fading into your skin, reminding you of different times. Times when those tattoos would've meant something. An eagle, a globe, and an anchor. *Semper Fi.* Nothing but blue lines now, wrapping around your arms like ivy overtaking a statue.

First time Benny saw the ink on my forearm, we were trying to keep each other warm while those teenagers broke beer bottles against the other side of our living room wall. Had to keep quiet, holding each other. That's when she noticed the lower fluke of the anchor, all fuzzy now, diving down deep into my skin. Gave her something to trace her finger along. Watched her run her pinkie over the lower hemisphere of the globe.

Bet it's cold there right about now, she said, pointing to where Antarctica would've been.

Colder than here—that's for sure.

We were in the thick of December by then, the temperature dropping off into the low thirties. It was only going to get colder the deeper into winter we went. That meant less visitors. Less dog walkers. Less joggers. Less families. Less of everything.

You know this used to be a prison camp?

Sure feels like one.

During the Civil War, I said. *Over five hundred thousand Yankee soldiers, right here. Couple thousand at a time, freezing their asses off in the open air.*

You're lying.

It's true.

The more we talked, the more our breath spread over each other. Good way to keep warm. Our mouths were our radiators now.

Since when did you become such a history buff?

They used to march prisoners over the bridge, I said. *Corralled them together like cattle. They went through the whole winter out here like that. Freezing. Starving.*

Sounds familiar.

Slid in next to her. Nestled my knees into the back of her legs, just where they bent. Had my face pressed against her shoulder, breathing into the bone.

They'd bring a surgeon out to check up on the men in the morning, figuring out which limbs he had to saw off from the frostbite.

Everybody in this city's a goddamn Civil War aficionado, she said, inching off without me. Figured that was the end of the conversation—up until Benny turned back around, asking, *So you gonna hold me, soldier? It's cold out here.*

Yes, captain.

Fell asleep first. I was always falling asleep before Benny— drifting off to the sound of her cough, these short retorts right at my ear, like some soldier in the trenches, the sound of musket fire just over my head.

Brought my daughter to Belle Isle once. Couldn't even tell you when anymore. Years ago. A different life. Packed a picnic and everything. Had to get there early, just so we could lay claim to one of the broad rocks resting along the river. We're talking prime real estate here. You ended up battling the sunbathers for the best spread. The Battle of Belle Isle.

Don't go out too far, hon, I said. *You've got to be careful about the currents.*

Benny always had to hold me when I woke up. Wrap her arms around me so I didn't buckle, bring me back to the present tense.

You're okay, you're okay, she'd say. *Just another bad dream, that's all.*

Everywhere you step on this island, there's another history lesson under your feet. Signs saying what happened at that very spot, almost two hundred years ago. Nothing but plaques in the ground. Never would've realized this place could hold so much pneumonia, so much dysentery. That's Richmond for you. Too much history for its own good. Whole city's a grave-yard. It's only when you have no home to call your own that you can see this place for what it really is. You're standing on the graves of men no matter where you step.

The prison camp had been directly below the highest mount on the island, overlooking the river. I remember bring-ing Benny up there, showing her the view for the first time. We could see the Capitol building up north. To the west was Hollywood Cemetery, on the other side of the James. Peters-burg wasn't but so far off, if you squinted hard enough.

Can't see why those soldiers wouldn't just swim for it, Benny said, shaking her head. *Lord knows I would.*

They'd try, I said. *End up getting shot right there in the water. Their bodies would drift downriver. Never set foot on dry land again.*

How do you know about all this stuff?

I just pay attention is all.

Pay attention. A good parent pays attention.

Let's go down there, she said, pointing toward the north side of the island.

Where?

Those big rocks—down there. Where the sunbathers all go.

I'm not setting foot down there, Benny.

Why not?

It's off limits to us.

There's a dam still standing, upstream, left over from the hydroelectric plant. Steers most of the water northward, around the bend and into the rapids. There are signs posted all around the island, warning families about the rapids. *Always have a parent supervising swimming children*, they say. *Don't let your kids go out too far unattended*. A bit of the river's funneled south through this concrete canal, into what's left of the turbines. Generated enough electricity to light up half of Richmond back in the day. Benny's body slipped around the south, into the canal. If she hadn't been dead when she entered the water, she was once she washed into the turbines. Her green paper gown was wrinkled, clinging to her skin like tissue. One sock on her left foot, nothing on the right. Reminded me of those sheep you see getting their coats shorn clean. Once the wool's been buzzed off their bodies, what's left behind seems so much smaller than what was there before. Pink skin. Thin frame. Legs don't even look real.

I'm staring at Benny, lying on her side in the turbine—and I can't help but remember her all bulked up in her jackets, a layer of long johns underneath. She'd just gotten another coat, three sizes too big for her, pulled it out from the lost-and-found at some church. Made her look like a little girl wearing her daddy's jacket, her hands swallowed up by the sleeves. Now she's naked. I'm noticing all the bruises I've never seen before, the abrasions. All the liver spots and melanomas that were hidden from me. Her wrinkles are full of mud, as if the river has tried washing the years away. I've never seen her face so smooth. I can almost imagine what she looked like when she was a girl, like in that photograph. The mud in her hair has dyed the white right out, back to natural brown. Chestnut eyes to match her new brunette curls.

I see the expression in her eyes, glassed over—those last few thoughts that passed through her mind as she wrestled with the river, fighting for dry land.

Afraid. She looks like she was afraid.

I'm imagining her numb hands thrashing through the water, reaching for anything that's going to save her. She's wearing some sort of ID bracelet, orange plastic snapped into place. Her arms are so thin, nothing but skin and bones. The bracelet slides all the way up to her elbow.

Have her listed as *DOE, JANE*. Bastards even took her name away.

She'd been complaining about a cough all week. Hacking up phlegm in her sleep. Sounded awfully deep. Whatever it was, it was rooted within her chest, beginning to block her breathing. The air couldn't reach her lungs without sounding wet.

Jesus, Benny. You sound terrible. Think you better have that looked at.

You my doctor now? Where am I gonna go?

How about a hospital? I asked, pressing the back of my hand against her forehead.

Hospital? Nah. Need to sleep it off is all.

It was easy to feel the fever burning through. Felt so warm, I couldn't help but keep my hand there a little longer than I needed to. Hold onto that heat for a while. Couldn't help but think about all those soldiers, sitting in the cold. Sickest prisoners were always taken to the hospital just on the other side of the island. They were made to stand and wait until their names were taken. Could've been hours before they got called up. If they survived that long, they were led to a ward already cluttered with dozens of others. Sheets were never cleaned. Beds full of vermin. These doctors would rush through the ward like it was a race, seeing who could finish first. I never blamed Benny for distrusting doctors. But there she was, sounding like she was drowning from the inside out. Running her finger along the anchor tattooed on my arm, only sinking deeper into her own lungs.

I'll go to the hospital if you let me ask you something.

Okay, I said.

Why'd we really come here?

I didn't say anything.

What's so important about this place?

I made something up. Something about Civil War relics buried somewhere around here. If we found them, we wouldn't have to worry over nothing ever again.

Hope you find them, she said, not buying it one bit, something pink making its way to her lips. *Whatever's buried here.*

Fell asleep first. I was always falling asleep before Benny did. Closed my eyes and found a familiar flame, this burning yellow one-piece, slipping off into the water without me.

Don't go too far out, hon, I'd said. *Only up to your ankles.*

We'd spread a blanket out across our rock. Lunch was behind us. All we had to do for the remainder of the day was rest next to the river. Take in the sun amongst all the other families. And swim.

But I want to go out there, Daddy.

Too dangerous, sweetie. You've got to be careful about the currents.

The what?

The currents!

Can't say how long I'd been sleeping. I didn't come to until I heard the family from the neighboring rock start shouting. I sat up, squinting from the sun. Couldn't focus at first, watching this flash of yellow disappear into the river.

Her body had turned blue by the time I reached her. I dropped to my knees. Pressed my lips against hers and breathed. I tried pushing the air into her lungs. Her chest would expand. Her rib cage was a pair of ambulance doors fanning open. But the air only seeped out, her chest sinking back down again.

The air wouldn't stay inside my daughter.

Benny didn't wake me up the following morning. Didn't ease me up from my dream like she usually does. I had to snap myself back. Woke up and found her just next to me, barely breathing. Her eyes were wide open, staring up at nothing.

Benny? What's wrong?

I carried her across the underpass, back to the mainland. Hefted her the whole way to the hospital, just praying we'd make it. Lost the feeling in my arms fast, but I held onto her the whole time.

We're almost there, Benny, I said. *Almost there.*

The sliding glass doors parted, welcoming Benny inside. I rushed her right to the front desk, all out of breath. The nurse took one look at us and froze. Stared at me like I was holding up the place.

You've got to help her, I begged. *She's sick with something.*

What's her name? Do you know her name?

Benny, all right? Now just do something!

Spent fifteen minutes in the waiting room. I quickly started to feel like I didn't belong. Looking over all the wounded, the sick. Everyone waiting for a doctor to call out a name. This little girl sitting next to me was as anxious as I was to get the hell out of there, scuffing her heels along the carpet. Her mom took one look at me and moved her daughter a couple rows over. Most folks were giving me a wide berth by then, sitting as far away from me as humanly possible. Then I caught sight of a couple of security guards coming my way. The nurse from the front desk was following right behind them, pointing at me. Panic set into my system, telling me I better act quick. But Benny wouldn't know where to go. She'd think I left her there, just up and abandoned her. The guards picked up their pace as soon as I stood. I cut them off at the sliding glass doors.

They followed me as far as the parking lot before giving up. All the while, I just kept saying to myself, *Belle Isle, Benny. Just meet me back at Belle Isle.*

Three days I wandered around. Took every nature path I could find, weaving in and out of the woods. I read every marker I stumbled upon until there wasn't a corner on the island where I didn't know exactly what had happened. Class was in session. Time for my history lesson. Get up on my Richmond. Wait for Benny to come home.

The dead were buried on the western slope of the island. That's what the sign said. Over a hundred prisoners of war dumped into the dirt. Nothing but burlap wrapped around their bones—the lice wriggling free, trying to hop out before the earth got shoveled over. The bodies remained on Belle Isle until 1864—not long at all. Just a few years in the ground before they were dug back up and reinterred on the mainland. Their bones were taken away, while their ghosts got left behind.

Corporal Edwin Bissel from Iowa. Company D, fifth infantry.

Captain Spencer Deaton. Company B, Tennessee infantry.

Lieutenant J.T. Ketchum. Company M, Richmond artillery.

And now Benny. Couldn't tell you where she was from. Couldn't say if she had any family around here or not. Never mentioned any kids of her own to me. But Benny was my friend. She's the only one buried on Belle Isle anymore, her grave unmarked, her body resting inside the vacant spot of some dug-up soldier. Only person who knows she's out there is me.

I stuffed her photographs into my pockets, layering up. Every jacket was padded with pictures, a Kevlar vest of Benny's memories to protect me. Hadn't left Belle Isle for over a week. The footbridge felt like it was about to snap, rocking under the weight of the traffic passing overhead. I was a bit wobbly at first, setting foot back onto the mainland, as if I'd been at sea all this time. First place I went was Monroe. Make an appearance for the police. Send a message that I was looking for them. When you're after the brass, it's better to let them come to you. So I just rested myself on a bench along the northern portion of the park, right under a magnolia tree. Couldn't have closed my eyes for more than an hour before I got my wake-up call. Nothing but a wooden baton in the ribs, two boys-in-blue encouraging me to move merrily along my way.

Time to get up, one of them said. *Sleep somewhere else.*

I'm looking for my friend.

Who's your friend?

Benny.

He loiter around here too?

If I was going to find out what happened to Benny I would have to go through it myself. Couldn't just waltz into the hospital and ask for a lollipop, expecting them to tell me what the doctors did to her. The only way I was slipping past those sliding glass doors was with an emergency. And for that I needed a little help from my friends. So me and the boys-in-blue did a little Civil War reenactment of our own right there in the heart of Monroe Park. Sure were looking like soldiers to me, more and more, anyhow. Their cadet-blue uniforms. Their Jefferson boots. One stripe on their shoulder for every five years of faithful service. I went ahead and shoved my elbow into the stomach of the closest artilleryman. He buckled over, leaving me and the other soldier to share a few fists back and forth. Got a baton straight across the face. Busted my nose right open. Wasn't long before the other soldier got his breath back, swinging right along. Some swift hits to the stomach came my way. Then the chest. Before I knew it, I was on my knees, this heat swelling up in my gut.

We catch you in the park again—next time, we're arresting you.

Where's Benny?

Fed a few loose teeth to the pigeons, spitting them to the ground like bloody bread crumbs. Watched the birds scurry up, pecking away. Must've been hungrier than me.

Not gonna tell you again.

What'd you do to her?

I blacked out after that. It gets a little patchy from here on. Memories begin to blend together; it was pretty difficult to tell whose history was whose anymore. I woke up in a waiting room. Could've been there for hours, staring up at the ceiling. Hum of fluorescents might as well have been flies buzzing about my body. Felt this fire inside my stomach. An oil lamp had busted open in my belly, kerosene leaking from my spleen. Nurses hovering over my head. None of them liked the smell of me.

One of them said, *Got another homeless here.*

Speaking like I don't understand English.

Humana? Unicare?

Acting like they couldn't hear me. *Where's Benny?*

Blue Cross?

What'd you do with Benny?

Kept hearing the same word, over and over—*Insurance? Insurance?*

All I had was an eagle and an anchor.

Another asked, *Name?*

I answered right back: *Lieutenant J.T. Ketchum. Company M, Richmond artillery.*

She called out, *This one's a vet, I guess.*

Damn right I'm a vet. I served my country. I fought at the Battle of Belle Isle. I have defended this city my whole life. I have given Richmond everything. My daughter. My best friend. I've got nothing now. What's left of me to give?

My colon, apparently. Had something hooked up to my side—I could feel it. A plastic bag. Reminded me of one of Benny's bags with all her junk. One of Benny's bags was attached to my abdomen, itching like a son of a bitch. Every time I tried scratching, some nurse slapped my hand away.

Just trying to help, I said.

Help yourself is more like it, she shot back, easing a needle into my arm. Suddenly the room went all soft. My tattoos felt fuzzy. The eagle on my forearm sank deeper into my skin, its talons dragging the earth down with it.

Just when you think you've got nothing left to give, there's always something more for this city to take away. Even your history. I'm back at the prison camp. Gangrene's lingering in the air. Rotten cheese. Got to keep the flies off—otherwise, they'll lay their eggs in my wounds. Neglected men everywhere, suffering from exposure. Fingers and feet lost to frostbite. Typhoid fever. Dysentery. My miserable comrades are dying all around me as the morning shift takes over, new nurses asking the same questions—*Anthem?*

What'd you do to Benny?

Carefirst?

What'd you do to my friend?

Clothes are gone. My shoes are gone. Got me in this green paper gown now.

Green paper gown. *Green paper gown.*

I'm in a wheelchair, rolled out into the parking lot. It's morning. Sun's just rising. An ambulance pulls up in front of me. I'm told to hold my colostomy bag as it drops into my lap. Feels soft inside. The guy behind the wheel's asking for an address.

Where you want to go? You got to give me an address, pal.

Only address that's coming to mind is Freedom House. On Belvidere.

There's no shelter on Belvidere anymore, he says as we drive off. *Shut that one down a long time ago.*

The ambulance stops. Back doors fan open. I'm met with the winter sun. I can see my breath fog up before me. I see the James.

I see the river.

Richmond could've cared less about Benny. She was just another blip of banal city bureaucracy. They dumped her along the river—up and dumped her as far away from themselves as they could, hoping the currents would carry her the rest of the way. What happened to her must happen in that hospital all the time. Because here it is, happening to me.

The driver won't let me keep the wheelchair. All I get is my colostomy bag. He tosses a Ziploc next to me, full of photographs. None of these faces look familiar. Can't tell if they're my family or not. I slip the edge of the pouch between my teeth, carrying it in my mouth as I crawl across the rocks. My green paper gown softens in the water, adhering itself to my body like a second layer of skin. The river's cold—but before long, all feeling is gone. I know I'm moving, I know I'm on my back. I can see my arms pushing through the water. My colostomy bag must be keeping me afloat, bobbing along the surface. Everything I own is inside.

A few photographs loosen themselves from the Ziploc between my teeth, floating along the water without me. Suddenly I'm surrounded by spinning pictures, swirling over the surface, moving downstream. One of them floats up in front of me. Black-and-white. Cute little brunette smiling for the camera. Reminds me of someone I used to know. Lost her in this river, long ago. Never been able to get her back. And here's history repeating itself again. Like getting caught in a whirlpool. Sucking me under. Looking at that photograph, bobbing through the water—I'm watching my daughter swim downriver with me, the two of us drifting along together.

That's Richmond for you. This city's built upon bones. What isn't buried simply washes downriver. It's a matter of hitting the right current. Ease myself to the southern side of the James. Keep to the right and I'll make it.

Got to make my way back to Belle Isle.

Got to head home.

A LATE-NIGHT FISHING TRIP

BY X.C. ATKINS

Oregon Hill

It was around the hour when the sun began to sink into the James River and the lights of downtown Richmond came on and made the city look as big and grand as it wished it could be. The air was warm and thick. It made me think of maple syrup. There was a small breeze that picked up when I pushed my good foot on the accelerator. One arm hung out the window, the other with a hand on the wheel and a smoke between the knuckles. I was driving into Oregon Hill and I wasn't happy about it.

Denby and Reggie Baker had just moved into the neighborhood. Cheaper rent, they told me. If you happened to be meandering through on a shiny afternoon you might see why. Oregon Hill was a dirty place and it was a nasty place. It was a place where stray cats could raise families. The gaunt houses were packed together and looked like the trees out in front of them: old, tired, and resentful. The porches sagged into themselves like wet cardboard, and Confederate flags hung with no wind to give them false glory. The lawns, if they had anything growing in them at all, grew wild and unkempt. Random objects stuck out from these yards, rusted machinery that had long since ceased to operate, children's toys. There were families here, white families, that hadn't yet moved out into the depressing alcoholic counties beyond Richmond, and they had a hell of a chip on their shoulders. The nights were deathly quiet but there was always something moving, shadow-to-shadow, and whatever it was knew when there was someone in the neighborhood who didn't belong. It was the feeling I had every time I paid a visit. And every time it felt like I was sneaking in.

I made a right onto China Street and parked a half a block down from where the brothers lived. I got out of my beat-up burgundy Dodge slowly, with my wrapped left foot in the air. I pulled out a pair of aluminum crutches, stood up, also very slowly, locked the door, and moved onto the sidewalk.

Many of the red dusty bricks that made the sidewalk were broken or missing and in between them grass sprouted. I tried to step quickly on my crutches without looking like I was in a hurry. Denby and Reggie might have been all right in the neighborhood initially because they were white. But it was their visitors who were going to end up getting them in trouble.

As I was coming up to the brothers' house, I could make out two people sitting on the porch of the place next door. No light illuminated the porch and I couldn't see their faces. Two men, from the looks of them. They sat in their chairs, smoking cigarettes, as silent as the neighborhood around them. I could tell by the direction of their heads that they were staring at me. I didn't stare back. This wasn't anything new. My skin couldn't help but get that crawling feeling, a feeling that made me very aware of that same skin's color. The two men could have been a part of the house if not for the smoke twisting into the air and the rising and falling red dots of cigarettes held by invisible hands. Behind their screen door, past the darkness, I thought I could hear something growl. It was a low growl that sounded like it came from something big. Maybe it was the house. I kept going and got to the place I meant to get to.

Denby and Reggie's house didn't put on much of a front.

A pair of beat-up sneakers sat next to the door that had no screen and the address was missing one of its golden digits. I was coming up the three steps of the porch when the door flung open, smacking against the rail of the porch. A girl came stomping out.

It was dark so I couldn't quite make out the hue of her eye shadow but I could tell it was Ebone and she wasn't happy. It was all the swearing that gave it away. I'd always found it amusing to hear people with British accents swear.

Her hair was short and sleek and a golden bird shook violently under each earlobe. She wore a zebra-print tank top and black hot pants, all of this showing a lot of the dark smooth skin I had found myself admiring the one night we had gone out for drinks with some mutual friends. That night, she'd been dancing on top of a bar with a drink in each hand. Now, her heels ground into the porch wood and she came down the stairs and went right past me without any word I took as directed to myself. She headed on down the block and didn't trip once.

When I turned back to the door, Denby Baker was standing there.

"Hey, bo." His voice was raspy, as if it'd been rubbed raw with a Brillo Pad. It matched the beard on his face and the Newport hanging from his bottom lip. He readjusted his Yankees cap, adorned with the brothers' trademark golden fish hook on the bill, and showed a perfect row of teeth while he held the door open for me to come through.

"Hey, Derb," I said, and passed him on the way to the kitchen. I leaned against the counter in the middle of the room next to an empty sink and a large microwave. The only thing on top of the counter was a set of jade dice. "Thought you were done with her."

"I am. That's why she was all in a huff. I can't even stand to listen to her talk. The accent lost its charm probably around the third time she scammed me. Ain't no way I'ma hook her up with nothing. Told her to beat it. It's nothing. Hey, how's life on the crutch though, Levy?"

"Hell on the armpits. But at least now I can grow out my beard like you two bozos seeing as how I can't work. I try to be a glass-half-full kinda guy."

"Speaking of glasses half full, how about a beverage?"

"Night's getting better already."

He stepped past me and opened the fridge. All that was inside of it was a twelve-pack of Milwaukee's Best, a jar of mayo, a loaf of bread, and a very large plastic bag full of marijuana. He grabbed two cans of beer, opened one, and handed it to me.

I took a healthy sip out of the can and said, "Your neighbors aren't creepy at all, by the way."

"Yeah. They're backwards as hell. But they're all right. Just sit on the porch and drink. See some dogs in the backyard here and there. Big boys." He took down practically half of his beer in one extended gulp. "Crazy thing is though," he continued, "me and Regg see girls come over there every now and again. Half decent too—I mean, no peg leg or hook at the wrist. It's suspect, real suspect."

"Kiddin' me?"

"Nope. Ain't no gun to their heads neither."

I gave him an unconvinced, "Huh."

Reggie came running down the stairs. He looked almost identical to his brother except his hair came down to his shoulders, he was taller, and he was lighter in the paunch. He entered the living room wearing a ridiculous outdoorsman vest and no shirt underneath, long jean shorts, and sneakers with socks pulled up right under his knees. In his hand he had a plastic container with what looked like dirt in it.

"Let's go fishin', boys!"

"Where to?" I asked.

"Docks on the James."

"I'm with it," I shrugged and looked at Denby.

"Lemme grab the kush." He took a small plastic bag out of a drawer and went to the fridge, filling it with marijuana from the larger bag. He stuffed that in his pocket, grabbed his beer, and we were out the door. The neighbors were no longer on the porch smoking.

We took their car. I kept my beer can low in my seat as we made a left onto Belvidere. In five blocks only six police cars passed us. We made a right onto Cary and slid down hills that brought us downtown. The streets and buildings looked like a world inside a lightbulb, all yellow and empty. Further down, past all the buildings occupied by suits in the daytime, the road became cobblestone.

Hotels and restaurants provided a different kind of light in Shockoe Slip. A group of brightly dressed young people stood outside of Tobacco Company contemplating where to get their next cocktail.

We made a left onto 14th and then a right on Main. The train tracks were raised into the sky above us, along with I-95. They created a dark ceiling, illuminated dimly by streetlights to give everything the grainy look that always made people from the West End reluctant to visit. When they did, they had to get drunk, and fast. The droves weren't parading the streets this night, however. It wasn't yet the weekend. But the traffic was still heavy.

We went past downtown, riding east on Main Street, past

Church Hill, away from the city. Everything became very dark and the night lost the sounds that people made. There were more train tracks down this way and the James River became visible as we passed through or under a large building that must have served as a kind of gateway at some point in history. Now, it was only a shell. Richmond had a lot of that kind of history.

A large white yacht was harbored on the docks. During the week it gave tours. Tables with white cloth draped over them could be seen inside the yacht through the windows. We parked the car a little ways down from where the boat was docked and unpacked the fishing rods, tackle box, bait, and booze. In the daytime it was fine to fish next to the yacht. People from all walks of life came out, set up chairs, and spent long hours fishing amiably. We wouldn't fish there though. Several lights set next to the boat and in the parking lot made the whole area very bright. There weren't any other cars out there, which wasn't any surprise, considering the hour. Still, it was too out in the open for what we had in mind.

Reggie took us away from the yacht toward where the trees came in and the river narrowed. We could hear the current rushing past in the dark. There was just enough light from the moon to make out a path. It wasn't a long walk before we got through the trees and had to work down a thin path that took me awhile to navigate on crutches. The path led to a smaller dock with no one else in sight.

We set everything down on the dock and I started on a new beer. The brothers began to rig the rods. They used a Carolina rig, which had a weight on the line that would sink to the bottom of the river. There would be enough line after the weight that the bait we put on the hook would float up several inches. The moon was bright over the moving river, causing the rocks that protruded from it to glow. It seemed like the arrangement of the rocks changed every summer.

We could see to the other side of the riverbank almost clearly, but where we were, with the trees hanging over us, shielding us from the moonlight, we were practically invisible. I guessed I could hurl a potato across the river and reach the other side. Maybe.

Reggie pulled out the plastic container of dirt and began to pick through it. When his hand came out he had a squirming night crawler.

"I got a feeling about it tonight, bo," Reggie said to me.

"Yeah. A big catfish maybe?" I said between sips, watching Denby pack a bowl with what I could already smell was strong weed.

"That'd be great. Reel one of those big boys in. Yep." Reggie stood up, his rod set and the worm dangling from the hook. He swung back gently, one finger holding the line, and then cast. It went out very far and made a good-sounding splash. Denby and I both commented that it was a nice cast.

"So what happened with your foot, Lev? Derb told me you jumped off a balcony or something?" Reggie asked, looking over his shoulder in my direction.

"Derb, damn, man. No. I didn't jump off any balcony."

He grinned, though I couldn't see it. I could just tell by how the words came out of his mouth. "Who were you running from?"

"I didn't jump off any damn balcony!"

"Whoa! Easy there, buddy. Just inquiring, just inquiring. What is it, Sensitive Tuesday?"

"It's Wednesday, you idiot," Denby said.

"What is it, Sensitive Wednesday?"

We laughed and the freshly packed bowl began to circulate. After I'd taken my first turn, each proceeding cast I made into the river became worse. I didn't care very much. We were laughing and I forgot about my foot and the other things that troubled me and became comfortable on the dock in the dark. Several times I lost my bait, either in a terrible cast or getting snagged by the brush on the bottom of the riverbed. I slowly became more concerned with drinking, if only to balance myself out. I felt the rig finally pull loose from a failed cast and was reeling it in when we heard a single scream. It came from the other side of the river. It came from a girl.

The rod almost fell from my hands. Across the river we could see a girl skidding in the leaves and dirt down to the bank. She got back on her feet and started running along the bank. She wasn't wearing much of anything. Her dark hair was long and looked wild in the moonlight.

Seconds behind her something came crashing down from the trees and almost rolled itself into the river. It was a dog and it was the size of a small bear. It got back on its four feet quickly and started chasing the girl. It didn't take long for it to catch up to her. The girl's screams were cut short but the few that she got out were the most terrible sounds I'd ever heard. Sounds that would stay with me for many years and echo inside my deepest darkest dreams. It was at that moment that I dropped my rod.

First it fell on the dock with a thud that shook all of us back to life. The metal of the reel clattered. The rod tipped over the edge and since I hadn't reeled it in completely, the current took the weight and pulled the rod in as quickly as a vacuum sucking up a dust bunny. The splash shouldn't have been so loud.

I looked back across the river and saw two men standing on the bank. We couldn't make out their faces but we could tell they were facing our direction. Lights were suddenly beaming toward us where we stood on the dock. They had flashlights. Then the dog jumped into the river with a splash that told us exactly how big it was.

"Go! Go! Go!" Denby was half yelling, half whispering. The brothers were grabbing everything they could. The tackle box wasn't latched and half of the lures and hooks and weights came spilling out when Denby tried to scoop it up. He left the spilled items there and put the box under his arm, with his rod in the other hand, and started running up the path into the woods. I was in front of Reggie and tried following Denby when I realized that was impossible, my heel was still broken. My leg twisted on the path and I went down. An incredible pain lanced up my leg. I grabbed at it and tried my best to be a tough guy.

Then Reggie was pulling me up and had his arm around my waist and we were moving. We couldn't exactly run but I was skipping furiously. It didn't make any sense that the dog had jumped into the water. I couldn't believe it would make it across the river, and even if it were strong enough, the current would take it much further down than where we'd been spotted. It would never catch us in time. All that logic did little to ease the incredible measure of fear pounding inside of me.

We stayed on the path through the forest, more or less. I felt my legs being ripped by shrubs and branches as we stumbled along, made blind by terror and adrenaline. I couldn't hear anything; I was breathing too hard.

The trees cleared away once again and there was still another hundred or so yards to the car. We could see Derby already at the car with the trunk open, throwing whatever he'd managed to grab inside. He slammed the trunk and then jumped behind the wheel. Instead of bringing the car to us, he sat inside and screamed from the window, "Come on! Hurry up!" I really didn't want to keep him waiting.

Reggie got me to the door, opened it, and all but threw me in. Then he jumped in next to me, not even bothering to run around the car to sit shotgun. The vehicle started moving before Reggie got the door closed.

"Roll up the fucking windows!" Denby was screaming.

Reggie and I both looked toward the trees. If we could have rolled up the windows with a handle we would have. But all any of us could do was put our finger on a button and wait for it to come up at its own pace. The monster of a dog was moving full speed from the black of the trees. It had a savage way of running. I could see dirt hiking up from where its claws were tearing the earth. The lights in the parking lot showed us that the animal's thick fur was reddish-brown and, even with the water it had just swam through matting down most of it, already beginning to puff back out. Its tail had a peculiar way of curling. Its face, which I could barely see, was stretched back across its teeth. We couldn't see its eyes.

Denby put the car in reverse and we swung back wildly. By the time he shifted gears again we heard the dog smash into the back of us and felt the car dip with its weight. It clawed against the metal and started crawling forward. We screamed at Denby to start driving. He did. The dog was on the roof of the car then. The tires made a horrible sound as they went over the train tracks we'd passed to get to the docks. Then Denby came to a sharp stop. Reggie and I almost kissed the windshield with our foreheads. The dog didn't have any windshield. It went flying in front of the car. Denby stomped on the pedal. We heard a piercing whine and felt the car thud viciously over something much larger than a speed bump. I turned in my seat and looked back out the window. The dog lay very still in the street. It still looked huge.

"What the hell just happened? Does someone want to tell me?" Denby was yelling from behind the wheel.

The brothers began talking over one another heatedly, each with his own theories. I sat quietly for a moment, trying to catch my breath. I felt like I had asthma. I needed a bellows shoved down my throat. We didn't realize we could put the windows down until we were halfway to the brothers' house. My shirt was soaked in sweat. It dawned on me I only had one of my crutches.

I wasn't very vocal during the ride home. The brothers were doing enough talking. I was trying to wrap my head around what we'd just witnessed. A girl running around in her underwear next to the river. Sure, it was warm enough. So what about Cujo? More importantly, what about the guys who'd sicced him on the girl? The thought put a miserable taste in my mouth and I didn't know how many drinks it would take to get it out. I wanted to take my throbbing foot and throw it out the window.

"Sorry about the fishing rod, guys."

"Did the dog rip the throat out of that chick? What the hell do we do now?" Reggie was leaning forward, clutching the seat.

"I don't know what all we can do. Call the cops, I guess." Maybe the body would still be there. Maybe both bodies.

"Do you think they got a good look at us?" Reggie asked.

"No shot in hell. No way. Not from all the way over there," Denby said.

I thought briefly about how easy it was to run into somebody you didn't want to see in Richmond. An asshole, an ex-girlfriend, a murderer. The city could be awfully small.

We turned into Oregon Hill. We'd been driving very fast up until then, but when we came to where the neighborhood started, Denby pulled it back to a crawl. I couldn't make up my mind about whether this was the adrenaline leaving him or because he realized we were coming back into Oregon Hill. I would've felt safer driving around Richmond in the car or, even better, out of the city altogether, but I kept my mouth shut. It was very late by then. A few kids passed us on bicycles as we got out of the car. The bars were closed. We stood still until they rode off the block.

The living room held a large collection of DVDs and a flat screen on the wall. The television was a gift from their mother. Several framed posters of horror flicks hung on the walls. I sat on the leather sofa and took out a cigarette and lit it. It didn't taste right in my mouth. I put it out in one of the empty beer cans on their glass coffee table. The room was cold, even in the summertime. Denby sat next to me on the sofa and Reggie took a seat in the corner of the room. We all stared at the floor or the wall or our shoelaces but avoided looking at each other. No one had anything to say, so we just sat there in the silence. Then we heard the kitchen door open. Reggie and I looked at Denby, as if it were his responsibility to lock the door. My eyes were all but bulging out.

Heels were clicking on the wood, followed by heavy boots. Ebone walked into the room. Her legs looked very nice in heels. Behind her was a black guy with a shaved head, a low-hanging gold chain, and wrists about as thick as my neck. He was only about seven feet tall.

"You really should lock your door, boys. I wouldn't exactly rate this as a safe neighborhood," she said. Her smile had as much venom as a King Cobra.

"This isn't really the time, Ebone," Denby started.

"I'm here to get that bag off of you, Denby. That's why I brought Maurice here. I hate to get nasty but you know how I am when I don't get what I want. I guess I'm spoiled."

I stood up. "Now listen here, you crazy—"

Maurice took a step toward me. I sat back down. Ebone laughed.

"What the hell are you going to do? You don't even have two crutches," she sneered. "Tough guy on one foot." She turned back to Denby. "So? Where is it?"

"Ebone, we already had this talk. I got nothing for you. If anybody should have anything for another body, it oughta be you. You swindled me, remember? Where do you get off?" I could tell he wanted to sound hard, but with the recent course of events and the present size of Maurice, his voice was strained and borderline soft. Though I wasn't exactly in a position to judge.

She came up close to Denby and played with his ear. "You're really gonna hold that against me, Denby? I thought we were friends?" she purred.

"Maybe if you make right."

"I tried to do that earlier tonight. You didn't seem to like my deal then."

"Discounts are out, Eb."

"Well . . ." She started walking away from him then. "I guess you and Maurice are going to have to play. I really think you'd have liked playing with me better though, Denby. We had fun once."

Maurice walked further into the room. I grabbed my crutch, almost holding it as if it were a bat. It's what I had a mind to use it as.

From behind Ebone we heard the door open again. Everyone froze and turned, looking toward the hallway leading into the kitchen.

Ebone started to back into the living room with us and came to stand next to Maurice. Two men walked into the room. One of them was very thin with a flat ugly nose and a trucker hat. The other was taller but had a beer belly that stuck out from under his white T-shirt and a full reddish beard. The thin one held a crutch he didn't need that looked very familiar to me. The tall one had a gun in his hand.

"We havin' us a party?" the thin one asked. He smiled and showed us his bad teeth. He raised the crutch. "I think you lost something."

"Hey, neighbor, now isn't exactly the best time . . ." Denby said.

No one seemed to care about Denby's schedule.

"Normally, we don't like to meddle, even if we do see folks we don't particularly like to see in our neck of the woods, ain't that right, Greg?"

"What, you mean niggers, Walt?" Greg, the taller one, replied.

"Precisely precise. And hell, we can even respect most anybody who enjoys the sport of fishing. I guess you boys just happened on a bad spot."

"A little further up by the bridge ain't bad fishin'," Greg said.

"Who the hell are you hillbillies?" Ebone demanded. The sound of her voice made me wince. The timing was off too.

Greg motioned the gun at her and Walt barely had time to grab his wrist before it fired. It didn't stop the shot but it did save her life. Instead, the bullet caught Maurice in the belly. His shirt began to show red quickly and he took a step forward. He made an awful sound. Greg fired two more times at the big man. Neither of these shots missed.

Maurice fell on his face and he was as heavy as he looked. The crash made almost as much noise as the gunshots.

"Jesus H, Greg! What'd you shoot for?"

"I didn't mean to, but he looked like he was making a move, man!"

"Yeah, cause you shot him!"

"I thought we was gonna to shoot 'em anyway!"

"Yeah, but you was aimin' at her! Be a waste to pop her here. We can play the game with her. She ain't a bad piece, even she is a nigger."

I had a bad habit of talking before I thought better of it. Maybe two people getting murdered right in front of me made me act stupid. "Is that what you were doing down there? Playing a game? Siccing a dog on steroids to rip a girl apart? What kind of fucked-up country bastards are you?"

Greg's face twisted up at that, but Walt just started showing us his teeth again.

"We love our dogs. They get bored just like we do. 'Cept they can't drink no beer. Or at least they don't like it all too much. And I do love to see a girl go for a run. Now, on your feet, gimpy. We gon' take us a field trip."

No one had been paying much attention to Reggie. It was a mistake not to pay attention to a man in an outdoorsman vest. No one had seen him unsheathe a machete in the corner of the room. Without a word, he swung it into Walt's arm. There was a shrill scream, like an elementary school fire alarm. Greg pointed the gun at Reggie but I'd already consented to their previous command and gotten to my feet. I swung my remaining crutch into Greg's face with all the muscle I had. The bolt I used to adjust the height of the crutch must have hit him right between the eyes. Blood spurted out everywhere and he fell to the floor, clutching his face, dropping his gun.

Ebone started screaming. She ran out of the room as fast as her heels could carry her. Denby scooped the gun up and pointed it at the bleeding men lying on his floor. The two who were still alive.

"Where the hell did you get a fucking machete from?" I yelled. I didn't mean to yell. It just seemed like the only way anyone could talk at a time like this.

"I dressed as Rambo this past Halloween," he said.

I got my cell phone out and called the police. My asthma was back.

In minutes there were enough cops at the house to have a parade. They took Greg and Walt to get bandaged up so they wouldn't stain the backseats of their squad cars. We told our stories so many times it felt as if it were one of the movies in Reggie's DVD collection. The officers radioed someone to check if the body of a girl or a dog could be found down by the docks. In an hour they got a negative on both accounts but found a lot of blood in the location we'd described. They found all the stuff we'd left behind on the docks as well. They only mentioned the beer. To be cute. They guessed the body of the girl would be found in the river.

The cops gave Reggie some trouble about the machete but relented some when they saw he owned every *Rambo* on DVD and had a life-sized poster hanging in the upstairs hallway. In any event, they took the machete with them. The entire time the police were in the house, Denby was constantly talking and moving around. It wasn't surprising at first, since that was Denby's way. Then suddenly it seemed like something more.

"Does Derb seem nervous to you, Regg?" I whispered discreetly to him.

"Could have something to do with all the tree we got in the fridge," Reggie said under his breath.

I lit a cigarette and began massaging my scalp furiously.

They raided the neighbors' house and didn't find anything too peculiar, for an Oregon Hill residence, until they went into the basement. There they found three more dogs in cages, all different breeds, each about as eager to get its jaws on someone's throat as the one we'd run over. They searched the truck the neighbors owned and found the body of the dog underneath a tarp. Of course, they wouldn't leave their beloved pet behind. It was identified as a Chow but of considerably greater size than normal. So far the police had everything except the body of the girl. That would turn up. All we could do was wonder who she was.

When asked about the big black guy lying on the living room floor, we just said he was a newly made acquaintance we didn't know all too well, which was kind of true. That didn't sit well with them but there wasn't much they could do about it right then. They found identification on him, took him out of the house, and told us to skip any foreseeable trips.

No one said a word about Ebone. Denby was doing most if not all of the talking by then, which Reggie and I were happy to let him do. I didn't know why Ebone didn't come up, but neither did I care very much to add anything else that would keep the police around any longer. I wanted them out almost as bad as the brothers did.

The sun was well upon its ascent by the time they all left. I sat on the leather sofa, leaning forward on my two crutches. My foot hurt, my shoulders hurt, my eyes hurt. But I couldn't keep my good foot from tapping and my palms from sweating.

"So . . . why didn't we mention Ebone? Besides the irritation it would cause?"

"She did me a favor," Denby answered.

"How?"

"Before she left she must've took the kush out of the fridge. If the cops had found it, I'd be sitting between those redneck fucks for distribution."

"Wow. Ebone comes through in the clutch. By scamming you. Again." I leaned back, letting myself sink into the sofa as I closed my eyes.

"That bitch," Denby grunted.

"Who do you think she was?" Reggie asked.

"Who?"

"The girl. That got killed."

"Who were any of them? They probably all bought it. All the ones we've seen. All the same way. We've been living next to these guys for almost two months now. I'm getting sick thinking about it. What are we doing living here?" Denby said, smoking a Newport rapidly.

"The rent's cheap," I replied. The Baker brothers didn't say anything. I kept my eyes closed. I didn't go to sleep. I just kept my eyes closed. I was picturing myself walking out of the house and into my car and driving out of Oregon Hill. It was early so it wouldn't be too hot outside yet.

THE HEART IS A STRANGE MUSCLE

BY LAURA BROWDER

Church Hill

Rachel's beeper went off just as her back began growing numb, jammed against the pieces of broken and discarded furniture in the storage room. A second later, Bobby's went off too. She unwrapped her legs from around his sweaty back, pulled herself up to a sitting position, and groped through the jumble of clothing and guns.

Six squads, Church Hill, multiple gunshots.

"They're at it again, huh?" Bobby was already shoving his wilting erection into frayed boxers, reaching for his trousers. "No respect for a man's lunch hour."

Part of her training, Rachel could get into full battle rattle in two minutes flat. She slipped out the door while Bobby was still strapping on his holster, past the hedge of boxwoods that Vaughn loved for their evocative fragrance. To her they just smelled of cat piss.

She had moved to Richmond with Vaughn four years ago, his dream more than hers. He loved the Civil War, the relics, the history. They had spent hours together wandering the pretty streets up in Church Hill, the whole area looking like a nineteenth-century theme park with its gas lamps, wrought iron, and carefully restored brick houses. It was lovely, but for her money they could have stayed in Rochester.

She could say this for him: Vaughn always knew how to

make anything sound good. Even when she was in the same place with him, sharing the same moment, he could make her see it differently. Strolling with him through Chimborazo Park, through the alleys where small crape myrtles wilted and the bright claws of someone's abandoned steamed-crab lunch reeked in the August heat, Rachel could let herself relax into his descriptions of how things had been a hundred-plus years ago: thousands of wounded soldiers stretched out on the lawn under tents, surviving horrible injuries in the world's largest hospital. Now, thinking it over, Rachel couldn't imagine why he found the idea of all those festering wounds so romantic. But back then, she probably did too.

Romantic now meant late-night drives down by the river with Bobby. The kind of guy, actually, she'd had the good sense not to hook up with that whole year at Al Asad, though not for lack of opportunities. He was a big guy, knew how to carry himself, brown eyes, tight ass. Not super talkative, good guy to have around when things got rough, not given to whining, flirtatious.

Now she was actually sleeping with her partner, what Vaughn would have called fouling her own nest and Bobby would have called shitting where she lived. Except that he wouldn't: they both felt right now that they were exceptions to this excellent general rule.

Riding down Broad Street with him, their sirens wailing, Coke turning warm and slushy in her crumpling paper cup, she asked, "Where we headed, anyway? Gilpin Court?"

He cut her a look sideways, slowing down just a little for the light on 25th before blasting on through. "Nah, it's Libby Terrace."

"They didn't say who." Before she could stop herself. There was one door she had thought about putting a few bullets through herself during one of her unauthorized midnight drives—past Vaughn's new place, a renovated carriage house with a view of the old Libby Prison, where they used to starve the dysenteric Union POWs in filthy, overcrowded cells. Supposedly, Mr. Libby had built the giant corner house to give him a good view of what was happening there, and at a second, filthier prison down on Belle Isle. What he had hoped to see with his spyglass trained on the prison in the middle of the river, Rachel couldn't begin to imagine. On the other hand, she pretty much knew what she was looking for on her late-night drive-bys.

She had gotten the "Dear Jane" letter her third month at Al Asad, when deployment no longer seemed like some kind of sick joke but before she was completely used to it. She had joined the Reserves for the college education because her mom didn't have the money to help her out. It had seemed like a great idea at the time, but then there they were, sweating away in the 130-degree heat, on the base everyone called Camp Cupcake because it had a Burger King and a nice gym and KBR lobster tails and T-bone steaks once a week. Well, yeah, lobster tails, but they were also getting mortared just about every night that February she got the letter.

When the incoming began at night she would put on her Kevlar, roll under her cot with a flashlight, and read the letter again: *Dear Rachel, These are the hardest words I have ever had to write.* Like hell they were. The mortars kept coming. If they landed too close, they could jar your organs. You didn't even need to get hit with shrapnel to sustain permanent damage. When she got to the phrase she hated most—*the human heart is a strange muscle*—what the hell did he mean by that? Had he plagiarized it from somewhere?—Rachel didn't care how close the mortars hit.

Her sergeant had taken her over to JAG, where it seemed like even the air-conditioning worked better. Miserable-looking soldiers waited their turns to see the lawyers; Sergeant Mackey had stood with his hand on her shoulder, steady pressure, while the JAG lawyer—bland, smooth-faced, young—helped her fill out all the paperwork, professional, like everyone in that office, but bored like she had seen it a thousand times before, which she no doubt had.

Rachel's friends moved all of her stuff out of the row house she and Vaughn had shared in the Fan, leaving behind the carved Victorian sofa with the apricot velvet upholstery, the Queen Anne end table from his grandmother, the framed engravings depicting scenes from the war—not her war. When she had arrived home last fall, she'd had to MapQuest the new Northside apartment she'd rented.

Another ambulance screamed by them, then another, jolting her out of her memories. They were already way up Broad Street. The car was stuffy, the seat sticky against her legs. Early afternoon in May and it felt like summer was already getting started. Rachel could feel the familiar adrenaline rush building, better than sex, really, though sex with Bobby was pretty good. She loved the familiar pressure of her Glock against her rib cage, loved the way details seemed to jump out at her from the street rushing by: coffee shop sign, dressed-up toddler throwing herself facedown in a tantrum on the sidewalk outside, the blur of summer annuals in riotous colors.

"Jesus, that's a lot of action," Bobby commented.

"Hang a right here," she said as they got to the light on 29th.

"You been here before, huh?"

"Why you giving me that look?"

Bobby smirked at her. "We used to get calls from the

neighbors, complaining about some chick's bare feet pressed up against a car window."

"Wasn't me," Rachel replied.

"Can't beat the view," Bobby said. "We should take a lunch break here some time."

"What kind of a break do you have in mind?" Jesus, she was starting to sound like an idiot. So . . . high school.

He looked at her and reached out to tuck a stray piece of dark hair back behind her ear. He had great skin, freckled and translucent, a broad, slightly curved nose that she loved to trace with her fingers, brown hair that looked redder in the sun.

Behind the median filled with garish crape myrtles in bloom, Wehmeyer and Carlson were smoking a cigarette. Had they noticed? She'd be fucked if she kept it together for a year in Iraq, gave no one any reason for gossip, only to blow it now. Cops were worse than soldiers when it came to the rumor mill, and that was saying a lot. And once the rumors started, life would be no fun anymore.

"Nice place to eat a sandwich, talk."

"Sure, Bobby."

"Whaddya think, some rich drunk cleaning his antique guns?"

"Some loss," Rachel said, and looked out the window again.

Bobby pulled to a halt on Libby Terrace, behind a couple of other cop cars. She could feel him looking at her, but she didn't turn her head. "You ever gonna tell me what happened over there?"

"I always liked that you never asked," Rachel said, unbuckling her seat belt and swinging herself out the door. She stood for a minute peering out at the glittering river, listening to Bobby slam his door, then turned back to face him.

"Rach, I been thinking," Bobby began. In the harsh sun-light she could see his crow's feet as he squinted at her. "It's been what, six months, for Christ's sake."

"Yeah. Store rooms, lovers' lanes."

"Christ, Rachel, you could have me over for dinner. I could have you over for dinner. It doesn't have to be this way. See a movie, for crying out loud. Whatever normal people do."

"Cops aren't normal people. Didn't you tell me that the first day in?" Her chest was tightening. Maybe Vaughn was right, the heart was a strange muscle. She imagined hers as a tangle of veins leading nowhere.

"Is there a reason, something you aren't saying?"

Around them, the static of radios. To her left, Vaughn's carriage house with its linen drapes in the floor-to-ceiling windows upstairs. Usually he kept them closed, but once, late at night, she had seen him silhouetted there, a drink in hand, looking out over the dark river and the twinkling lights of the city. Behind him, was that someone moving in the back of the room?

Rachel glanced around, trying not to be too conspicuous. His car wasn't here, a good thing, otherwise the excitement would surely bring him out onto the street. She tried not to think about where he might be. When she was getting ready to head over there, during those four interminable weeks at Fort Drum, there was a second lieutenant always talk-ing to them about SA—situational awareness. When you're outside the wire, he would say, and you're thinking about getting to the end of the day, a cold shower and a trip to the chow hall, it means you aren't noticing the dead dog on the side of the road, the one with an IED hidden inside it that's gonna blow you up as you're driving past. Not that any of them needed to be reminded of that once they got to Iraq. But now: Bobby leaning against the car, popping his knuckles methodically, the faces of two little girls pressed to the window above them, a little white dog lying inert on the sidewalk. She felt her palms start to sweat, her heart thudding in her chest. Relax, she told herself, it's hot. The dog's just sleeping. Jesus.

If Vaughn saw her from the window, maybe he would think she was just another civil servant keeping him safe from late-night adulterers and drunks in the park. He probably didn't know where her money came from these days.

With his little trust fund he'd never really had to work that much—maybe his problem, but at the time very convenient. Because if he didn't have to work, she didn't either. She could have fought harder for support from him, but that wasn't really going to happen, not with a JAG lawyer. They were mainly there for the paperwork, and she couldn't stand the thought of waiting and coming home to a mess—to Vaughn's explanations and soulful looks, to tearful discussions over who got the Velvet Underground CDs and the Indian cookbooks. Besides, Vaughn's mother had made her sign a prenup, which she and Vaughn had laughed about, back in the days when they were so smugly sure that they would never need it.

She'd taken the check that Vaughn sent her out of guilt, mailed it off to the bank, and tried to forget about it. She wasn't going to be one of those fools pissing away her bonus on a Corvette. On the plane home from Iraq she had all these visions of flowers, grass, strolls in the park, drinks out with old friends. After two weeks sitting inside her darkened apartment, her staff sergeant—whose brother was a Richmond cop—called her about an opening on the force.

"Come on, Gallagher. Get over here, Barstow." They walked, shoulders nearly touching, over to where the other cops were clustered. Sergeant Harris—dark-skinned, neat mustache that would have been in style twenty years ago, gray around the temples—gave her a look, then Bobby. She stared right back at him.

"Any casualties?"

"Just a couple of stray bullets from Sugar Bottom. One of them went through a guy's door down on short 30th." At the end of the street, a few neighbors, coffee cups in hand, peered over the hill. "Can you get them the hell away from there, Barstow?"

Pristine restored row houses lined one side of short 30th. A tricycle in a yard, pink and green chalk flowers on the sidewalk out in front. On the other side, a tangle of brambles, weed trees. Bobby caught up to her.

"Is that all you want, a quickie in the supply room?"

"Let's just get these jokers out of here." She walked fast, already starting to bark out orders, her uniform feeling too tight, the air heating up, the damp cloth under her arms starting to chafe. Her voice mechanical: "Clear the site, please. Until we have determined that the danger is contained, we'll take any statements over by the park."

A middle-aged guy with a short white beard. Two girls in their twenties who could have been students. An older lady, shoulder-length hair, big glasses.

Through the tangle of honeysuckle and weed trees three cinder-block sheds were visible, one with torn plastic replacing the windows. Sergeant Harris came up behind her. "Shot went through this guy's door about ten minutes ago." He nodded his head back to where a splintery hole interrupted the varnished dark surface of the wood. "Then another one heard

a few minutes after that. We got the guys down there searching the area."

One of the girls, cute, long blond ponytail, said to the sergeant, "I only wish you all were here as much during the day
as you are at night. I mean, don't get me wrong, it's GREAT
to have you by the park, but then this happens."

Rachel stared at the girl, inscrutable-cop look on her face,
mainly so she wouldn't have to feel Bobby watching her. She
didn't think she was here all that much, anyway. But it was
still too much.

"We do what we can to protect the citizens, ma'am," Bobby told her, and Sergeant Harris, weary, shot him a dirty look.
"It's not safe right now," he told the girl. "Go inside."

A bullet pinged against a tree on the hill and Rachel felt
that familiar energy surging through her veins, time slowing,
colors brightening. Head down, she ran in a low crouch to
take cover behind a red minivan, gravel crunching under her
feet, Bobby breathing hard behind her.

"You come here at night to see him, don't you?" he said.
"You still sleeping with him?"

From down the hill, a single cry, and then a burst of fire.
She could smell Bobby, his sweat an acrid mix of sex and fear,
next to her.

"If you know so much—" she started to say.

"Where's the fucking SWAT team?" someone yelled behind her. From down the hill, silence.

"You've been following me," she said. A woodpecker drill-
ing the tree above them, the whirring of wings.

"Nah, I just wanted to know where he lived. In case he
gave you any trouble."

"What were you planning to do, pay him a visit?"

"Something like that."

"What the hell's that supposed to mean?" Bobby: yeah, good in bed, quick with a joke, but what else? All the hours spent together bored on stakeouts, riding around the city, busting poor jerks for running stop signs. Had she been paying attention to anything these last months? She had spent all those hours looking out the window, letting the sights of the city entertain her like it was TV. *I've got your back*, he was always telling her. Whatever that meant.

Bobby peered behind the van's rear bumper. "That blond girl? She's the one he's fucking."

"Like I'm supposed to care." Squabbles: high school again. Nothing from the bottom of the hill, then the sound of cop cars squealing to a halt down there. "Can't we talk about this later?" Smelling herself now, that familiar sharp odor stronger than any of the spring flowers and damp earth. Who the hell was she kidding?

She looked past the splattered bumper of the van. On the left, quick low motion through the leaves. She turned fast, weapon at the ready: a black cat.

Bobby saying, "Surprised you didn't know that, all the time you been spending here." Sweating, urgent. In the side mirror of the van was a face framed in a glass transom, staring out, too dim to see. Rachel kept looking, hearing the rustling of a squirrel rushing through thick leaves and up a tree, her eyes adjusting. It was the girl with the blond ponytail, staring out through her door. Behind the girl, a man approaching. Vaughn. So why hadn't his car been on the street? Was the Mercedes in the shop again? Situational awareness. It meant being right here, right now, the daily noise of life stripped away. Rachel wanted Vaughn to open the door, just so she could scream at him to get the fuck down, enjoy the startled expression on his face.

The window of the minivan shattered, and a shower of glittering fragments fell to the street. Absurdly, Rachel thought of her wedding day, holding hands with Vaughn, ducking their heads and laughing as they ran beneath a cascade of rice. In the mirror, she could see Vaughn staring out. She wanted him to stay there, forever stuck behind glass, watching. She wanted to be away from him, not caring. From the bottom of the hill, another gunshot exploded.

"I'm going down there." Already on her belly, inching forward.

"Rachel, they're drug dealers, who cares, the guys've got it covered." She could picture the dark shapes moving through the cinder-block buildings down there, shadows. Picture herself closer now, uniform ripping on the thorny underbrush, her own breathing quiet, feeling alive, time slowed to that single moment. All those nights wasted up here, peering out at the lights of the city. Hip bones grinding against Bobby's, his rough neck against her face, their muffled exclamations. That wasn't wasted. She glanced back at him leaning toward her, looking hurt. She had liked it that he never asked, but now he was going to start. And there was so much, really, she just didn't want to talk about. In the morning, she knew, she would call her recruiter.

"Jesus, Rachel, get back here." His hand gripping her arm, a surge of feeling coming through her body. For a moment she paused, hesitated. She couldn't afford to look back.

Then she pulled away and was moving again, already halfway across the street, her knees scraping against the gravel, heading for the impenetrable tangle of weeds ahead.

THE FALL LINES

BY DEAN KING

Shockoe Slip

Based (loosely) on a true story

1807

It was a tobacco-stain of an August night in Shockoe Slip, so humid a body seemed to drizzle when it moved. Stench from the outhouses on the canal bank behind the hotels and shop fronts and the sweet fug of flue-cured leaf tarred the air. Inside the Eagle Tavern, bourbon whiskey and rouged cheeks shimmering in smoky lantern light raised a man's threshold for swelter.

The General was down to his last few dollars. He held only a pair of deuces and a single bullet in his hand now. However, his eclipse had been a long time in the making. That it should happen here was ironic. He had been in many worse places.

An army officer since his youth, he had long understood he might perish of thirst in a deep Texas oak thicket or be pierced by an arrow on some damned buffalo plain. Many times over, he could have been gut-shot on the dunes of North Africa. By contrast, no matter how loudly the falls clattered, the bustling banks of the James, in the bosom of Southern plantation hospitality, did not seem an obvious threat. He was forty-three. His weaknesses included whiskey, women, and cards, but even more a liberal constitution, a vivid imagination, and not just a lack but an absolute rejection of caution. These last had once made him a force of nature and a charmer—a man who could lead a horse to water and make it beg for a drink.

The General's aide-de-camp, Mustafa, sat across the room, measuring the crowd and meditating on the gold medal recently awarded to the General. It hung just out of sight around his neck, like a cursed scarab. Mustafa had followed the General to the United States from Egypt. As the General's fortunes languished, he watched his behavior grow more erratic. The General, fearless at the worst of times, now drank as if to extinguish a fire and gambled as if to obliterate the past.

Mustafa understood what was eating at him, a man who had battled the longest of odds in the Barbary War and won. He had been biding his time, waiting for the General to figure out a way to set things right again. So abysmal were circumstances at the moment that Mustafa had begun to crave the scorch of bourbon too, a betrayal of his religion and a thing unheard of in his family.

The trial of Aaron Burr had gathered an impressive group of politicians, salesmen, gossipers, and whoremongers to the Virginia capital, at the fall lines of the James. Above the miasma, on Shockoe Hill, not far from Patrick Henry's church, rose the state's neo-Roman capitol, designed by President Jefferson. It was both a symbol of the city's vanity and a beacon of hope to its Episcopal citizenry, who still enjoyed the full cornucopia of humanity's sins.

In the Eagle, just down from Shockoe Hill, the din of pressmen, gentlemen farmers, lawmakers, slave traders, merchants, and unattached ladies was considerable. Their prosperous city of 6,000 souls had recently received its first bank charter, and a public library had opened. Their talk ranged from the price of tobacco leaf and the prospects of rain to the European war, but most of all to the trial being presided over by Chief Justice John Marshall and of particular interest to President Jefferson.

The General was a player in the drama. Prior to his exploits in North Africa, he had entertained a proposal from Burr involving the territories stretching west of the Mississippi and down into Mexico. The scheme—to hew a new kingdom out of this wilderness—had collapsed, and now the General was called to bear witness against Burr on charges of treason.

The General had testified that day. As he sat in the stand, a military hero, in a place, at last, where that seemed to matter, his luster had returned. That evening, when he took his seat at a gaming table in the Eagle, he felt fresh again, his battered confidence restored.

Across from the General, the gentleman from Shirley Plantation, a broad raw-boned man who was the largest property owner and slaveholder in the state, dealt, his massive fingers barely able to distinguish the cards. To the General's left sat the principal of Southside Plantation, a man whose bald forehead was speckled red by the sun and whose teeth approached in color his few strands of brown hair. To the General's right, a legislator from Maryland, a smart silver chain dangling from the fob of his waistcoat, observed the table with darting eyes.

"So you were the hero of Derna?" the legislator asked rhetorically, looking at his hand, an eyebrow raised. The General, still in possession of his instincts, instantly sensed this man to be a threat.

"The Marines were instrumental," he replied, not looking

up. "But it was my notion, so I received the shiny medal to show for it." Any man who read the newspapers knew that he had, in fact, orchestrated the coup of a particularly inimical pasha, recruiting an army of cutthroats in Egypt, marching across Libya, and taking the Mediterranean port. The sudden and extraordinary blow had shocked the piratical Barbary dictators, who had immediately treated for peace. The General had effectively won the Barbary War.

"I raise a glass to you, sir," said the Shirley man, with earnest admiration.

The others raised theirs, filled with Thorp's corn liquor—bourbon—invented by an Episcopal priest at Berkeley, well before Kentucky was chipped off her mother state. "The Gen'ral," they said.

The General neither smiled nor reacted. The twirl of a dress in the glint of lantern light had caught his eye. His mind leaped the sea. The pasha's older brother, the rightful ruler of Derna, whom the General had found in Egypt and installed in place of his usurping younger sibling, had just as quickly been abandoned by the U.S. government, deposed, and beheaded. The General had used his persuasive arts to induce the man to risk his life in the cause of another man's nation. Then he had walked out on him at the insistence of that nation. A lifelong soldier, the General still struggled to swallow his indignation. Though outwardly sure, he had come to despise himself.

The General laid down knaves over deuces, a lady high. Looking away, he gathered in the pot as if it meant nothing. He was a virtual chameleon when he wanted to be—having once, it was sworn to by good and sober U.S. Army officers, learned a certain Indian language, stained his skin to infiltrate the tribe's village, and returned with intelligence that caused its destruction.

* * *

The General's aide-de-camp sat in a dark corner.

"Do you know what they'd do to you?" Rosy O'Sharon said, when his eyes met hers.

"I am not a black man," he countered in his bass voice. "My name is Mustafa. I am an Arab." Rose's head tilted a notch. He was tall, over six feet, square-shouldered, café au lait.

"Liar," she spat. "A-rabs don't drink."

"They do not dwell in the devil's lair either," he responded flatly, eyeing the Marylander, who he noted wore a blade in his boot and a carefully concealed shoulder holster.

"Well, I seen slaves lighter'n you, doll," she warmed, "but none as handsome."

Mustafa watched her feet as she walked away. "Can you dance?" he called to her.

"I'm Irish," she answered.

"Can your friends?"

The youngest brother of the feuding pashas, Mustafa had crossed Libya with the General and fought at Derna in his ragtag army, which numbered a dozen Americans, forty-odd Greeks and Italians, and some five hundred Turks, Mamluks, and Arabs. When the General requested that Mustafa continue in his personal employ, he had considered it an honor.

The General returned to the U.S. to great fanfare. In Washington, Mustafa had stood proudly in the background in his flowing white haik and a black turban. He took in his new country with glowing eyes, as he would a sumptuous meal of camel.

In New England, the General's wife, however, received his two aides-de-camp—one Arab, one Italian—coolly. "William, with all due respect to your men," she had stated, "they shall bed down elsewhere."

"But, my darling, I need them nearby," the General insisted, though with nothing of his usual force. "Gilo is a superb amanuensis. You can use his services."

"That may be so, but they will be comfortable enough in the barn."

As the weeks wore on, the two men had begun to realize that the daring leader they knew in Libya was not the same in this cold place. Over time, as the General's plans stalled, the Arab and the Italian came to despise one another. Gilo mostly smoked and sneered. Mustafa furtively courted the servant of a neighboring farm, meeting her at night in the woods to soothe her fears with cold fingers.

"You will only ruin her," Gilo had chastised Mustafa.

When the General's wife asked her husband to leave, Mustafa found that Gilo had been right about the girl. It wounded him far more than she knew when he revealed that he was leaving, far more than the elbow she delivered to his jaw, which chipped a tooth.

Gilo had found ways to twist the knife. "I won't be missing nothing here. How about you, Mufti?" he prodded as they set out with the General. "No, this place is like a punch in the mouth." When they reached New York City, Gilo, who served as the General's purser, deserted them, taking along a good deal of the General's cash.

A man with two tankards in his hands teetered up to the card game. "You shoulda seen the Gen'l today," he crowed, slamming a pint down and sloshing it on the table. "For you, sir, a real hero, not one of them quill scratchers. Damn fine testimony today." The Hall of the House of Delegates had been filled to capacity. The prosecution's first witness, the General had slipped back into character, a field commander again, not to be toyed with by legal men. He described a conversation with Burr in Washington during the winter of '05–'06. "I listened to Colonel Burr's mode of indemnity," he declared, "and as I had by this time begun to suspect that the expedition he had afoot was unlawful, I permitted him to believe myself resigned to his influence that I might understand the extent and motive of his arrangements." The General, who had admired the scale of the former vice president's ambition, if little else, paused for effect. "Colonel Burr laid open his project of revolutionizing the territory west of the Allegheny, establishing an independent empire there; New Orleans to be the capital, and he himself to be the chief." The courtroom had been transfixed.

The General quaffed the tankard in two large gulps and chased it with a shot of sailor's rum from another admirer, delivered by a plump lass with wet lips. As the Eagle filled with smoke, the General regaled the men at his table with stories of his military affairs. The Shirley and Westover men listened intently, he noticed, while playing cautiously. When the stakes started to rise, they folded. They attended to their pipes while the General and the Maryland sharp traded financial blows. At length the Shirley and Southside men were replaced at the table by new money, Willcox—"two Ls, sirs"—of Belle Air Plantation and Wilcox—"single barrel, my friends"—who had married an heiress and restored Flowerdew Hundred.

As the hour grew late and the smoke and din intensified, the fortunes of the General and the Marylander seesawed back and forth. For the Marylander, this was sport—or was it? The General wondered. He had every penny he owned on the table. He felt a sudden sense of doom, a keen feeling in the pit of his stomach that he had been played. He had enemies in high places, he knew, in Washington, where he had browbeaten more than one feckless politician. The medal he wore under his vest bore the tarnish of those who had betrayed their allies in Derna.

The presence of working women had slowly increased as they trickled in through the back door at intervals. They caught the General's eye, like flashes of fish striking flies in the afternoon light. The pressmen huddled together at the bar. The merchants and plantation owners mingled, clapping backs, laughing heartily, drinking, and puffing their long pipes. Some furtively pawed the women with leathery hands, maneuvering toward dark recesses. Others watched the card game. After several hours, it was winding to its conclusion, tension high as the final pot rose. The Marylander seemed to be forcing the bids. First Willcox swallowed his bourbon, shook his head, and folded. Then the single-barreled Wilcox threw down his cards in disgust.

The General eyed the pot with apparent serenity. It could keep him for weeks. If he lost, he would not be able to pay for his room the next day.

As if on cue, the back door crashed open. In danced a mulatta in bedouin robes, her face covered, her hands and hips swaying rhythmically to the strings pining in the back corner. A hush spread across the room, as the glassy-eyed dancer twisted and spun through the haze toward the card table.

The woman sashayed over to the General, whose fondest conquest had come in Rabat, where he had learned Arabic and donned robes, going native in every discernible way. She beckoned to him, and he rose as if in a trance, with a thin smile. She swayed around him, and he bit his lip. His eyelids sagged while he became lost in the music of her body. The men, clinging to their mugs and pipes, were mesmerized. The women, gathering up their tips, looked on, whooping encouragement. The dancer stroked the General's collar. When she popped free a button on his coat, a cry of encouragement went up from the crowd. She allowed her robe to fall open until the men could see nearly her entire breast. The General leered. The crowd clamored, circling inward around the pair. The General was back in his element, the center of attention, the commander. He maneuvered behind the dancer, swaying, his hands groping.

Mustafa kept his eyes on the Marylander, taking in the smirk on his face, rising abruptly as the man swiftly raked in the money on the table and headed for the door.

"Inshallah!" the General groaned. "Inshallah."

The pressmen would report the scandal in the papers the next day. The General, a national hero and star witness in the Burr trial, had copulated with a woman in front of a crowd at a downtown tavern. The General would not know whether it was true or not. He would remember the white robes. And he would discover that his congressional medal had been taken from around his neck.

Rosie met Mustafa outside the back door. Shockoe Slip—a place stolen from the Powhatans and gilded by the slave trade—lay on a mosquito-ridden flood plain. The bloodsuckers swarmed at dusk. She led him across the alley into the brush near the johnnies on the bank, where the women met when they needed to discuss their private affairs. She showed him some bills and the glinting gold. He showed her what he had and lit a cheroot. Beneath the dappled stars and a crescent moon that lit both the Old and New Worlds, just above the river's fall lines, the two talked briefly about getting out of town and danced in the Southern stink.

PART III

NEUROSIS

The whole infelicity speaks of a cause
that could never have been gained.
—Henry James, on Richmond

PLAYING WITH DABLONDE

BY TOM DE HAVEN

Manchester

They'd finished having sex, Tacko and DaBlonde, but her husband Louis (you couldn't call him Lou, she called him Daddy) was still taking pictures with a small silver Canon PowerShot. He'd circle the bed, crouch, loom, even push in between DaBlonde's open chapped thighs. She'd threaten to trap him there, scissor him, and they'd laugh. Weird shit. Very weird shit, thought Tacko.

Louis was a big guy, obese, and whenever he'd kneel on the bed for another shot, it crunched and sank. He had on a tent-sized black T-shirt and gray Nike sweatpants. He always kept his clothes on. Well, both times so far. "That's enough pictures, Daddy." DaBlonde shook a foot at him, making short flicking motions with her toes.

She was at least fifteen years younger than Tacko, who was forty-eight. She might have been still in her late twenties—slight, almost skinny, a pretty face that looked dairy-maid wholesome when she took off her glasses. Just now, though, she'd kept them on through everything, fellatio included.

Louis was nearer Tacko's age. A friendly, blunt-talking fat cuckold. Tacko didn't use the word in mockery, merely as description. So the guy enjoyed watching his wife do strangers—so what? Other guys enjoyed tramping out in the dark and bitter cold to shoot at deer. And as far as Tacko could tell, DaBlonde loved the variety. She loved it, Louis loved it, therefore no problem. Weird shit, though. Tacko was in the presence of people the likes of whom he'd never come upon before. They were like TV Martians, human-looking but deeply different underneath. Being with them was exhilarating.

Till now Tacko had been a pretty standard guy, suburban youth in the '70s, ever-rising, ultimately tiresome career straight out of college. He went to church, Episcopal, till he was thirty-five. All told, he'd had nine sex partners (including DaBlonde), considerably less than the national average for men, which he'd read was thirteen. With his first wife, but certainly not his second, he'd watched porn, but always the tame and corny stuff. *Deep Throat. Devil in Miss Jones.* He'd never been to an orgy, a strip club, a live sex show, or known any swingers or fetishists, that he was aware of. So yes, hooking up with the Amboys and balling her while the husband filmed it—that was extreme sport for Tacko.

"Really and truly, Daddy, no more pictures. Do you know if there's still coffee to reheat?"

"Should I look?" Louis tapped the camera's on/off button and the snouty lens retracted with a tooting whir. It amazed Tacko how agreeable the guy was, like a new boyfriend or a seasoned butler. "Mr. Tacko?" he said. "If there's coffee, do you want a cup?" Louis only called him Mister. DaBlonde, come to think of it, never called him anything. "Or do you want another glass of wine?"

"Coffee sounds great."

After Louis went out, Tacko turned on his back, pulled the sheet over him to mid-chest, and folded his hands behind his neck. He could hear it raining, a sleety, hard-ticking persistent March rain. He could also hear muffled sax, drums, and bass surging up from the art gallery below. Some kind of fund-raiser there tonight. Noticing a photograph in a pewter frame on the dresser, Tacko did a stomach crunch to have a better look. When he lay back down, DaBlonde loomed over his face. "What?"

"Just checking out the picture."

"That's our wedding."

"Really?" He looked at it again, Louis in a dark-blue suit, DaBlonde in an Easter-pink cocktail dress. Outdoors on bright green grass, a flowering tree behind them. "How long ago?"

"Last spring." Tacko watched her remembering, her mouth shifting into a private smile. "We're still newlyweds. Year in May."

A year in May, and practically from day one, they'd told Tacko, DaBlonde had been fucking strangers with Daddy's blessing. *Hot Wife/Husband Watches But Doesn't Join In.* That was their lifestyle niche. They'd started playing strictly for thrills, because they wanted to and could, but then Louis and DaBlonde wondered if they might earn some income from it as well. They recorded so many videos and took so many pictures, what were they supposed to do with it all? And frankly, they could use the extra money, what with their two divorces, which they hadn't gone into in any detail about with Tacko. A website seemed worth a shot.

Louis, who was living on permanent disability (apparently he had twenty things wrong with him), was a seasoned entrepreneur. Before he'd hooked up with DaBlonde (they'd met online, each in a miserable marriage), he'd owned a small chain of video stores in the Petersburg area, and during the dot-com boom a website where he marketed things like patio misters and mosquito lures. He'd run that business out of the family garage in Chesterfield County while holding down a good job assessing and purchasing liability coverage for a residential building contractor. It wasn't hard for Louis to do the research, stake out their domain, take care of all that technical stuff.

The site went hot six months ago. The original version was amateurish and skimpy, offering only a few dozen nude-slash-action pictures of DaBlonde and a handful of short clips. Over time it got better, easier to navigate, and grew to include thousands of photographs and more than eighty videos. About two thousand subscribers signed up, guys like Tacko paying $23.95 per month with automatic credit card renewal. Subscribers from all over the country, she'd proudly told him. Europe, Japan, Australia, Brazil, even the Middle East. "Arabs and blond women," Louis said once, meaningfully clenching his jaw, and let it go at that.

Tacko had never intended to contact DaBlonde, even though as a member of her site he was encouraged to. But ten days ago—the same day that Dave Sandlin of the Eury Agency telephoned out of the blue and asked Tacko to fax over his resume—he'd impulsively written her an e-mail. Saying how much he enjoyed her newest video, adding that he'd been in the same bar dozens of times, the bar where she'd picked up that stringy Jamaican guy with the white teeth. It was the Tobacco Company, wasn't it?

She'd e-mailed him back, using emoticons and *u* for *you*, which Tacko loathed. Would he like to meet? Tacko didn't reply. Fantasy was okay, but actually *doing* something? Very damn unlikely. DaBlonde persisted. She wrote Tacko again, and included two cell numbers. When he didn't call, she wrote a third time: they would be at Siné Irish Pub in Shockoe Slip on Wednesday evening at 8:30. It would be so great if he joined them.

By ten past 8 last Wednesday, Tacko still hadn't made up his mind.

He'd been so nervous when they met that his lips kept sticking to his front teeth. He just nodded and smiled, sipped his beer, and let DaBlonde and Louis do most of the talking. This was their dog-and-pony show. Not that either of them had dressed to impress. Louis, in need of a beard trim and a haircut (his full beard was salt-and-pepper; the hair on his large head gray, thin, and wind-blown), had come to the pub wearing khaki pants and a plum-colored knit shirt stretched over his big stomach like a drumhead. He hadn't worn a coat. Twenty degrees out and no coat. Louis was about five-eight, but his bulk made his presence overpowering; he took up so much room! They'd stood, all three of them, talking at the bar for more than an hour. Tacko wondered if they stayed there because the tables and booths were too confining for the guy.

DaBlonde introduced herself as "Ann-dray-ah but spelt like Andrea," and Tacko thought she looked dowdy, a little drippy, in person. At any rate, in clothes. Charcoal slacks and a pale gray blouse, black vest hand-decorated with colored glass beads. A dobby four-button jacket. She'd dressed like a third-grade teacher out for a drink—a non-alcoholic margarita—on a Friday afternoon, even though it was a weeknight, and she drank a White Russian, then a second. This is what they liked to do, she said. She looked Tacko straight in the eye. He smiled back. There was their marriage, she said, and then there was this. She gave a happy shrug. This was just a hobby they shared.

But it was a business too, said Louis. Tacko would have to sign a consent form. They would try not to show his face in videos. Louis was careful about that. However, if Tacko were recognized, they could not be held accountable.

He had to think it over. What would happen if he *were* recognized? What *could*? Tacko wasn't married, and his friends and professional acquaintances were universally unlikely to surf into DaBlonde's "hot wife" site, although you could never know anything for certain. His parents were deceased, so was his brother, he didn't plan on running for public office, and he'd been laid off from his job, so he couldn't be fired.

Fuck it, he signed the waiver.

"That your real name?" said Louis Amboy.

Tacko blushed. Had he done something wrong? Was he supposed to make one up? "But nobody calls me Vincent," he said. "Vin sometimes, but not so much. Never Vinnie. Usually either Tack or just Tacko." Shut *up*.

DaBlonde had put her hand on his leg, right thigh, underneath the bar ledge. She moved it back to his crotch. At that moment her cell phone started playing Van Morrison's "Have I Told You Lately?" and she withdrew the hand to root though her bag. "Excuse me." She turned away and answered, frowning.

"Look, I'm in a restaurant. Because I am, that's why." She planted an elbow on the bar and slumped in dejection. "Nice. *Classy*. And I'm supposed to listen to this crap? *Scott*. I'm not listening to you. No, Scott, you may not speak to *my husband*, either. Because that's who he is, Scott. And now I'm going to hang up. Same to you, asshole." She listened a few more seconds, then snapped her phone closed. Flipped it back open and turned it off. Then she raised an eyebrow significantly at Louis. "That was Scott."

"I gathered. And?"

"You heard me. I wouldn't listen." She looked testy, then didn't. She widened her eyes, doing mock-waif, and smiled at Tacko. "Scott's my ex-and-I-couldn't-be-happier-about-it-husband. And I'm especially happy that he lives in Greensboro. He makes cheap furniture. And empty threats." After a shrug, DaBlonde leaned forward and kissed Tacko on the mouth, with tongue.

"Well," said Louis, recovering abruptly (he'd paled at Scott's name) and paying for his and DaBlonde's drinks with a twenty, "shall we continue this somewhere else?"

They'd gone to the Omni since they could walk to it from the pub, Louis explaining to Tacko on the way how it was standard practice for the single guy to pay for the room. Tacko thought, *Standard practice.* In the Amboys' world it was standard practice for the single guy to pay for the room. In the Amboys' world, and in Tacko's world now too.

He'd felt a knot of fear when they arrived at their room and he unlocked the door with a magnetized card. (What if they robbed him? Tied him up and tortured him? What if—?) Then it was gone. DaBlonde threw off her clothes like it was nothing. White cotton underpants, white undershirt with spaghetti straps, no bra. Tacko was delighted by her smooth skin, her small breasts, impressed by her intensity. The more DaBlonde carried on, and the louder she got, the more Louis enjoyed it. That was demonstrably evident. All told, they were at the hotel for about an hour and a half.

Afterwards, Tacko felt conscience pangs. He'd wondered if he would, and he did. He felt like some kind of crazy amoral heathen, and as big a pervert as Louis Amboy. Well, maybe not quite as big.

He was surprised when the Amboys e-mailed him and suggested another get-together. He'd been flattered too by the follow-up invitation, but uncertain how to respond. He'd met them just to say (to himself) that he'd done it, to actually do something outrageous for a change. But what was the point of seeing them again? Sure, *that.* But did he really want any more of the Amboys? No. Yes. No.

Eventually, he decided to see them again, and then to his further surprise (and slight discomfort) they'd invited him to their condo on Decatur Street, just south of the Mayo Bridge. Tacko knew their pay site well, and all of the videos and pictures there had been shot in hotel rooms or in public or semi-public places, never their home. Till now they'd not so much as hinted at where in the city they lived. For all Tacko knew they actually lived somewhere else and just played in Richmond. No, it turned out they lived on Decatur and Third.

A few of the red-brick early-twentieth-century buildings in the old Manchester district still operated as factories (Alcoa had a plant, there were a couple of box companies), but most were either derelict or had been gutted and refurbished into work space for artists, art galleries, or luxury condos. Where the Amboys lived had once been the United States Cardboard Company and still bore the name chiseled above the entrance door.

They owned one of the few residential units that had been sold in the building. Two or three cooperative galleries, a banquet hall, a café, and about fifty artists' studios comprised the ground level. Louis and DaBlonde lived on the third floor, a wide-open industrial space, exposed brick, timber columns and trusses, everything else chrome or glass or bleached canvas, Ultrasuede or black leather. The place was furnished, Tacko thought coming in earlier tonight, like a full-page design collection ad in the *New York Times Magazine*—except for all of the computers.

There were desktops and laptops, Macs and IBM PCs, and monitors either shining a dead blue light or playing explicit videos Tacko recognized from the pay site. DaBlonde with the Sports Bar Guy, the Sharp-Dressed Man, the Man in the Woods, the Cowboy Trucker. In the restroom at Chesterfield

Towne Centre, on a farm, on a different farm, behind the Ashland Wal-Mart, at the Virginia State Fair. All of the monitors had the sound turned off. Even so, it was disorienting, porn everywhere you looked, and the actual woman, the "hot wife" herself, standing right there, dressed in herringbone slacks and a white fuzzy sweater, urging Tacko to sit down, then sliding onto the sectional beside him.

They drank red wine (Louis poured) and smoked half a joint (Louis rolled, Louis lighted, Louis declined to partake, same as he'd passed on drinking wine). DaBlonde pulled up her sweater and exposed her breasts, then slotted her tongue at Tacko while Louis talked geekishly about a new camcorder he'd bought that took higher quality videos. They required more time to load, he said, but it was worth it.

Once they'd moved into the bedroom, the sex was better than last time. Not so bing-bang-bing or as impersonal. They were learning each other's moves, adding finesse. Tacko forgot about Louis and his camera, except for whenever the husband asked DaBlonde how she liked it so far and urged Tacko to come wherever he wanted, externally, internally, whatever struck his fancy. Unlike last week, Tacko wasn't impelled by a flight reflex immediately afterwards.

"Tell me something," DaBlonde was saying now. "You a cheater? You can tell me, I don't care."

"Cheater?"

"Married."

"Jeez, no. I've been divorced since ninety . . . seven."

Louis stuck his head into the bedroom. "There wasn't enough to heat so I put on a fresh pot." Then he was gone again.

DaBlonde flung herself upright as if suddenly and willfully were the only ways she could ever force herself to move again. She laughed when she almost bounced Tacko off the mattress, then swung her legs around, grabbed her Chinese robe (black and red with a firecracker dragon on the back) from a chair, put it on, and cinched it. "Do you want to take a shower first?"

"If you wouldn't mind."

"No, you go ahead."

But Tacko felt like dawdling. "Do . . . do a lot of guys you meet say they're not married?"

"You're kidding, right? Because I'm not even sure I believe *you're* not." She laughed and came back and sat down on the bed. "You're all a bunch of genetic liars."

"Harsh."

"Except Louis. Otherwise you're all cheaters, if you ask me. Not that I give a damn."

"I'm really divorced."

"I believe you. No, seriously. I was kidding." DaBlonde's expression changed again, her long face looking placid, her gray eyes vacant. "But most men are cheaters. You know they are. And worse. Like my ex? Was just con*vinced* that I screwed around, and I never did, not once in seven years. But meanwhile Scott's out knocking off new stuff every other weekend. *And*—and carrying on with my best girlfriend, maid of honor at our wedding." The corners of her eyes crinkled and her smile returned. "Louis is probably hovering out there right now, hoping we're having sex again, and here we are having a regular conversation."

Tacko thought, *A regular conversation?* That's maybe not how he would've described it, but they were having . . . something. Something Tacko was okay with. That he was here for, *present* for. He was good with all of it. It was just—he still had a hard time convincing himself he could *do* something like this, weird shit like this, and get away with it. He'd probably get AIDS. Or maybe Louis was right that second dropping a diamond-shaped purple roofie into his cup of coffee, he'd end up with a ball-gag in his mouth and dangling from a ceiling beam. Jesus. Had he lost his mind? Had he lost his mind since he'd lost his job? He wondered.

For almost nineteen years he'd worked at Greene and Scivally Advertising, the last eleven as a group creative director. Then: new management, and out he went. Week before Thanksgiving. One day he's brainstorming a new campaign for a national brand, the next he's emptying his desk with a security cop standing by in case he goes berserk. But Tacko wasn't the excitable type.

It was scary carrying away his carton of personal items, but also a secret relief. He'd been in career burnout a long time, he just hadn't let on. In recent years, movies and novels and TV series about characters who found the courage and/or the foolhardiness to abandon stifling lives had held great appeal for Tacko.

The first two months he didn't do much. Got out to the gym more regularly, subscribed to Netflix and caught up on the third season of Lost, scheduled and kept doctor and dentist appointments before his company health insurance lapsed, and worked on his screenplay, the one based on a botched kidnapping that happened in the early 1990s. But the story got trite as he was writing it, not basing it closely on the real case at all, and he gave it up again. He knew he wouldn't go back to it.

During this period Tacko wasn't dating, by choice. He'd had an on again/off again friends-with-benefits thing with a married secretary who used to work with him and now worked for the Virginia Bar Association. But when they didn't get in touch over the Christmas holidays, Tacko wondered if maybe this time the off-again was permanent. Upon consideration he discovered that possibility not even slightly painful. Thinking about Connie Agnew and how insignificant she had become in his life was the first inkling Tacko had that he might have left more behind recently than his job.

People he knew well, whom Tacko considered friends, called and left messages. *Tack, a bunch of guys are getting together for poker tonight, we'd love to see you. Vincent, my man, you at all interested in seeing a movie? Tack? I sent you an e-mail about Robin's birthday party. Call me. Vin? Nikki and I were saying how we haven't heard from you. Vincent? Tack? Tacko?* He didn't get back to most people. It just wasn't anything he cared to do. After a while there weren't many calls. Tacko had no problem with that.

At the end of December his brother died suddenly, but he didn't fly out to Salt Lake City for the funeral. They'd been estranged. Their personalities, their politics, their dad's will. His brother, though. Jesus Christ. Heart attack. And he was younger than Tacko by four years! His brother Kenny's death shut Tacko down for weeks, well into the new year. Except for paying bills online, he mostly slept and moped around the house. He watched four seasons in a row of *The Wire*. Grew a beard and shaved it off.

He'd received a good severance package, and had significant savings, even some excellent technology stocks, so money wasn't an issue. The rest of his fucking life was. But even deep into January his future remained a subject Tacko felt he couldn't deal with yet. If something great, some fabulous new direction, didn't happen or present itself by the first of February, he'd look for another job in advertising. First of February. February the first. He marked it on his calendar.

Often Tacko woke in the night and lay awake for hours. He couldn't turn his brain off. One night, but just the one, he pondered ways a reasonable man might realistically kill himself, but otherwise he just thought about how much he didn't want to resume his former life. Is that what it was already? His *former* life? What he wanted, what Tacko most needed, was something different, a fresh possibility, even the merest glimpse of one.

For a about a week he considered writing a novel, one set in the cutthroat world of advertising. He actually outlined one on the computer. But when he read over what he'd done, it sounded like every other story ever written about an ad agency, so he deleted it and looked at Internet porn instead.

Honestly, Tacko could not recall how the habit started— from boredom and curiosity, probably. But he'd also recognized just how infrequently (hardly ever) he thought about women these endless unemployed days and nights at home, and so it was possible he was using the stuff as proof he hadn't lost interest in sex. Porn gradually became a daily routine, and one of his favorite pay sites (by the middle of February, he'd subscribed to six) was DaBlonde's. Not *only* because she was located in his hometown, although it surely played a major part. (Finding her site had been a sheer accident, serendipity, link to link to link to link . . .) No, what he liked best about her? The woman seemed utterly reckless. Fucking men in stairwells, hallways, at highway rest stops. Behind the Museum of the Confederacy. That took guts. Her site biography (which Tacko figured was probably all bullshit, but he chose to disregard his cynicism) stated that she'd been raised in a strict household and had never even kissed a boy before she was twenty-one. And look at her now!

"You seemed like you were going to say something."

"No," said Tacko. "Just thinking."

"What?"

"I don't know."

"Sure you do," said DaBlonde.

"Who came up with your name?"

"It's what my ex used to call me, but that's not what you were thinking. He'd call me that when he called me a slut. So what were you really thinking?"

"All right. I was just wondering—you and Louis met on-line? At a chat room?"

"Yeah . . . ? I was in North Carolina and Louis was living here. Well, out in the county. So?"

"I was just wondering. Was there, like, one day, one particular day, when the two of you just said that's it, *enough*, and then packed your stuff and walked away and—got together?"

"I guess. But it's not exactly an *original story*. It happens all the time."

"Well, maybe."

"It does. People walk away, Tacko. And the world doesn't end. You can do whatever you always wanted and nobody can stop you. Is that what you're asking me?"

"Yeah. No. I'm not sure." He was babbling now because he realized this was the first time she'd called him by any name, and she'd chosen his last name, the least familiar, even the coldest, of the possibilities. His heart sank a little.

DaBlonde got up. "Go take your shower."

"Yeah, sure." Tacko rolled out of bed and started collecting his clothes from the floor (shirt, briefs, jeans, one sock, Clarks boots, second sock) while DaBlonde fingered apart two thin blinds and looked out the window. That side of the condo faced a gutted brass foundry covered by construction company signage.

"It's still raining," she commented. "Listen to that."

"It's supposed to stay like this till midnight," said Tacko, just to say something.

He picked up the Amboys' framed wedding picture. They were both laughing with their toothy mouths open. He set it down and thought he might not shower after all, just get dressed and go home. But since he was already standing naked at the bathroom doorway, he went in and turned on the faucet in the tub. This was so weird. The whole thing. Being here. Taking a shower now. Using their shampoo, their liquid soap, their scrubby.

As soon as he turns off the water, Tacko hears voices raised in an argument. The Amboys quarreling? But no, the man's voice isn't Louis's. Tacko can't make out what he and DaBlonde—it's definitely DaBlonde's voice—are hollering about. Then he hears the guy shout either "disgusting" or "disgust me" and feels a spurt of jangling dread. He starts to put his clothes back on without drying himself.

That's a shot. Fuck.

Somebody just fired a gun, out there. Beyond the bathroom door, beyond the bedroom, out there in the loft.

And that's a second shot.

He's fully dressed now, but paralyzed, unable to decide whether to move—to investigate, to implicate himself—or to stay put.

He opens the door a crack and Louis Amboy's hysterical voice carries in.

"Scott, please. Scott, please. Please, Scott."

He makes cheap furniture. And empty threats.

"Scott, please, for God's *sake*!"

Why isn't DaBlonde saying anything?

It's still raining hard and downstairs the band is still

playing. Tacko quietly closes the door and locks it.

Three more shots in a burst. Silence, and then another shot. Then silence.

The first slap against the bathroom door is percussive enough to shake it; the second is the merest scratching tap.

Now a spot of dark red glistens in the narrow gap between the bottom of the door and the saddle. The spot widens, liquefies—blood. In its flow, carried along, comes an inch-and-a-half-wide sodden strip of black silk.

A tie end from DaBlonde's Chinese robe.

Straddling the pool of blood, one foot planted on either side, Tacko unlocks the door, eases it toward him, and her huddled body insistently pushes it open the rest of the way. He glances down for only a moment, but long enough to register DaBlonde's fixed eyes. His head goes groggy, and he wills it clear, staring through the bedroom and out into the living area, seeing part of the black-and-white sectional and a row of blue screen monitors on a molded glass table.

The only sound now is the rain lashing at the building, the windows, the roof. The band has finally taken a break.

Now Tacko is standing at the bedroom door, now he's creeping out into the loft, and now crouching beside Louis Amboy sprawled on the floor, a bullet hole at the base of his skull. Blood runs down the back of his neck into his collar. Tacko's mind fills with strobing light and he bolts for the front door.

"Hey!"

It's a young guy, thirtyish, full head of brown hair, filthy tan barn jacket, short barrel revolver clutched in a fist streaked with mahogany wood stain. He steps out of the kitchen, or glides from behind a bank of computer monitors (sound on, DaBlonde groaning), or just leans forward in a flexible mesh chair, and says, "You're disgusting." Or maybe, "You disgust me." And squeezes the trigger. A hundred times, like it's a fucking machine gun.

"Hey! Tacko!" DaBlonde: tapping on the shower glass. "You want to leave me some hot water?" She pulled open the door, shed her robe, and stepped into the spray, smiling as she nudged Tacko from under it. "Can I have the shampoo?" He plucked it from the caddy, Elizabeth Arden, and handed it to her. "You can stay. We can share."

But he was already out. "No," he said, "I'm done."

Louis Amboy was conveying a French press and three ceramic mugs on a service tray from the kitchen to the coffee table when Tacko came out of the bedroom fully dressed and grabbed his leather coat from the sectional.

"You're not leaving, I hope."

"I should."

Louis carefully set down the tray. He cocked his head. "Well, if you have to."

"This was fantastic."

"Tell me something, Mr. Tacko. Would you be interested in making it a regular thing?"

"Sure. I guess. I don't know."

"Ah," said Louis, seeming abashed. "Can I loan you an umbrella?"

"No, that's okay."

"Well then. Good night."

"You too." Tacko would've had to walk all the way around the mammoth sofa to shake hands, so he just waved to Louis. But it wasn't like he *wouldn't* shake hands. It wasn't like *that*. Even so, riding the elevator down, he felt like a real shit, then had an abrupt impulse to push the button again and go on back up, saying he'd changed his mind, he'd wait out the rain and have that cup of coffee now, if they didn't mind. Because you can do anything you want and nobody can stop you—wasn't it true?

He'd have to think about that some more.

"Vincent!"

Tacko flinched. He'd flipped up his collar, hunched a little, and stepped outside into the gusting rain, but hadn't gone three steps across the sidewalk before someone hailed him. Shit.

It was Dave Sandlin, a VP at the Eury Agency, wearing a tux and smoking a cigarette in a doorway not ten feet down the block from the Amboys' street entrance. Tacko felt he had to go over. Had to? Had to.

"How you doin', boy? Haven't seen much of you lately." Sandlin transferred his cigarette to his left hand and they shook. "Keeping busy?"

"Not really." Tacko glanced past Sandlin into the gallery, saw the musicians picking up their instruments again, the drummer sliding behind his kit, an all-white, dressed-up crowd drinking and talking, and large abstract paintings, black the dominant color, hanging on the walls. "Just enjoying life."

"Fuck's that mean?" Sandlin laughed but looked skeptical. "I thought I'd hear back from you."

Tacko, who'd been standing in the rain like an idiot, finally stepped under the overhang. "I've had a few personal projects I've been taking care of."

"Yeah, well, you don't want to stay out of sight too long, Vinnie. People forget you. Look." Sandlin tossed away his cigarette and pulled out his wallet, extracted an embossed card. "Give me your hand."

"What?"

"Put out your hand." He placed the card in Tacko's right

palm, then tapped it. "Fax me your damn resume. What's to-day, Friday? I want it on Monday. All right? Okay?"

Looking at the card, looking at Sandlin, looking at the people, many of whom he recognized, dancing now in the gallery, Tacko felt disgusted. *You disgust me. You're disgusting.* "Thanks," he said. "Monday. Promise." Pocketing Sandlin's card, he put out his hand again. "Well, let me run."

"What the hell're you doing down here anyway?"

"Visiting friends."

"Fax me."

Tacko dashed across Decatur Street and walked along the chain-link fence to the parking lot entrance. When he'd ar-rived there were only about a dozen vehicles, now there must have been close to a hundred, most of them Beemers, Lexuses, and SUVs, and he couldn't immediately remember where he'd left his. Rain drilled on a diagonal through the vapor lights. As he peered up and down the lanes, then jogged to a red Cooper he thought was his but wasn't, Tacko noticed a man sitting in a parked Saturn that was at least ten years old and badly dinged. The interior dome light was on. The man was rummaging through a leather satchel on his lap, but glanced up at Tacko. He looked about twenty-five, had stringy long dark hair and a soul patch. Tacko nodded. The man did not.

By the time Tacko found his car, he was drenched and his shoes and socks were infused. He got in and just sat there dripping. Then he glanced up and there were DaBlonde and Louis Amboy gliding up and down in front of their wall of windows, DaBlonde in that Chinese robe, her hair in a blue towel turban. The pair of them moving forward and sideways and back, box stepping.

They were dancing. Her tiny, him huge, they were dancing,

waltzing—not gracefully, shamblingly, but still. Still, they were waltzing alone in their little weird-shit world.

Tacko turned the car on, and the heat, then just sat there watching.

He had his cell phone, he could call them, invite himself back. Nothing to stop him, if that's what he wanted to do. He took it from his coat pocket and Dave Sandlin's business card came out with it. He glanced at the card—exquisite printing—and then opened his window and tossed it out.

They were still waltzing up there, and Tacko started scrolling through his stored numbers—*Abbott, Bill; Adler, Ed; Agnew, Connie, Alman, Foster & Meeks; Amboy, Louis & Andrea.* Thirty-two on Tacko's speed dial. He hesitated, then was startled by a car door slamming nearby.

The guy from the Saturn stood alongside of it now in the downpour staring at the Amboys' brightly lit condo, staring up at them as they danced their mechanical waltz. Then he strode toward the open fence gate, satchel swinging in his hand. He crossed the street, passing a few people departing the fund-raiser under voluminous black umbrellas. He walked directly to the building's corner entrance. Tacko glanced back up at the Amboys' windows, but they were no longer in view.

When he looked back down, his eyes tracking past where it was chiseled *United States Cardboard Company*, the young man with the satchel had opened the door and was going inside. Had they buzzed him up? Had they invited over another "friend"? Or thought Tacko had come back?

He turned off the car, opened his door, and got out. Stood in the rain for perhaps a minute, but still didn't see anyone in the windows.

Dave Sandlin, he noticed, had gone back into the gallery.

A middle-aged couple hurried by under umbrellas, squealing with laughter as they hit puddles.

Tacko started to get back into his car, but changed his mind and jogged up the line to the Saturn.

North Carolina plates.

And now when he looked back up, the Amboys' condo was dark, except for an ambient blue wash that came off the computer monitors.

On his way back to his Cooper, he stooped and picked up Dave Sandlin's card. Then he got in, tossed the card on the other seat, restarted the engine, and drove home.

Did he even *have* a fucking resume to send?

MIDNIGHT AT THE OASIS

BY ANNE THOMAS SOFFEE

Jefferson Davis Highway

Dedicated to the memory of Saleem Hassan

Things were bad, real bad, when I went to bed that night. Coming up on one month without smoking rock meant having to deal with the mess I'd been making of my life since I first picked up the pipe. No job, hardly any money, and a real pisser of an attitude problem—not that I'd started with the friendliest personality, but you work with what you've got.

"For somebody so young and pretty, you sure are awful hateful, Kim." This was something Beau said to me once while we dragged the stinking corpse of a harvest-gold Frigidaire down the steps of a trailer I was cleaning for the Arab. But that I could deal with. This particular night really started to suck when the sun went down and two of Ivan's girls walked over from the City Motel to give me a gentle reminder about the money I owed.

"Ivan's lonely," the one with the broken teeth said. She grabbed a fistful of my hair and jerked my head to the side.

"He don't miss you," sneered the one with the gimpy arm. "He just miss his *money*." She reached out with the good arm and smacked the side of my face, hard. The other girl let me go, and they stood there and looked at me with as much disdain as two twenty-dollar whores could muster.

"Ivan knows they fired me from the diner," I told them, rubbing my cheek where it stung. "Tell him I'm looking for work."

"You think he cares?" Teeth reached for my hair again but I stepped back. "You better get that pretty little ass out on the corner and *make* his money."

"Just don't do it here," Gimpy-Arm warned. Then the two of them headed back out to Jeff Davis, where a car had already pulled over to meet them.

They didn't need to worry about me horning in on their territory. I was already pissed off at myself for being a trailer park stereotype, what with the waitressing and the crack rocks and all. I'd only moved to Richmond from Christiansburg that spring and already I was like something out of a bad indie movie full of trailer park caricatures. Beau told me not to worry about it, that it happens to a lot of people when they first move into Rudd's, but that hardly made me feel better. It'd almost been a good thing that the diner fired me and Ivan cut off my tab, because it did for me what I couldn't do for myself.

I went to bed with my cheek still tingling, worrying and thinking about the money—a thousand dollars, not that much to some people but a hell of a lot to one unemployed teenage waitress in Rudd's Trailer Park. I'd heard about things Ivan did to people who owed him less, and it wasn't anything I wanted to be a part of. He'd told me stories, casually, while I smoked on his dime at the City Motel. At the time I thought he was confiding in me because I was different, like he could see the light behind my eyes. In hindsight, he was probably just issuing a warning. When I finally fell asleep, I dreamed of box cutters, of socks full of rolled nickels, of the gimpy-armed whore's hard little eyes.

So you wake up from a night like that and you figure there's nowhere to go but up, right? You figure you'll make a pot of black coffee, warm up the old Emerson record player that came with the place, put on *Metallic KO*—Iggy Pop being the Patron Saint of Trailer Parks—and shake it out, clean a trailer or two, and go on with life. That's what I figured until I opened my door and found a random crackhead on my steps, or what looked like a random crackhead until I realized he was there for a very specific purpose.

"Ivan says you gotta pay him before Saturday," he said without looking up.

"I can give him something on Saturday, not all." Realistically, there was no job, no legal job, that would make me that much money by the weekend.

"Ivan says he needs it all by Saturday." He picked at a sore on his hand. "Or else you're gonna fall off the Lee Bridge." When he looked up I could see that he wasn't telling me because he wanted to. He turned away. "Ivan says nobody would miss you."

I like to think that I'm tough, but when he said that, it stung worse than the gimpy-armed whore's slap.

Ivan's messenger skulked out of the trailer park, and I sank down and sat on the step where he'd been, picturing my waterlogged remains floating down the James River, wondering how long I would lie on a slab at the city morgue before somebody claimed me. If anyone ever did.

To say the trailer park governs itself would be true, but the real truth is that the place is run like a kingdom, the Arab's kingdom, and he is a benevolent ruler. If you follow the rules and pay your rent, you're a subject in good standing. If you follow the rules and can't pay your rent, you're afforded leeway because you're trying. If you don't follow the rules and you can't pay your rent, he'll cuss you out in two languages, but he'll let you stay because you *might* be trying. And he'll probably slip you a twenty when you leave, because *Allah forbid* you go hungry. Really, as long as you don't smoke crack or steal anything, the Arab has your back.

A lot of the folks in the trailer park don't work; the Arab keeps about half the residents on a casual payroll, with salaries and titles that vary depending on how bad you've managed to fuck up lately. Take Beau, for instance—because he's the biggest guy in the park and is always being called on to break up fights or scare off crack dealers, he's designated Trailer Park Police. The week he tried to move a trailer without permission and destroyed the Arab's old Ford pickup, he got demoted to Raccoon Wrangler. Bill Baldy is the Arab's assistant, and as far as I can tell that job involves drinking beer and doing crosswords in the office—which is actually just a trailer with *OFFICE* written on the door. Bobby Harvey's been here the longest, so he's Senior Manager, but it's more like *Señor* Manager, since that job is mostly steering drunk Mexican dudes into their trailers on Fridays. And Judy is the Arab's secretary even though she doesn't read or write. Her job qualification is her diabetes; unsupervised, she'll sneak to the 7-Eleven and eat herself into a coma on Bama Pies. The Arab made her his secretary so he could get her into the office and keep an eye on her.

Ever since I lost the diner job, the Arab had been letting me clean trailers whenever somebody skipped out and left one full of junk. My title was Home Improvement Expert. He paid me a hundred bucks a trailer. He had at least one every rent day. But not lately. When things get tough all over, the trailer park business booms. Folks were beating down the door to get into Rudd's. To make a little more room, because *Allah forbid* somebody gets left in the cold, the Arab offered to pay me double to clean out the big trailer on the property's back edge. Nobody had lived in it for decades. I was grateful for the chance to make double pay; at least I'd have something to try and buy time with on Saturday—but that was between me and Ivan. The Arab just thought he was giving me grocery money.

"Sure, I'll clean it," I said, taking the keys from him and sticking them in my jeans. "How long has it been vacant, anyway?"

"Ain't nobody *ever* lived in that goddamn thing," he told me. "Not as long as I been runnin' this shithole, anyway. Most of what's in there probably came out of the house, when they tore it down." The house was where the Arab's aunt had lived, a rooming house on Jeff Davis, which used to be part of the biggest travel highway on the East Coast. When Interstate 95 came through in 1958 and the tourists dried up, the rooming house was left to fall to pieces until the city finally made the Arab tear it down. He put up the trailer park in its place. It's that whole Islamic revenge thing.

The Arab said I could keep whatever I found in the trailer, but after I got through the first room it was pretty obvious that there were only a bunch of dusty old ledger books and guest registers. I pitched box after box of ledgers and files out the front door for Beau to load into the dumpster. Then I pitched one that clanked instead of thudded. I figured it was office supplies—pencil sharpeners and staplers, you know, more useless crap. I wasn't expecting a passport from Beirut, Syria, for Saleem Hassan, born 1890. Tucked under that a stack of letters, written in Arabic, mostly postmarked in the 1930s and 1940s. And sepia-toned pictures of the man from the passport standing with a woman I recognized as the Arab's aunt, whose picture hung in the office. In the bottom of the box was a thick layer of Arabic newspapers, and between every couple of sections there were records, old 78 RPM ones, with Arabic writing on the labels. And, in the very bottom of the box, the source of the clank—wrapped in a handkerchief, four brass cymbals the size of Oreos.

Since the Arab said I could have anything I found, I took it all home with me that night. I brewed myself up a pot of coffee and put on one of the records. I never thought I'd see the day that I'd need the 78 setting on the old Emerson, but then I've done a lot of things I never thought I'd do. While the stereo went through its ancient ritual of dropping the record onto the turntable and situating the needle in the groove, I unfolded the letters. Not that I could read any of them. I wanted to take them to the Arab, but then again I didn't—I figured he was related to Saleem Hassan, and who would want their family reading their letters, especially ones so personal they were saved in a box? The passport revealed that Hassan had traveled a lot—mostly back and forth from Lebanon to New York. His last stamp was for entry to New York in October 1960. His picture was grim—gray hair and a droopy, permanent frown that pulled his whole face toward the lapels of his black suit. I squinted and tried to see my Arab in his face, to no avail. There was nothing there but something that felt like loneliness, radiating off the page.

The records were the opposite of the picture. Between the crackles and pops there was a celebration, shrieking and ululating and drumming and the rhythmic clanking of finger cymbals, *tek-tek-tek-a-tek!* I unrolled the handkerchief and took out the cymbals. They didn't have any handles or straps, just two slits in the center, like buttonholes. I held one in each hand and tried to hit them together, but they made a muddy sound, not a bright chime like on the record. I rolled them back up in the handkerchief and set them on the table.

That night, when I went to sleep, Saleem Hassan came to me in my dreams. Droopy frown and all. It was just his face, black-and-white like in the passport photo, surrounded by a gray haze, cheesy, like in the movies. The Arabic record was playing in the background.

Rubber bands, he said. He nodded and pointed his finger at me through the haze. *Get you some rubber bands.*

The next day I got up early. When you might only have a few days left on the planet, you want to make them last, even if they are spent scrubbing down old trailers on Jeff Davis Highway. You just have to appreciate life for what it is.

When I stopped by the office to report for duty, the Arab asked how it was going. "You find anything good yet?" He was eating his usual, meat and eggs with sliced onions on the side. Judy was tending to her secretarial duties, watching *Jerry Springer* and painting her nails. No one else was up, seeing as it was the crack of 9.

"Just papers, mostly." I opened his desk drawer, pulled out a handful of rubber bands, and slipped them onto my wrist like bracelets.

"What do you need out my desk? You need money?"

"No, I'm good." It was pointless to even answer because when the Arab asks if you need money it isn't really a question, it's a statement of intent. "You said it was your aunt's stuff in there?"

He shrugged and bit a big wedge of onion. "*Mumkin.*

I don't know whose it is. Just get it out of here." Then he reached in his pocket and pulled out a roll of bills. Peeling off a twenty, he threw it on the desk and pointed at it like it was a cockroach. "And take that and get you some goddamn food. You're gonna blow away." Which is what he says to everybody when he gives them money, even Beau, who weighs three hundred pounds easy. Then he added the footnote that comes when you don't reach for the money fast enough, "Take it and *kul khara!* Eat shit!" I took the twenty. Saying no was not an option. I tucked it into my pocket and headed back to tackle the old trailer.

Day two of cleaning didn't bring any more mystery boxes. Old sheets and towels mostly, some dishes, all of them covered with fifty years of dust and grime. The first thing I wanted to do when I got home was take a shower. I stripped off my filthy jeans and T-shirt right inside my trailer door and was slipping the Arab's rubber bands off my wrist when I saw the cymbals on the table. I remembered my dream from the night before. *Get you some rubber bands.*

I took one of the cymbals and looped a rubber band through the slits in the middle, making a slipknot underneath. I did the same with a second cymbal and stuck my finger and thumb through the bands. *Tek-tek-tek-tek-tek!* They rang clear and true, just like on the record. I rigged the second pair and put them on and then, just because why the fuck not, I carried my butt-naked dusty self over to the record player and started up the music again. I danced like a whirling dervish in my eight-foot-wide living room, clanking my cymbals and shaking my hips, moving ways I'd never thought about moving with muscles I didn't know I had, until Bobby Harvey threw a bottle at my trailer and yelled at me to shut up the noise. Looking at the clock, I realized I'd been dancing for hours. I fell into bed, filthy as you please, and closed my eyes—only to see Saleem Hassan's grumpy face. But where the frown had reached almost *past* his chin the night before, this time it stopped just before it got there. He was nodding, like he approved.

Tanoura, he said through the haze. *At the top of the kitchen cupboard. Tanoura!* He lifted a cigarette to his lips and drew on it, then blew out more gray haze. Then he was gone. The music kept playing.

In the morning I went straight to the old trailer. I hoisted myself up onto the red Formica countertop and opened the kitchen cupboards. In the first three, nothing. In the last one, there was a rolled-up Thalhimer's bag stuck way back on a shelf. Inside the bag was a single piece of fabric, a black mesh diamond-patterned linen with strips of silver woven through. Unfolded, it ran the width of the trailer and the length of the kitchen. I stuffed it back into the bag and walked over to the office. The Arab was watching CNN and drinking red soda out of a plastic mug.

"Hey, who's Tanoura?"

He snorted. "Did somebody call you *Tanoura*?"

"No, I just heard the name somewhere." I wasn't sure what he'd think if I told him about Saleem Hassan.

"It's not a name. It means *skirt*." Where'd you hear it?"

"I don't remember. Somewhere. Maybe a song."

I rushed through the afternoon cleaning session with the help of Iggy Pop and a lot of coffee. Then I took the Thalhimer's bag back to my trailer and laid the fabric out flat on the floor, calling on all the Christiansburg Middle School Home Ec knowledge I could muster to convert that wrinkled old linen into a *tanoura* that would do Saleem Hassan proud. It wasn't anything fancy, just an elastic waist and some high slits up the sides, down to my ankles and gathered up at the hips for some flounce. I had enough of a piece left over to crisscross into a skimpy halter—a trick I remembered from the trampy girls back home, although they'd used bandannas or Confederate flags. I checked out my getup in the mirror, fluffed my hair, and put on my finger cymbals. Then I played my record and danced, spinning and undulating and *tek-tek-teking* until the bottle hit the trailer and signaled me to stop. I took off my *tanoura* and cymbals and lay down on the bed, awaiting my next mission from Saleem Hassan. This time he was smiling. Just barely, but it was definitely a smile.

Inti jamila, ya habibi. He nodded, puffing on his cigarette. *So pretty! And now you are ready to go back to the diner. Go tomorrow. Bukrah. At night.*

What did the diner have to do with anything? I woke up wondering if maybe I wasn't getting omens, just going crazy. Saleem made more sense when he was talking in Arabic. Still, he was right about the rubber bands and the fabric—I was willing to take my chances on the diner. With Saturday coming fast, I didn't have many options.

The next day I cleared the last boxes out of the trailer and gave it a good scrub with bleach water. It passed the Arab's inspection with flying colors, so I had two hundred dollars in my pocket, plus the twenty he'd given me. Stepping out on faith, what little I had of it, I packed my new outfit in a backpack, borrowed Bobby Harvey's bicycle, and headed up Jeff Davis toward the Lee Bridge. Just before the bridge, as I waited for the light to change at Hull Street, Gimpy-Arm loped across the parking lot of Church's Chicken and screamed my name.

"You better make that money, *bitch*," she called, flinging a Styrofoam cup of Coca-Cola that exploded next to my tire.

Fortunately, Jeff Davis crack whores are like vampires in that they can't cross moving water. She didn't follow me toward the bridge.

Once I was halfway across, I stopped to smoke a cigarette and get my nerves back. The view from the Lee Bridge that night made Richmond look sparkly, more like a city than it really is. It was beautiful against the dark sky. Looking down, the glistening water was beautiful too, until I started seeing visions of my lifeless body floating in it. I forced myself to raise my eyes to the skyline. The city had seemed so big to me when I first got here. Now it was way too small.

I finished my cigarette and headed to the diner.

Only when I got there, there wasn't any *there* there. To be specific, there wasn't a River City Diner there. The neon clock was out front, and I could see the grill of the Cadillac sticking out of the wall inside, but the sign had been covered with a hand-painted banner that said, *BUBBLING*. In the window, rows of hookah pipes like the one the Arab kept in the office stood at attention, and the booths were full of smokers, mostly men—young, swarthy men—smoking hookahs and scooping at plates of food with flat bread. I understood now what I was supposed to do. Of course Saleem Hassan hadn't steered me wrong. I felt bad for doubting him. I locked Bobby's bike to a parking meter and walked inside.

At the grill, a dark-haired man scurried to fill baskets with kebabs, fries, and pitas. He muttered as he worked, snatching order tickets from the carousel as fast as the waiters could tack them up. "Have a seat anywhere," he barked. He turned his back to me and began shaking a basket of fries over the deep fryer.

"I'm not here to eat," I said, then screwed up my courage and pulled a pair of cymbals out of my bag and slipped them on. "I'm here to dance. I mean, if I can, if you'll let me." I clanked the cymbals once for punctuation and he wheeled around.

He squinted at me through the grill fumes. "You bring a costume?" I nodded. "You bring music?" I shook my head. Saleem should have mentioned that. "*Ma fi mushkila*, it's no problem, I have music. You change in the ladies' room. But I no pay you! You dance free! If I like, next time I pay!"

Dance free? The doubt crept in again. What the hell was Saleem thinking? And, really, the bigger question was: what the hell was I doing, about to belly dance in a hookah bar because a dead Arab told me to? As Iggy said at the last Stooges show, I never thought it would come to this.

After I got changed and combed my hair out with my fingers, I put both pairs of cymbals on and closed my eyes, calling on Allah, Jesus, Saleem Hassan, and whoever looked out for crazy trailer park girls who needed money bad to help make this whatever it was supposed to be. Then I slipped out of the ladies' room and stood in the dark corridor until one of the waiters came back and asked if I was ready.

"Muhammad wants to know your name so he can introduce you."

"Kim," I told him. He looked at me like I stank and walked away. A minute later he came back and said, "Muhammad says your name will be Jamila. It means *beautiful*."

I nodded. Over the chatter and clatter and bubbling hookahs I heard Muhammad yell something in Arabic, and then he called my new name and the lights dimmed. The opening strains of an Arabic song I'd never heard poured forth from the vintage Wurlitzer. I danced down the aisle fast, giving everyone a quick taste, twirling in great cursive loops and clanging the cymbals together over my head like an ambulance siren, clearing my way through traffic. Then I made my way back up the aisle more slowly, stopping at each table for an undulation or a stomach flutter, teasing, flirting, and charming the men, flirting more with the few women there just to show there were no hard feelings. They ululated as I spun, and each time I presented a piece of myself to a table—a bobbing hip, a shrugging shoulder, or a beckoning arm, someone would tuck a bill into my costume. As I *tek-a-teked* to the music on the Wurlitzer, the men got up one by one, leaving their hookahs to dance with me for a measure or two, showing off to their friends, snapping and clapping and blowing clouds of fruity smoke around me. Through the smoke I could see Muhammad in the kitchen, nodding along with the music and shaking the fryer basket to the rhythm of my cymbals.

When the instruments fell away and the song was nothing but drums, two waiters cleared the backgammon boards from the front table and hoisted me up without asking. I stood, covered in sweat, dollar bills lining the waist of my *tanoura*. I translated the beat of the drum into motion, hips snapping left left right, up up down, circle around and back. Whenever the drums paused, I answered with my cymbals, clanking in syncopation. The longer I danced, the more bills the men stacked on their tables, and as the drums built to a crescendo that I followed with my hips, the men leaped up to flick the piles of bills at me like dry leaves. They fluttered down around my feet for the waiters to scoop into a paper bag.

When the song ended, I wiped the sweat from my eyes, blew kisses, and bowed, then grabbed my paper bag and hustled back to the ladies' room to see if I had enough to save my ass. The bag was stuffed full—I had to have enough, after all of this craziness with the dreams and the *tanoura* and the dancing and all, right? Isn't that how stories like this end?

I was confident, giddy. I pulled handfuls of ones, fives, tens, and twenties out of the bag and piled them on my lap. Sitting on the toilet and stacking bills on the sink, I counted three hundred and forty-two dollars. Three hundred and *fifty*-two, after someone slid a ten under the door. Which put me at five hundred and seventy-two dollars. Four hundred and twenty-eight short of what I needed.

Pulling my jeans on and folding the money into my pocket, I felt betrayed. By Saleem Hassan, by Saint Iggy, by my own stupid-ass choices and bad decisions. I was a cliché. I was going to be a dancing girl who gets murdered in a trailer park on a Saturday night over crack money. Fuck irony. All the way from Christiansburg to Richmond and this was what my life had become. I might as well have stayed a waitress and called everybody *honey*.

A knock on the bathroom door pulled me out of my self-hating trance. I opened it a crack and saw nothing, then looked down and saw an Arab guy, a kid really, a head shorter than me, in a black shirt and a silver tie.

"Jamila, right? Jamila." I nodded. "I'm Marwan. Can I talk to you for a minute? All business, I promise."

What did I have to lose? I followed him to his table. Marwan's heavy, copper-colored eyes locked on mine as he pulled from the hookah.

"Jamila. You're a good dancer, Jamila. How much you make tonight, two hundred, three hundred?"

I shrugged. "I don't talk money with strangers."

"Good policy. Smart girl. Hey, Jamila, I'ma be honest with you. I run a club. A *nice* club. What you call a gentleman's club. The *best* one. I can tell you for a fact you could make a thousand dollars a night there, easy. You dance like that, *Ma fi mushkila*, no problem. Only just a different costume."

He leered a little and licked his lips. "So what do you say you come by tomorrow and work for me? I put you on the main stage, none of this *tables. Inti Jamila.* You so pretty."

I reached across the table and took the hookah tube from him and sucked in a deep draft of gray smoke. I held it in my lungs and considered my options. I could be one kind of cliché and end up dead in the trailer park on a Saturday night. I could be another kind of trailer park cliché and dance around a pole with my tits out for money. Or I could go back home tonight and see what Saleem Hassan's next piece of advice was for me, with a couple of hundred dollars in my pocket for which I had him to thank. That looked like the best choice. If dancing around a pole was what he wanted for me, I'm sure he'd tell me—though from what I'd heard the Arab say about girls who did that, I had a feeling it wasn't what Hassan wanted. I blew the smoke politely toward the floor and shook my head.

"I appreciate the offer, Marwan, but I don't think I'm cut out for that kind of dancing. Thanks anyway."

Before he could argue, I threw my backpack over my shoulder and walked out. As I unlocked Bobby's bike, I could see Marwan scrambling to throw money on the table, but I was down the street before he made it out the door. There are men you trust and men you don't, and there was something sketchy about that little dude I just didn't like.

Back at Rudd's, I locked Bobby's bike to his porch and walked across the gravel road to my trailer. I could see Beau through his window, drinking a beer and watching wrestling. I went inside and sat down at my little kitchenette, wondering what tomorrow was going to bring. I could stay and try and reason with Ivan, giving him what money I had, or I could just disappear—but to where? To do what? Although it felt strange to even hear myself think it, the idea of leaving the trailer park filled me with sadness I'd never felt when leaving Christiansburg.

For once, I realized, I was living in a place where the list of things I didn't hate was at least as long as the list of things I did. I didn't hate the fact that I shared my walls with no one, thin and aluminum though they were. I didn't hate the way outsiders avoided our potholed roads that were occasionally blocked by the Mexicans' work trucks and junker cars, because that meant I didn't have to deal with anyone I didn't want to. I definitely didn't hate the cheap rent. And, though it'd taken me awhile to trust him, I didn't hate the Arab. The more I thought about it, the more I realized that Rudd's was the closest thing to a real home I'd ever had, and the Arab was the only person I'd been able to count on in my whole life.

I knew that if it came down to it and I told him what was going on, I would have sanctuary in the trailer park as best he could provide it. I'd watched him pretend not to speak English and stall the *inmigración*, the cops, and the dogcatcher long enough for Bill Baldy and Bobby Harvey to hustle folks—and dogs—to higher ground. And when the people from Social Services came to take Judy to a group home, he'd chased them all the way out of the trailer park and up Jeff Davis, spitting and cussing in two languages. "*Neek hallak!* She already lives in a goddamned group home! What the fuck do you think this is?"

I had no plans to ask the Arab for help, but the more I thought about it, the more I realized I wasn't willing to take my chances anywhere else. This was where I belonged. Whatever was going to happen would just have to happen here.

A knock at a trailer door after midnight is never good news.

Sometimes it's crack whores, sometimes it's drunk Mexicans, and occasionally it's Bobby Harvey coming home to the wrong place after too many sips of Wild Irish Rose. But tonight? Since it was technically tomorrow, it must have been *the* knock. I took one more sip of coffee and one more drag off my cigarette. At least I would get it over with now, without the dread. It's the dread that kills you. Well, the dread and the four hundred and twenty-eight dollars in old crack debts that you didn't make back belly dancing in a diner.

I stood behind the closed door and said a quick prayer of intercession to Jesus, Allah, Iggy, Saleem Hassan, and whoever else might be listening. I hoped that it would be Ivan himself, and not one of his lackeys, so that maybe memories of all the good times might buy me another day or two. Or less cruelty, at least. Not that there had actually been any good times.

I opened the door and looked out, and then down, to see not Ivan but Marwan standing on my step, his low-slung champagne-colored Mazda as out of place as he was in Rudd's Trailer Park.

"Jamila, *habibi*, I followed you here. Look, I want to talk to you for real, because you're making a mistake."

"There's no mistake," I said, angry that he wasn't Ivan. I had already gotten psyched up for getting killed. "I'm not going to work at your club and I don't like being followed, so get lost."

"No, seriously." He placed his hand on the door to my trailer. "Lemme talk to you because you're making a *big mistake*."

"I think you're the one who's mistaken," I said through my teeth, leaning my weight against the door to keep him out. "I don't want anything to do with your club. Now get lost."

"Fuck you. I drive all the way to the *Southside* to a fucking *trailer park* to give you a job and you don't have no manners?" He stuck the toe of his Italian leather shoe against the door and kept it there. "You fucking piece of trash, you should be *grateful* I even talk to you!" His breath came through the crack of the door, hot in my face, smelling like fruity tobacco. Over his head I could just see the window of Beau's trailer. Beau stood up slowly from the sofa, looked my way, and turned out his light.

"Fuck you, *sharmouta!*" Marwan spat once, twice on the steps of my trailer. "You're not even beautiful! *Kelbeh!*" After his last insult, he smacked the side of the trailer hard with his open palm. The vibration made the cymbals on the table chime faintly, like a distant call to prayer. Marwan wedged his arm and shoulder into the crack of the door and grabbed a handful of my hair. I leaned back to pull myself loose, but I couldn't get far enough away and keep the door shut, so instead I tried to twist around and bite him. I had just gotten a good toothhold on his wrist when his body jerked up like a marionette. Through the crack of the door I saw Beau's big arm hooked around Marwan's neck. Beau pulled him out of my door, off my step, and up into a standing camel clutch that would have made the Iron Sheik proud.

Beau held Marwan like that for a good thirty seconds, just long enough to scare him, and then flung him loose onto the ground. It was a short fall, broken by an errant cinder block. Every trailer park has them. Unfortunately for Marwan, this one happened to be exactly where it was, and its corner made a sickening *thud* as it connected with his temple.

Beau and I stood there for a long time. Looking at Marwan, looking at each other, feeling bad, but not as bad as we might have.

Bobby Harvey came wandering through after a while, making his last evening check of the trailer park.

"I didn't see anything," he said to us. "Did y'all?"

We both shook our heads.

"Good. Now get on inside before somebody does."

There are some things that don't warrant much investigation. A dead strip club manager in a shiny tie on Jeff Davis Highway is one of those things. Particularly if nobody in the trailer park heard anything or saw anything. And, not to gild any lilies, but just suppose there was a crack rock or two in his hand when the police got there, well, these things happen in trailer parks *all the time.* Such is life. I'm sure the Arabs have a saying about it, and it's probably close to what my Arab said when he realized that the body he'd been called out of bed for was one of his guys. *"Rahimahullah!* His daddy should have beat him harder."

The police took a report, but beyond that there was no investigation to speak of. The man's wallet was empty. According to the girls at the club, he usually kept about five hundred dollars in cash on him—*usually* meaning on the nights he didn't drop seventy-two dollars at a hookah bar on baba ghanoush and shoulder shimmies—so robbery was the obvious motive. The police made a point of coming around and reminding us to lock our doors. They were especially concerned about me, what with it happening right outside my place. I told them not to worry, that the Arab was letting me move to a bigger trailer in the back of the park. Same rent, more room—and with nobody next door, I could play my cymbals as late as I wanted every night.

Now, instead of waiting tables, I dance two nights a week at the hookah bar for better tips than I ever got slinging eggs when it was a diner. Word's gotten around and the place is usually packed—Muhammad actually pays me now, and he's even put a picture of me in the window, next to the picture of his famous kebabs. I still clean a trailer for the Arab every couple of months, not so much for the money but just to keep my title and help out. Because that's what I guess family does. Saleem talks to me in my dreams every now and then, mostly to call me *Jamila* and ask me when I'm gonna get married. And sometimes he tells me I should eat more, I might blow away.

UNTITLED

BY MEAGAN J. SAUNDERS

Jackson Ward

To my mom, who showed me strength

An uneasy silence engulfed him. Occasionally, he would glance toward the driver's seat and stare at Janie, who still wore her factory clothes. She didn't look at him. Sighing, he moved his eyes back to the window. They flew past abandoned buildings, past Ebenezer, where he found God, and Armstrong, the school where he discovered Janie and everything else. Men sat on curbs heading nowhere, complacent. He knew them intimately—knew their stories, their fears, and their delusions. "So you ain't gonna talk to me?" he asked, finally.

She hesitated. "What you want me to say? You don't wanna hear what I gotta say. I ain't ready to talk to you yet."

"Well, you could say *somethin'*." Her eyes narrowed. Still, he pushed the conversation: "How'd you pay the light bill?"

Words flew from her mouth like venom. "You ain't gotta worry 'bout that, Jayden! I found a way. Not that you helped me. Not that you care." The silence lasted until she pulled onto Marshall Street. She slammed her car door and pushed past him, through the overgrown grass and the trash people constantly threw into their yard. He followed close behind.

Once inside, he rushed to the back room. He opened the door. Nothing.

"Janie!" he screamed. He found her on the living room floor peeling potatoes into an aluminum bowl. He could barely breathe. "Where's my piano?!"

She didn't look up. "We need to do somethin' 'bout all these holes in the roof. Don't make no sense. I wake up every mornin' and start my day covered in—"

He squatted in front of her, lifting her chin until their eyes met. "I said, where's my piano?"

She smacked his hand away. "You ain't gonna put your hands on me. You better get that idea out your head right now." Her voice intensified. "Don't you dare disrespect me, Jayden. Today is *not* the day."

He paced, hands shaking. A lump grew in his throat.

Janie sighed. "Naw, I ain't sell your piano. Things hard but they ain't that hard. All these damn holes in the roof. I had to move it."

"Where?"

"Back there." He raced to the bedroom, where he saw it pressed against the window. He collapsed beside the doorway, smiling. But his smile didn't last long. He walked back into the living room, dragging his feet. Janie looked up momentarily, then continued her work.

"I'm sorry," he stumbled, "guess I overreacted a little. Who helped you move it? Quincy?"

"It got wheels."

"Guess it does. So how'd you pay the light bill?"

"That was Quincy."

His eyebrows rose. "Really?"

"I called my mama, Jayden."

"Oh. You want help with them potatoes?"

She shrugged. Jayden grabbed a knife and sat beside her. They peeled together in silence, the tension building with the rhythm of the wall clock.

Then she exploded. "Where were you, Jayden? You couldn't call me and let me know where you were?!"

"I was over Charlie's place."

"For a week? Tonya told me she saw you over on Belvidere talkin' to Angelo. Called me all frantic, told the whole neighborhood, making me look like a fool. I rush from work, drive up and down the street tryin' to find you, beg you to come with me, and for what?"

Jayden gawked but said nothing.

She slammed her knife into the bowl, producing a harsh ring. "You ain't gonna say nothin', Jay? You gone for a muthafuckin' week and you ain't got nothin' to say?"

"It was only five days."

Tears fell, but she wiped them away. "Don't you know how worried I was? What am I supposed to do with you? What am I supposed to do?"

"I'm sorry, baby—"

"You're sorry?"

The words slid off his tongue as if rehearsed. "That was the last time. I promise. You know I got that big audition comin' up soon—"

"It's always the last time. Always for some reason or other." Their eyes met. "It's always a lie."

He dropped the knife and hurried down the hall. He made his way to the piano, tracing the contours of the keys before he pressed down. A minor chord rang out. He exhaled, then modulated. Notes at first, then the sounds became something deeper. Ellington. "In a Sentimental Mood." After some time, he sensed Janie in the doorway watching him; sensed her anger, her sadness, and her love. He played harder, letting his soul seep through the music. "I'ma change, baby. You wait and see."

"What are words?" she replied, and walked away.

"Don't forget I got you booked at the Hippodrome. The gig's tomorrow." Quincy mixed bacon into a sea of hard-cooked eggs. He barely swallowed, yellow bits sprinkling an unkempt goatee. He wiped it away, greasing crisp sleeves.

Jayden tried to lift coffee to his lips but his hands shook uncontrollably. Coffee spilled down his shirt before the cup finally made its way to his mouth. He gulped, then placed the cup back on the table. "I'll be ready." He smiled uneasily. "Ain't no thang, you know? I was born to do shit like this."

Quincy leaned back in the booth and laughed. "Fuck. You can't even drink coffee, let alone play some keys." He pointed his fork toward Jayden. "I can't have you embarrassin' me, man. I have a reputation."

"I said I'll be ready!"

"You got a song, at least? Know you've been strugglin' to find somethin' that works."

Jayden wiped sweat from his forehead. "I'll have somethin' by Thursday."

Quincy dropped his fork on his plate, the metal clanging obnoxiously against the porcelain, drawing the attention of the other restaurant patrons. He moved to the edge of the seat, folded his arms on the table, and looked straight into Jayden's eyes. His voice lowered. "What happened to you, Jay? What are you thinkin'? You tryin' to go cold turkey right before the Hippodrome? The Apollo of the South. Ella Fitzgerald, Duke Ellington, and Billie Holliday all played there. You know how many people get discovered."

"I gotta," Jayden said defensively. "If I don't, Janie'll leave me."

"So what? You gonna let some bitch destroy your dreams? Never knew you as a pussy." The bell on the door rang furiously as a young man entered the diner. He wore a button-up at least two sizes too big; still, he stood confidently. Third Street smog mixed with the smell of bacon, but the harmony ended as the door slammed. Quincy's eyes sparkled. "Tré! Tré, over here."

The boy approached them briskly, a saxophone case in hand. His hair was conked, he whistled loudly. He looked no older than fourteen.

"Tré, I'd like you to meet Jayden. With some development, I think Tré's got a future." The young man extended his hand. Jayden reluctantly took it. "Jay here's playin' at the Hippodrome tomorrow night. He's gonna sit at the piano and stare at the audience. It's revolutionary."

"I'll have somethin' composed," Jayden mumbled.

"How's it comin'?" Tré asked.

"It'll come."

"He's goin' cold turkey."

"Damn!" Tré looked around the restaurant nervously. Satisfied, he reached into his coat and took out a small plastic bag. "Here."

Jayden examined its contents, then pushed it away. "Naw, man, can't do it. My girlfriend would have a heart attack."

"And so will I if you fuck this up!" Quincy growled. "It was real nice of Tré to help you out." He leaned closer. "You'll stop shakin' and you'll get a song. Win-win, you feel me?"

Jayden paused, staring at the bag on the table. He wrapped his hand around the plastic and placed it in his coat pocket.

"Now you're thinkin'." Quincy smiled. "That's my boy! I'll see you tomorrow."

"Tomorrow," Jayden replied. He placed a few dollars on the table. "Thanks for the chance, Q. Nice meeting you, Tré. You're real generous."

"Ain't nothin'," Quincy replied, finishing off his potatoes. He looked up. "Just don't mess it up."

Tré nodded in agreement. Jayden walked away.

He tried to find his song; tried to find that brilliance—that excellence—everyone said he had, but the more he played, the more frustrated he became. He wanted to play more than music—wanted to give the world something deeper than a beautiful arrangement. He wanted to play his life in song. But this tune wouldn't come, no matter how much he tried. He pressed his fingers hard against the ivory, filling the room with dissonant noise.

Gingerly, hands embraced him from behind. They made their way across his shoulders, then traced his spine.

"You know, when I was a boy, my daddy used to play all night long," Jayden said. "I'd listen from my bedroom as my Mama cursed and cried, but he'd keep playin'. Like she was just singin' the words to his songs. After she fell asleep he'd come get me; sit me down on the bench and teach me. Then he'd put me on his lap and play poetry with glazed eyes. I wanted to be him, baby."

Janie sat beside him, running her fingers down his thighs. "It'll come. You're just puttin' a lot of pressure on yourself, that's all."

"I got a reason to be nervous, don't I? This can make or break me—set us up for life—and I ain't got any ideas. I can't stop shakin' and I'm sweatin' all the time." He looked into her eyes, asking for understanding; asking her permission for the easy way out. Instead, she wrapped her arms around him.

"It's late. Come to bed."

"I can't. I ain't got no melody. No song—"

"Yeah, you do. It's inside. You just gotta let it go."

"What if it don't come in time?"

"Then it just isn't time. Not the end of the world. There are other gigs, other clubs—"

"Of course there are other gigs and other clubs, but you only get one shot at the Hippodrome."

Janie moved from the piano bench to the side of the bed and patted the mattress. He hesitated. She frowned. "Look, baby, you've been playin' all day. I don't think your song is gonna break through tonight." She grabbed his arm. "Let it go."

"A little longer, Janie."

She sighed. "Maybe tea will calm you down. I'll be back." She left the room.

Jayden fumbled with the keys a little more before finally giving up. He shifted to Miles Davis's "My Funny Valentine," played half the song, then stopped, his muscles tensing. He took the plastic bag out of his pocket and held it, running his fingers down the smooth shaft of the needle. Frantically, he searched for a lighter.

"What you looking for?" Janie asked.

Jayden shoved the bag back in his pocket. "Nothin'."

"I love it when you play that song." She handed him a steaming cup.

"Thank you." He drank quickly. She watched intently from the bed.

"I want you to know that whatever happens tomorrow, I'm proud of you." She tugged on his arm, gently but with persistence.

Reluctantly, he moved toward her. Without wasting

time, she kissed his cheek. She moved her lips down to his neck while unbuttoning his shirt. He ran his hands down her curves. His body shook. He tried to push past it—tried to take control—but there was no use. Janie moved away from him.

"I'm sorry, baby—"

"Don't be." She laid her head against the mattress, pulling Jayden to her chest. She wrapped her arms around him, gripping him tighter when the shaking grew more intense. He stayed in her arms all night.

Streetlights illuminated the stone exterior of the Hippodrome. Ivy covered the building; portraits of Jackson Ward adorned its façade. The marquee read: *Come See the Stars of Tomorrow.* Rain fell like the notes of a sonata, but that didn't stop people from coming. Smooth lavender music filled the air, blending with the sound of rainwater. On most nights, people only danced on stage. Tonight, however, bodies trickled down the aisles, whiskey perfuming conversation. Women swayed their hips to syncopated music and men smiled because they knew it was all for them. The vast majority dressed casually. Janie and Jayden stood out, she wearing a tight red dress and he dressed in a five-button suit. They grabbed a booth against the back wall.

"This place used to be classy," Janie said.

"This whole neighborhood used to be classy." He fiddled with the plastic bag in his coat pocket. "I don't know what I'm gonna do, baby."

"Play something old."

"I need something new."

"Improvise."

An announcer in a bright white penguin suit marched to the center of the stage and grabbed the microphone. "Are y'all ready for live music?" he called out.

People clapped and yelled in excitement.

"We'll start the show in about ten minutes. Until then, enjoy the piccolo, get loose, and relax."

Janie placed her hand on Jayden's thigh. "You're gonna do fine."

He smiled uneasily. "I gotta run to the bathroom. I'll be back." He made his way through the crowd of staggering people. In the haze he saw Tré sitting at the bar. The kid lifted his glass. Jayden nodded in acknowledgment. Once inside the bathroom, he headed straight for the stall. Muted music leaked inside. He took out the bag, mouth watering, hands shaking in anticipation. Thoughts of his father, his dreams, his future overwhelmed him. The music shifted from the jitterbug to classic jazz. "My Funny Valentine." He pressed his head against the cold metal of the door, fighting. The room spun. Jayden leaned against the toilet, nauseous. He breathed hard into the bowl until the feeling went away. Slowly, he made his way back out of the stall; stared at his blurred image. "I can do this," he whispered, splashing water on his face. He reentered the club, body shaking once more.

"Jay! Jay, over here!" Quincy sat in a booth surrounded by beautiful women. Grudgingly, Jayden approached him. "You ready?"

"It'll be the best you ever heard, man."

Quincy smirked. "Took your medicine, ay?"

"Naw, don't need it." Quincy's smirk turned to a frown. Jayden headed back over to Janie. She took his hand.

"You gonna be wonderful, baby." Her eyes sparkled, confident reassurance.

He believed her.

But the moment of truth came too soon. The announcer reemerged. People dashed to empty booths and chairs. "I got a real treat for y'all tonight!" he exclaimed. "This first act comes to us from the business management team of Quincy Freeman. Now, y'all know Quincy only works wit the best." Jayden's heart pounded through his chest. The world moved in slow motion but the announcer's words blared with the intensity of a thousand trumpets. "I want y'all to give a warm welcome to that most excellent, that most gifted, the fifteen-year-old sax phenom himself, Tré Andrews!"

Jayden's world came crashing down. The kid marched onto the stage wearing a light blue suit and top hat that almost swallowed his eyes. He took a bow, and started playing.

Janie rose from her seat. "Come on, baby," she said softly. "Let's get outta here." He followed her in disbelief.

Before they got to the door, Quincy jumped in front of them, sweat dripping from his forehead. He started talking fast.

"Look, man, it's nothin' personal. It's just that the kid is marketable and he got looks and he dances real good. That, and he's ready. Don't be mad. It's just business."

Hot anger rose from the depths of Jayden's soul. It took everything he had not to swing his fist. Instead, he reached into his pocket and pulled out the plastic bag. He threw it at Quincy, then walked away.

The two wandered down 2nd Street, silent. Graffiti covered most buildings, others were boarded up. The few businesses that remained opened were deserted, the owners sitting alone, watching people pass by. Janie walked close to the buildings while Jayden dragged his feet on the far edge of the sidewalk, unmoved by the world. Relentless weeds grew in the cracks of ragged streets. Jayden focused on the smooth emerald of each blade basking in the moonlight. The rain had stopped falling.

Janie finally broke the silence. "Look, I look too damn fine not to do somethin' tonight. I at least want a drink. You wanna get a drink with me, baby?" Jayden shrugged.

They found a scarcely populated lounge, indiscriminate save the red neon *OPEN* sign on the window. They walked straight to the bar.

"Two rum and Cokes," Janie said, leaning against the counter. "And make one a double." Scuffed wood paneling covered the lounge floor. Posters of Charles Mingus, Charlie Parker, Dizzy Gillespie, and Thelonious Monk decorated the walls.

Jayden watched a man in a sharp black suit flip chairs onto empty tables; watched him grab a broom and start sweeping. On stage, a grand piano shone in soft blue light.

"Y'all close soon?" he asked the bartender.

"Closin' now," the bartender said back. "Last call."

The man in the suit looked at his watch, then dropped the broom. He took slow, exhausted strides to the stage and grabbed the microphone. He jumped when it screeched. Once the noise stopped, he began: "We got time for one more performance. So if anybody out there wanna do a poem or sing a song or play somethin' up here, then you're welcome to it." He jumped from the stage and went back to sweeping.

"Get up there, Jay!" Janie exclaimed. "You know you wanna!" He hesitated. "Go on," she persisted.

Slowly, absentmindedly, he made his way onto the stage. He looked through the blue haze out into the audience. He saw his lady. She smiled. Slowly, he sat.

"What ya playin'?" a lady in the audience called out. Slight laughter hummed throughout the room.

Jayden pulled the microphone close. He paused, contemplating. "This is untitled," he said finally.

He pressed down. Notes at first, then, to his surprise, they turned into something more. He moved between major and minor chords—modulated between his joys and his pains; his past and an uncertain future. First major and he tasted his mama's lemonade—remembered makeshift water parks on hot summer days and his first kiss. Then minor and he re-lived cold winter nights with no heat and no love. He saw the look on his daddy's face, those glassy eyes, and feelings took over. His fingers moved, pumping life into music. They told his story; his life in song.

He asked no questions, simply let go and was. He played an unknown melody, forgotten once he touched the keys. Memories he'd never experienced danced through his fingers, scenarios that had never crossed his mind, but two things were constant, his love and his lady, moving together throughout time.

Then the final chord. He struck it hard and didn't move. He was afraid to move. The sound resonated throughout the room, blending with the pitter-patter of the rain against the aluminum roof. An eternity before he lifted his hands from the keys. After that, silence. Smoke stood in its place, refusing to rise, and people stared, not breathing. He squinted through the haze and saw his lady. She wiped away tears.

MARCO'S BROKEN ENGLISH

BY CONRAD ASHLEY PERSONS

West End

Meredith Lewis, housewife, mother of three, sat watching her second hour of television on a cloudless morning in Virginia. Dressed in a pink robe with matching slippers, she wept furiously. One of those advertisements, from Oxfam or Greenpeace or *some organization like that*, ran and ran and implored her to help the starving denizens of some small nation in Africa whose name Meredith didn't even dare try to pronounce.

The situation there seemed tenuous. She couldn't tell whether the government was a victim of imposed circumstances, whether they were especially corrupt or just poor. The camera panned across another woeful scene, and more buffalo tears welled as Meredith realized how fragile everything was. The most permanent of fixtures was nothing more than a well-built tent, houses shoddily constructed of canvas, threadbare schools with throwaway books, scantily dressed children in scantily fed bodies, and dust everywhere. Everything was so thin she knew that one brave gust of wind could push this tiny civilization into the sea.

But there was hope. Development could come into existence and be sustained, but it wasn't going to be easy. It was going to take money. It was also going to take fundamental changes in politics, collective amnesia about colonialism, and faith. But the money was what they needed now. Some busty celebrity came in from camera left and made the final plea. Her chest heaved from grief. The situation was as follows: no food—ribs bravely protruding through skin, thirsty flies who, finding no safe ponds, feast on eyes instead—vague, beige bags of rice flown in from the good guys, seven cents could feed seven children, no clean water here, the heat: unbearable, the wind off the vast sands: bitter, the great rivers: gone dry. Simply put: this was not fair. Meredith Lewis, help us, help us help these children. Cry for the horror of this world, for its depravity, for its interminable thirst for entropy. Help us now.

She thought to light a cigarette, didn't, and chewed her lips instead. She shuffled to the bathroom for a fistful of tissues. Like the rest of the house, this room was modestly appointed, with a lavender ribbon pattern running from baseboard to ceiling. A bowl of potpourri rested by the sink, a medley of dried purple flowers. She took a fluffy towel, also purple, and used it to cover her face. And suddenly the sweetness of the room, its scent, its color—each piece a cute counterpart to another—it all seemed unbearable: a morbid lightness amongst so much horror.

Staring into the mirror, with its gilded frame, she was utterly confused by her appearance. A housewife all cried out in the suburbs. With no mascara, the tears did little to disturb her face. But they made her eyes raw and red and searching. Were her tears for Africa? Or were they for that feeling, deep in her belly, a sad expectancy that any day now she would find lipstick on her husband's collar, or that he would rush through the door and make straight for the shower, with no explanation save a liar's grin?

She had not looked at herself for a very long time. She viewed her face shyly at first, then with immodest intent. Meredith had medium-length brown hair, which was burnished by the naked light. Her green eyes were as flat and clean as a newly clipped lawn. Her cheekbones were substantive, but not pronounced, which made her appearance delicate and accommodating. She had once been beautiful.

She rarely flattered her appearance with the many products she spotted in other women's cabinets. Meredith's morning routine consisted of the same old foundation and blush she'd first bought the night before prom. She had always clung to simplicity like some familiar womb. But she could feel things unwinding, felt some loosening that precedes a clamor.

She'd spent time in Lyon looking at churches when she was a student, and had once even skinny-dipped in Interlaken on a dare. But adventure was a short-lived pursuit; she loved the cozy streets of the West End and the circumstances of home best. She had never wanted to be anything other than a mother, and since she had birthed her boys she thought of nothing else. She sighed, said her name, and turned her head from the mirror.

To her left was a window. Pear trees were heavy, threatening to bear fruit. Local university boys walked by all dressed in khaki, their hair wet, books shoved tightly in their cases. There was no breeze; not a single branch stirred.

Stepping into the living room, she realized that half an hour had passed. *Could I have spent that much time in dumb contemplation?* Or was it like all other days when tasks ate her time like corrosives? The commercial was still running on the television. The number on the bottom had been there so long she feared it would burn its impression into the screen: a *1*, an *800*, and a reminder of suffering in some part of the world she would never, ever want to visit.

Meredith gave Harry's sixteen-digit credit card number

with expiration date, was promised future mailings and a picture for her refrigerator of a darling black girl, and in exchange received relief, temporary relief from *all this shit*.

The rest of her day spread before her. She had watched her boys go to the bus long ago, and recalled their three heads in single file as they walked: capped, small, anxious. Harry had left this morning quietly. He tiptoed in the mornings, his thin black socks barely touching the hardwood floors. Lights flickered on and off in quick succession as he made his way from room to room. And the way he left the bed was an elaborate, silent ceremony, sliding off in an awkward balancing act so that he wouldn't wake Meredith and her desire.

The house was empty and ready for more of her tears. She decided to leave it. She went to her closet and decided to not wear much. She donned a white sleeveless crochet dress that finished just above her knees. She wore white shoes with modest heels. Around her neck hung a cheap Spiga necklace that had the pin and sprawl appearance of a bolo tie. She got into the station wagon and, as if seeing it for the first time, thought it old-fashioned. She drove north to Monument Avenue without thinking, jerking the stick, switching gears, the mindless radio playing songs she already knew, or thought she did. And soon, without any recollection of her journey, she was at Hash and Mash.

Hash and Mash occupied a low-slung building walled with windows and topped by beaten-up brown shingles. The day's specials were painted on the glass, inventive and banal interpretations of the diner's muse: the potato. Meredith walked in and heard the loud crackle of a sizzling grill, smelled the sharp hint of fried onions. Will, the manager, had droopy eyes, which looked at her, then directed their gaze to his right, where an empty booth sat. He never moved, just walked patrons to their seat with those eyes, which always seemed on the verge of bored tears. A waitress came and took her order, never looking up from her pad.

Pennants and posters of athletes lined the walls. All the short order cooks wore paper chef hats and grease-stained white polos. The local radio played music but was occasionally interrupted by news bulletins, Harry's news bulletins. He had been reading the news for seventeen years now, his voice the city's voice; he had delivered Richmond new presidents, used car sales, and the impending doom of market indicators. It was the voice that sent them to sleep, and got them up at an hour when everyone was dreaming except for maids and truck drivers. Here was Harry, on the radio, only a voice, a faceless bogeyman, as he was at home.

She could hear that voice and imagine him at his desk, a packet of Pall Malls beside him, reading the wires, breathing down a ribbon microphone, all the better to catch his timbre, which was querulous, slightly frightened at what the AP might send him next. Privy to too much war, too many fires, too many car crashes in the night. All of it had made him tired, just as something was making Meredith tired, making her fear that she wanted something more.

Harry never came to Hash and Mash. It was local, and cheap, and he said he thought it was the sort of place where you might run into someone you'd always hoped you'd never run into again. For Meredith, this made it sweet.

Her hash browns arrived like a mountain of steaming flesh. She wished she was wearing sleeves, so that she might roll them up in order to properly enjoy this meal. She devoured it, nothing but streaks of ketchup left on the plate. She left a five-dollar tip, left Will in his dependable stupor, and drove to Short Pump. To paradise.

For Meredith, the American mall—with its anchor stores and boutiques, its cacophony of sing-along music, its sheer level of harmlessness—had always been a world unto itself. For Meredith, this was the ultimate escape. She bought lots of things. First Bouvier glasses too big for her face. Then a dress covered in sequins that made her look like she was coated in the eyes of sea monsters. And finally she went to the counter for a makeover. She wanted to make over her face—make it new again, wipe out that carrot-shaped birthmark beneath her chin, the slight wrinkle that had erupted on her brow, and the permanence of worry that she never asked to be there. And after the formulas and approving looks from the makeup girl, she believed it was gone. She critically gazed into the mirror, and unlike this morning she was utterly pleased. With her face fixed and her donation made, she felt downright cheery: about Africa, about herself, about everything.

She returned to the car and did what she never did: she ventured to the Tavern, a place she hadn't visited in three careful years. This was a rare treat, but with the way the morning had gone, with this rare and acute sensation all over her like a happy rash, she pulled the wagon out and headed down Broad Street toward a once familiar bar and its reliable disrepair.

Inside the main entrance, she pushed through the set of saloon-style louvre doors, practically made of plywood, weighing nothing. They made a clatter, which meant her entrance was noted by the patrons. Her white dress was the only unsullied thing there, as everything else was worn but handsomely dirty. The bar was full, but there were no groups, no polite chit-chat, only the friendly haggling over life's minutiae that preoccupies barflies at midday. She found her second booth of the day and sat down.

The music on was known to her; she could not be sure but it sounded like Elvis, the voice muffled by the crowd's screams, while little girls at home bemoaned the fact that he was only filmed from the hips up. She had two glasses of Pinot Gris and smiled as the wine opened in her mouth like a flower. She sat in the quiet corner and tried her best to think of nothing. When she departed, the bartender stood up and doffed his hat.

She got into her car, turned the ignition, and prepared to head home. The front of the wagon peeked out of the road like a turtle's head and was smashed, mercilessly and with great violence, by a roadster. The last thing Meredith Lewis ever saw was an old Mustang speeding toward her. She did not see three-by-five shots of her little boys—John, David, and Robert—in her mind's eye, nor did she see the wrinkled and cavalier face of Harry; she saw red, coming at her all too heavily and too soon and she was dead.

The driver of that red roadster was Marco Dogliotti, on his way to Atlanta to deliver three suitcases to two sweaty men who wore open collars. He had a belly full of vodka, what looked like paper cuts all over his face, and a wrecked auto—but he was alive.

It was just after dusk south of New York City and Marco had the swagger of a man with a country. America, it was like a song on his tongue, each new detail embellishing this embarrassment of riches. Here he was, behind the wheel of a convertible, registered to his many-syllabled name, tumbling down a highway so fast the windows shook, hatless, with his brown, thinning ponytail tousled by the wind.

Route 78 was a four-lane highway. Traffic lights interrupted its flow only every few miles. On each side was the detritus of a country with too much land: gas stations, junk shops, car washes. Otherwise just concrete trying to squash grass—so nothing to visit but a lot to see. The monotonous scenery thrilled him because this was *American* soil, and American boredom was a new sort of boredom—bigger, more of it to study, somehow pretty in its unnaturalness.

Mother of God, how far am I from Naples? Only two months and he was already forgetting its sooty port and oranges. Its gawking visitors, pickpockets secreted in the very cracks of walls, unruly traffic, and girls' skirts that never lifted an inch above the knee. Its rituals, its thievery, its charm. Here in the U.S.A. everything was too new, hung too loosely. One moment it all seemed too transparent and simple to read. Other times he saw only tops of icebergs, understood only parts of meanings—things slipped away in translation. He would think *e* but say *or*, bow his head in thanks as locals eyed him queerly. He could not yet trust his tongue.

In his car he drank heavily from a thermos. His sunglasses had white frames and had come free with his last tank of gas. He straightened his ridiculous posture and grinned for no other reason than it was morning. This hour was often accompanied by a giddiness that would die just before lunch, that could somehow never be sustained. Today, though, he would find out what this giddiness ate, and would feed it luxuriously: pollute it with rich foods, regardless of the cost. Today he would genuinely try to be happy. For he wanted, very badly, to be a smiling American, and make this place's incorrigible sweetness a daily habit.

He mouthed the names of gas stations, fiddled with his dial, ignored the speed limit, and waited, as he always waited, for something significant to happen to him, for a simple change of luck. Engrossed, he didn't see the red light until it was flush upon him.

His foot flattened and the car groaned to a stop. After the shriek of the brakes died down, he heard that rapid and aggressive sort of chatter that reminded him of talk radio. To his left was a bearded man in a big white make. The man rolled down his window and screwed his face. He said something so angrily that spit flew from his mouth and speckled Marco's closed window.

He was unable to interpret the English fast enough, only picking out words here and there: *mother, dumbest, cunt, ugly*. He felt unsure and unwanted and as if a door to a very comfortable room was being closed before him. The stranger stared, shook his head purposefully, and finally pulled away.

The shadow cast, his mood soured, Marco pulled to the shoulder of the road and sat quietly. The rearview mirror had been affixed to the front window by glue and wire. But the heat, which made dreamy lines rise from the asphalt, had melted the adhesive, so that the mirror had started to come off, and was attached only by a thin, naked wire. So now the wind pushed the mirror back and forth like a pendulum. In it, Marco saw flashes of his face, seesawing so as to make him slightly nauseous.

It was olive-skinned with slim features. His hair was the color of assorted, processed tobacco and his eyes were doleful but prying. His mouth was tight and dry, as if his face was in pincers. He viewed the reflection in the mirror, and was disappointed that this new country had done nothing for his appearance. He frowned at its smooth, unblemished contours, wishing a scar or some other mark of distinction might emerge, thinking America at least owed him that. He felt that in this nation of so many, he might never be able to distinguish himself. And surely not with a face so plain it was rendered blank.

He started the car again. He drove seventy miles an hour for as long as it took both sides of a Sam Cooke album to play on CD. At the sight of a sign that read, *Middletown,* he turned off the highway and went to the first bar he saw. It was just before noon but already raucous inside—tight, big-hair riffs came from the juke box, while boys in baseball caps raised hell and screamed in shorthand. A girl sat alone at the bar. She was his type—destitute—so he crawled over and asked if she liked the vodka.

"That and anything else," she said, so he ordered two, and two again, and it didn't stop until his vision was so blurred it was like seeing the world through tears.

When they got to the hotel she silently disrobed. He offered her his white bag, and she unfurled a line long and thin as a snow corn. She took the scraps and applied them to her gums, which made her wince, then blush.

Twelve hours later they hadn't slept. Unaccustomed to attention, she was talkative. He learned that a perm couldn't tame her hair and she liked waterfalls. She'd traveled. Done a tour of Texas, where her ex lived. Farthest she'd ever been from home. Sick on the plane. In a monotone voice she listed cities visited like exotic but affordable items from the market: Plano, Dallas, Argyle, Cee Vee. He pretended to be impressed, widening his eyes each time a name left her lips. But all he was thinking of was if she would lay him again, and if not, what he might do to keep her quiet.

She said they had a bond, but the bond wasn't forever, because when the coke ran out so did she. Her possessions looked like trash, but she put them in her purse anyway, and then shuffled out, scrubbing her nose. She left the door open, letting a ruler-straight line of light into the room.

Feeling unclean, he showered, and when he returned there was less money in his wallet than there used to be. Inwardly he shrugged his shoulders: so life would be as life was. This land did not want him but he wanted it, could already taste a new existence. He slept like the dead and promised himself that he would cross the Mason-Dixon the next day.

He woke up wet from the heat. Sometime in the night the air conditioner had given out. The hotel robe was thinner than a paper napkin, but he wore it anyway. He put on a ragged pair of sandals too, and came out of his room looking like a forlorn Jesus, all disciples up and gone, no one but he and the Bible out here in a forgotten-about America, lost counties abutted by lost counties, weak radio signals, shabby concrete, and long highways, the very end of some backwoods called Earth. He wanted to say a prayer but could think of none.

He went out to the car, tiptoeing on the hot asphalt. The key entered the trunk's lock, pricked the spring, and he heard the satisfying pop. It yawned open, revealing three gray suitcases. One would be innocuous, but three, lined so neatly, sitting so idly—made him think of gravestones in an abandoned field. He staggered back—awed yet again by his smallness and the sheer stupidity of his task. It had sent him north, south, and sideways. They told him to never go in a straight line, to never give the appearance of making sense, to always take the circuitous route of a phantom or an idiot.

He cleaned up in the shower, then returned to his car and drove the speed limit forever. Delaware looked no different to his eyes than Pennsylvania had, and Maryland was but a field of grass. To Virginia then, with a red cardinal on its welcome

sign, and the instant and confused surety that he was no longer North.

The buildings were suddenly squatter. There were advertisements for grits, pancakes, and cobblers. A hotel offered
rooms for twelve dollars a night. Pines crowded oaks out of
the landscape and hawks flew in wide arcs over the crown of
his thinning head.

A few hours in and he neared Richmond. He got flustered
though, and when 95 and 64 split, he choked. The simplest
decisions flummoxed him, and at the last minute he went
west on 64. Then came the sense of stupidity that follows such
an error. He called himself horrible things. Impatient, he got
off the highway. He followed the Broad Street exit and pro-
ceeded to drive in circles. Finally he parked his car, preferring
to use his feet.

Walking, he came upon a restaurant called Dune, standing two stories tall. Its first-floor windows were closed to the
heat, blacked out by plantation shutters. The second floor had
French doors that opened onto a short patio, with a sturdy
guardrail protecting the diners. He sensed something closed
about it: colloquial, clubby, but full of black sheep. He decided
that it might be a pleasant place to lunch.

But instead of lunch he had five vodkas with tonic water.
The day was clear and the view from the second floor laid
the town out like a canvas. He was confused by the sprawl's
repetitiveness, how, in an effort to be neat, people could make
things ugly.

He settled into his seat. He settled into the voice of his
waitress because it too was a place—a lazy hammock in the
sun. The hours passed with his eyes closed not in sleep but in
something like mental dawdling.

He felt an angel touch his shoulder and tell him the restaurant closed between lunch and dinner, and so he was asked to leave so that they might clean up. The pretty waitress chatted to him amiably, said she wished he could stay. He heard her but didn't hear her, for they spoke differently down here, vowels stretched like rubber, the pitch nasal and too sweet.

He left Dune and got into his car. Stationary, he turned the dial and fished out a college radio station. The song was one of the Stevie Wonder numbers from back when he was called "Little Stevie." The crackle of an old record like fat in a pan. The instruments made noise first and the singers followed. The tune featured gospel-style call and response. *Little Stevie lets go an outrageous howl that sends the piano jumping.* The engine turned over and purred. He put the car in reverse and swung it to the left real easy. He started to navigate his way through the parking lot. *The call comes like it deserves an answer; the singer pleads for assurances.* He edged forward at a slow pace and the gravel went crunch underneath. He pulled into the long line waiting to leave the lot. Shifting the vehicle into neutral, he hopped out and rolled the canvas top down. The interior was flooded with light. He pushed the car forward. *The response comes: six women, six women with thighs like hams sing a chorus.* Finally at the front of the line, he turned his head left to address the attendant. A lanky boy with pimples and a bowl haircut told him that it was five dollars. He went to his wallet and handed over the first thing that his fingers found, producing an enormous tip. He wanted to congratulate himself for this, for having made this kid's day. *The song slows now, not with an abrupt bang but with one of those old-school Detroit fades.* Turning right out of the lot, he gathered speed as he crossed over Glenside. The outdoors was all around him. With few cars on the street he felt alone. Then something timidly pulled out on his right-hand side. His foot just could not find the brake, and then the sound of metal going through itself. He had crushed her.

The road is closed and the cops' lights blaze brightly. Shrill whistles direct traffic elsewhere. The ticket boy says the man slurred, "Good afternoon," and the Italian is rabid and gesticulating wildly. He is sweating and looks like a tortured, bleeding child. A helicopter makes awful noise overhead. A man with aviator shades looks down and tells the city how to crawl around the accident. There are so many people crying that it is like a wake. But the woman is newly dead and her body is still warm. Three newspapermen drive up in town cars and all smoke cigarettes in the same deliberate way. And the corner of East Broad and Willow Lawn has now become the city center.

In his office miles away, Harry dreams of making love to his secretary, which he has lately had the pleasure of doing. She peeks her head through the door and raises an eyebrow. She's too young, and her come-hither gestures are unschooled, sophomoric. But she gently rubs her calf against the door and Harry feels like he is breathing pure air, like everything and everyone outside this room is as dour and sluggish as church. She has long bangs and a porcelain face. Her lips are red and easy. But she hasn't come here to give him satisfaction. She says in a voice that is mock professional that he should go to the newsroom right away, that there is something coming off the wires that needs to make the 6 o'clock feed.

Harry walks over to the wires and sees what is there. There is one scroll of paper, bright yellow. The ink is applied by a machine that runs back and forth over the paper like a cross-cut saw. The effect is that these stories come in line by line, inadvertently making revelations tortuous, overly long.

He sees that there has been a car crash. A man and a woman, and the woman is dead. An idea begins to form but tears start to swell in his eyes like blisters and the water washes the page. It is very sunny outside and he suddenly becomes aware of the immense noise of the tiny newsroom. His neck cranes and he looks toward heaven, but all he sees is a coffee-stained ceiling.

Harry gnaws his fingers, says the name of God, and all at once realizes his dirty, fitful prayers have been answered.

PART IV

NONSUCH

*But ere we had sailed a league our shippe grounding,
gave us once more libertie to summon them to a parlie. Where we
found them all so stranglie amazed with this poore simple assault as
they submitted themselves upon anie tearmes to the Presidents mercie:
who presentlie put by the heeles 6 or 7 of the chiefe offenders. The
rest he seated gallantlie at Powhatan in their Salvage fort, they
built and pretilie fortified with poles and barkes of trees sufficient
to have defended them from all the Salvages in Virginia, drie
houses for lodgings, 300 acres of grounde readie to plant; and no
place so strong, so pleasant and delightful in Virginia,
for which we called it Nonsuch.*

—John Smith, on the first English settlement at Richmond

THE THIRTEENTH FLOOR

BY HOWARD OWEN

Monroe Park

Jackson is what you'd call a lackey. He'd been at the paper longer than I had, and he wanted to stay there, which was a problem, because Jackson and I were part of what the new broom apparently meant to sweep clean. We were the Old Guard, and experience wouldn't get you a cup of coffee around here.

Jackson and I, we'd drunk plenty together, hung out. He'd gone to two of my weddings. But if he had one butt to hang out to dry, and it was mine or his . . . You get the picture.

I'd been covering the legislature for the last fifteen years. It was a sweet deal, with nobody really watching over me down at the Capitol. More was known than was ever reported. I always thought some of those country boys got themselves elected just so they could come to Richmond and party. And what was said and done at the parties, it was understood, stayed at the parties.

The new broom was being wielded by Hanford. Hanford the Hangman, they called him. Probably still do. He's a forty-something ex-jarhead and seems to be under the mistaken belief that he stormed Iwo Jima. They'd brought him in from some place where grace is considered a liability. He's the kind of stiff who's necessary so the guys at the top, the real money, don't have to get their hands dirty with firings and demotions and such. He'd been there a month when Jackson called me aside and told me, off the record, that Hanford had informed all the department heads that he wanted them to "work 'em till they drop."

Maybe Hanford thought I was too old, although he put me on a beat that would wear even a young guy down. Maybe he's prejudiced against smokers. Or so-called heavy drinkers. Maybe it was because I flat out refused to slip into our former lieutenant governor's hospital room and get a damn deathbed story from a poor sap who was dying of AIDS. Who can say?

At any rate, Jackson called me in to tell me there was a reorganization. Night cops. The night police beat.

"I do it to you," he told me, not quite looking at me with those tired, bloodshot eyes, "or he does it to you, after he fires me." I appreciated his honesty. And I figured Jackson would probably be gone before me. He made more money. Everybody around that sinking ship knew the bottom line. The publisher's favorite saying was, "It is what it is," code for, *Shut up and keep rearranging those deck chairs . . .*

So, it was a Friday night. We knew it was Pearl Harbor Day because, in a private e-mail sent to everyone who worked at the paper, from receptionists to pressmen, Hanford reamed out the poor night guy who'd failed to run a story on A1 to that effect.

Around 10:30 I heard, over the cop radio, turned up just loud enough so it didn't disturb the copy desk watching an NBA game on one of the overhead TVs, that there'd been a shooting at 612 West Franklin.

I stopped playing solitaire on the computer.

"Isn't that your . . . ?" Sally Velez asked me from the metro desk.

"Yeah," I said, and was on the elevator in about a minute.

612 West Franklin is the Prestwould, where I was living. It hovers over Monroe Park like a dark angel, casting its twelve-story shadow across the college kids and the homeless. They'd brought a guy down from New York City in the late '20s to build it. Guess they had what you'd call delusions of grandeur. They finished it just in time for the Great Depression to punch in and end that kind of fairy-tale building. But it's something. The sick puppy who had the unit across from mine, halfway up, said that if the 9/11 bastards had flown those planes into the Prestwould, they'd have just bounced off and killed a bunch of bums in the park.

The place has a lot of characters in it, but mostly of the midnight-and-magnolias Old Richmond type. The majority of them, to my knowledge, do not pack heat.

I was there in ten minutes. The night photo guy was out covering a fatality on the interstate, so I'd grabbed one of those moron cameras even reporters can use. They'd trained me how to use it the previous week. There wasn't much crime-scene photography at the legislature, although maybe there should have been.

I saw Gillespie as soon as I got out of the beat-up company Citation and put out the Camel I wasn't supposed to be smoking in it. He was leaning his fat butt against the patrol car. He'd been a young cop when I was on my first tour as police reporter, more than twenty-five years ago. He recognized me.

"Black," he said. It wasn't a greeting, just a confirmation. "I heard they kicked your ass back to the curb. You've put on weight."

I mentioned that he seemed to have cornered the Krispy Kreme market.

He gave me the finger, but otherwise didn't seem to take offense as we braced ourselves against the wind.

"What happened?" I looked up the side of the building. Most of the lights were out. The residents of the Prestwould were so used to sirens screaming by on Belvidere and Franklin that most of them wouldn't know what had happened until morning. Only the twelfth floor, the Randolph unit, was lit.

"We got a call from the night security guy," Gillespie said. "He got a call from some guy on eleven, saying he'd heard gunshots up above him."

Nobody had really lived in that apartment since Taylor Randolph died in October. Far as anyone knew, her nephew, Mac Constantine, was her only living family, other than her sister Jordan, who the nephew had moved into an adult group home. Said it wouldn't be safe for Aunt Jordie to be there by herself. He was a jerk, but maybe he was right. The nephew inherited the unit, and he stayed there sometimes. I'd been to one of his parties. I figured he would put it up for sale or just move in permanently, if he could afford to. The Randolphs were Commonwealth Club from way back, knew all the right people, but I knew Taylor had been hard-pressed to pay a four-figure condo fee, assessments, and seven grand a year in property taxes.

I'm renting, thank God.

When they went up, Gillespie and the other two cops, they found the door cracked. Inside, they found the nephew. It was a mess, Gillespie said, and when they let me up, I could see that the carpet looked like somebody had spilled a gallon of cheap Pinot Noir all over it. Pieces of indeterminate matter that probably used to be part of Mac Constantine's brains speckled the rug and white walls. What was left of his head was, like the rest of him, under a sheet that was getting stained from beneath.

"You don't wanna see," Gillespie said before I even asked.

"So where . . . ?"

"We figure the service elevator. Didn't take the main one, or the guard would have seen him come out. Down there, up the stairs, out the back door. He must have took the gun with him."

I walked through the rest of the unit. A lot of Taylor's clothes were still in the closets. A half-empty bottle of Coke sat on the kitchen counter alongside the remains of a half-eaten pack of cheese Nabs.

I got the basics and was back at the paper in another twenty minutes, in time to get something in for the city edition. They even used one of the photos I took.

"Good job," Sally Velez said to me. "You might have a future in this business." I gave her the same one-finger salute Gillespie had given me.

I skipped the usual round or three at Penny Lane. Something was bothering me. It was like that piece of meat you realize is wedged between your molars after you've eaten a good steak. You know you can't stop until you find a toothpick.

Next day, I took my morning stroll through the Fan. People were out walking their dogs, raking leaves, doing all the crap people do. Kate and I'd had a town house over near the river, and we'd spend Saturday mornings like that, more or less.

Kate was my most recent wife. She was the one who'd wanted to move to the Prestwould. Said she'd seen it all her life and always imagined what it would be like to live there. We'd only been married eight months when we stumbled on a rare rental unit and did the deed.

I'm not sure Kate understood what she was getting into, marrying me. What might have seemed at least regionally exotic—hearing my stories of state senators acting badly, going to cocktail parties where the governor called me by my first name (he knew the janitors' first names too)—soon just became a pain in the ass. So did those long nights waiting for me. And then not waiting for me.

I could've drunk less, I'm sure. There were times when it would have been hard to have drunk more, and she wasn't the only one that was guilty of tippy-toeing outside the sacred bonds. Like our charming city's teenage drug desperadoes, who seem to believe that thinking might hamper their nerve or their aim, I have been known to not properly consider the consequences of my actions.

Because she's a lawyer headed for partner and I'm a half-assed, broken-down political writer turned night-cops reporter, she hasn't been busting my chops. I don't even think she hates me. Maybe she just sees me as a youthful indiscretion, something she can learn from and get over.

She surprised me by moving out of the Prestwould herself instead of telling me to. Said the place was pretty much ruined for her. It isn't exactly growing on me either, but it's a roof, at least until I can't make rent anymore.

The ten-incher I did on Mac Constantine's murder was on A1. Couple of black guys get gunned down in the East End and it's B6, maybe B1 if it's a slow news day. But Mac Constantine was rich and white. Since Taylor Randolph was descended from two presidents, I suppose Mac was too. And he had been on the city council.

At the end of my daily constitutional, I waded my way through the TV trucks and a couple of dozen reporters and cameramen who weren't allowed inside the Prestwould. They were waylaying every elderly citizen who tried to get past them and into the building. Good thing we have security guards. A couple of the TV folk, trying to save their well-tended hair from the wind that was bringing in the season's first real cold front, recognized me and begged to be let inside. I made sure the door closed all the way.

When I got up to the twelfth floor, I saw they'd padlocked the door and sealed it off with yellow crime tape. As I went through the door separating the lobby from the back stairs and turned a corner, though, I saw that Gillespie was the same fiend for detail he'd always been. The back door, the one that opened into Taylor Randolph's kitchen, was untouched, even though they must have gone out that way the night before to check on the service elevator I was standing alongside. The door was locked, but Taylor had entrusted me with a key. I think she'd given one to half a dozen other residents, just in case she needed help. She worried a lot, about her health and about Jordie.

Jordie wasn't quite right. One day, after I'd helped move some furniture, Taylor told me, over Scotch, cheese, and crackers, that she was afraid of what might happen to her sister if she, Taylor, went first. She didn't expect that, but she was still worried. Her nephew and heir had promised to take care of Jordie, but Taylor frowned when she said it.

Jordie was pretty much given the run of the Prestwould. She was close to eighty, I guess, about five years older than Taylor. They both had snow-white hair, although Jordie was fond of wearing a black wig that scared small children. Both seemed like they'd live to be a hundred. You never knew when you might suddenly run into Jordie, riding the elevator or walking from room to room in the basement, sometimes talking to herself, sometimes perfectly sane. The sisters had never married, and everyone said Taylor gave up everything to take care of Jordie, who'd started hearing those little voices when she was still in her teens. A combination of pills, Taylor, money, and an occasional visit to rest at Tucker's had kept her among the uninstitutionalized. At least until Taylor's heart suddenly gave out one Sunday morning.

I wasn't there when they took Jordie away, and was glad I wasn't, from what I heard. Jordie did not go gently into that good night of the adult home. Mac Constantine reportedly said that it was the only solution, that he wouldn't be able to take care of her, not even if he moved in with her. Evidently, Taylor hadn't made her wishes specific enough in her will to ensure that one of the last two surviving members of her old and tapped-out family did right by the other.

Jordie was, to say it plain, thrown out like bad meat.

I let myself in through the back door. Everything was pretty much the way it had been left the night before, including Mac Constantine's blood on the Turkish carpet, a dark brown Rorschach blot no rug cleaner was ever going to remove. The radiator was doing its usual version of the Anvil Chorus and filling the room with heat that smelled like rusty metal.

It didn't take long to confirm what I thought I'd seen the night before. Take a few memories, stir in a flash of color you glimpse from the corner of your eye, add one phone call. I guess you couldn't really fault Gillespie, sap that he is, for not knowing what he couldn't have known. Although I'd have plenty to blame him for later.

When I got to work, Jackson wanted to know where the hell I'd been and what was I doing about the Mac Constantine murder. It was all over TV, perfect for the good-hair people to get all breathless about, even if they didn't know shit.

I'd checked in with Gillespie and confirmed that the cops were grilling just about anybody who'd gone to one of Mac Constantine's parties. They'd been the talk of the Prestwould since he'd started staying there on occasion. There were some good leads, although so far everyone seemed to have a solid alibi. Constantine was a collector. What he collected was enemies. There had been a couple of fights, because that's what Constantine apparently did when he had too much to drink. Hell, that's why he wasn't on city council anymore. Nobody who watched council meetings on public access TV would ever forget the night he came straight to a meeting from the lounge at the Jefferson Hotel and wound up duking it out with one of his constituents. The constituent, who'd had truth on his side, had accused Constantine of being the hired boy of a developer trying to turn a block of Jackson Ward into high-rise condos.

"I'll have something for the first edition," I told Jackson, then advised him I might have something better for the metro. When he asked me what, I told him to wait for it.

"You know," he said, "it's crap like that, knowing stuff and not writing it, that got your ass put on the police beat." If it hadn't been that, I told him, it would have been something else. And walked back to my desk.

The newsroom seems like it's running on low power these days, and it isn't just that you can't make as much noise with a computer keyboard as you could with a typewriter, or that half the editors have wires coming from their ears so they can listen to music and not be bothered by such irritants as conversation. It's more than that, more than the weak-ass lighting suitable to computer moles but not to actual life on planet Earth. The problem is, despite the directives that we should be a twenty-four-hour-a-day news source, there just aren't as many bodies. Revenue is down, so expenses (meaning reporters and other such frivolities) have to be down too. Nobody admits to a hiring freeze, but there are icicles on the ceiling.

I saw Hanford hanging over the shoulder of one of the page designers. The headline read, WHO KILLED MAC CONSTANTINE? "Yeah," Hanford said, slapping his thigh the way you would if somebody told you the funniest joke in the world. "Yeah. That'll sell some damn papers."

Maybe, I thought, you'll have to rip that up before the night's done.

The moon was rising pale as a frozen ghost over the Hotel John Marshall when Gillespie picked me up in front of the *Times-Dispatch* building. It was almost 9, and my first story, the one that would hold a spot until later, had already cleared customs with the copy desk.

"This," said Gillespie, who didn't even know what a cliché was, "had better be good." We turned on 4th Street and then west on Grace. At the Belvidere stoplight, I looked up and thought I saw what I was looking for, barely visible from down below. Gillespie parked his cruiser in the loading zone in front of the Prestwould, and we went in.

Like Jackson, he wanted to play Twenty Questions, but I wasn't saying anything until we got up there. Gillespie was panting just from climbing up the front steps, the wind nipping at our heels. I was thankful the elevator was working.

When we stepped out on twelve, I finally told him what I was thinking, and about what I'd seen from his car. "You won't need it," I said as he reached for his Glock.

"Let me be the judge of that."

I led him through to the hallway where the service elevator was, and he actually seemed surprised to see there was a back door, which I unlocked with Taylor's key.

"I hope you haven't been snooping in here, compromising a crime scene," Gillespie said.

I didn't grace him with an answer.

It would have been funny if it hadn't been so sad. The Nabs were still on the kitchen counter, and you could follow the trail of orange into the utility room. It used to be a maid's room, back when everybody at the Prestwould had live-in help. Taylor had used it mostly for storage. Where the maid's postage-stamp toilet had been, there was now a closet.

I walked over to the closet and opened the door. The ladder was still there, the way I remembered it the time Taylor showed me.

"How the hell am I supposed to get through that?" Gillespie asked me, looking up at the two-by-two covering.

"Don't worry your fat butt. There's an easier way."

I led him back through the kitchen door, then another that led to the back stairwell. We climbed it and came to the locked door leading to the roof, Gillespie breathing hard. The building manager always had the key, and I had tipped him pretty well at Christmas. When I'd stopped by to see him earlier that afternoon, he remembered my generosity.

"Thirteenth floor," I said as I worked the key. The terrace. That's what they called it whenever somebody, usually a new-comer, would have the bright idea of putting a swimming pool or a garden up there. The old-timers would have to explain to the sap about the cost involved, plus damage to a roof that already leaked like a sieve whenever we had a tropical storm.

"Remember," I told Gillespie, "no gunplay." He grunted and I pushed the door open.

You could see why anyone would've wanted a garden or

something up there. Under the full moon, the downtown buildings were outlined in lights for the holidays. Richmond may have showed its age spots and wrinkles in the sunshine, but the old girl looked good at night in December. Directly below and across West Franklin, Monroe Park's lights winked up at us. It would have been a pretty place to have a bourbon or two on a summer night and put the day in a sleeper hold.

I wasn't much in the mood for sightseeing, though. For one thing, it was cold as a gravedigger's ass.

We tiptoed across the roof like it was a minefield. I couldn't swear we wouldn't hit a soft spot and fall through. Gillespie had his flashlight, and I glimpsed the rectangular shape I'd remembered, off to the east side. It was a kind of half-assed tool shed, built for who the hell knows what. A sliver of light, which I'd seen ten minutes ago from Gillespie's car, leaked out of it.

We were walking on a bed of loose rocks and couldn't have slipped up on a deaf man. We weren't more than five feet from the shed when the door opened suddenly. I heard Gillespie grunt and jump.

Jordie Randolph had never been a beauty. I've seen pictures. Now, she couldn't have weighed ninety pounds, and her eyes were like a couple of holes somebody had burned into a silk tablecloth. She was in the same shabby bathrobe that had been her preferred garb around the Prestwould. The black wig was slightly askew. She'd tried, for some reason, to put on lipstick in the recent past, with unfortunate results. Under better circumstances, it might have been comical.

She didn't say a word, didn't seem even to recognize me.

I said, "Jordie—"

"Put your hands in the air! Get down on the ground! Now!" Gillespie was kneeling as he shouted. He had dropped the flashlight and held his Glock with both hands, the way he'd been taught. In the moonlight, I could see that he was shaking.

I think I said, "Gillespie, don't," believing I could convince him that an addled eighty-year-old woman armed with a pack of Nabs didn't need the full monty.

Jordie looked from Gillespie to me and back again. She didn't seem at all fazed by the Glock.

"It's okay, Jordie," I said, holding my palms up, approaching her an inch at a time with all the caution I would have given a wild, cornered animal. "It's okay. We just want to help you."

She did something peculiar then. At first I thought she was crying, but then I realized otherwise. Jordie was not prone to laugh, or even smile, but she was laughing now. When she spoke—"Mac's dead"—she sounded as sane as I'd ever heard her. "He's dead." She wiped her nose and tried to quell a giggle.

I glanced at Gillespie, whose shake had subsided.

"Put your hands in the air!" he repeated.

Before I could do any more brilliant negotiating, Jordie sealed the deal. She raised both hands in the air as instructed, still holding the Nabs. Then she turned her back to us. She was two steps from the side of the building. As a cold gust of wind hit us from the north, she started moving.

Nobody said anything else.

She took three steps, spreading her upraised arms like she thought she might just float down. Before I had time to move, she was, as Gillespie had requested, on the ground. More specifically, she was splattered on top of Bert Campbell's Cadillac DeVille in the parking lot below, a dark spot we could barely make out, with little lines trickling from it.

"You stupid son of a bitch!" I screamed at Gillespie, and for a moment thought he was going to shoot me. I'm pretty sure I took a swing at him. I must have missed.

"She might've been armed," was what he kept saying, all the way down the elevator.

The next morning, I woke late from a very bad dream. I'd given Jackson his write-through for the metro, then set a personal record by eschewing Penny Lane's alcoholic charms two nights in a row. When I picked up the paper outside my door, I saw the picture of Jordie Randolph splayed across the top of the Cadillac. It took up five columns. The headline read: *KILLER'S REMORSE?* They had to put the question mark on the end because at that point they could only assume.

It wouldn't take long, though, for one of Gillespie's sharp-eyed associates to find the gun, half-buried in the rocks on the Prestwould's rooftop, like I figured they would.

One call to the New Horizons Adult Home the morning after Mac Constantine's murder was all it'd taken to find out that Jordie had disappeared two days earlier. By the time they got around to calling her next-of-kin nephew, he wasn't up to answering the phone, being dead at the time. New Horizons wasn't much on doing follow-up calls, apparently.

What I figure is this: Jordie still had her keys to the apartment. She came back and got in through the basement door, something the building's surveillance tape would show as soon as somebody bothered to look at it.

Maybe Constantine wasn't there when she entered the apartment. Maybe he came home later and she hid. I'm thinking he misjudged his aunt. He probably thought that because she was seriously deranged she also was retarded. But I knew Jordie was able to use a gun. Taylor told me once that their father had taken both girls to firing ranges when they were in their teens and made sure they knew how to shoot. Taylor had kept a gun around the apartment, and one time, years ago, Jordie supposedly got hold of it and threatened to shoot herself over some imagined wrong. Taylor talked her out of it.

Everyone knew Mac Constantine carried a pistol. The one party I'd been to at his Prestwould unit, I was appalled to see that he left it sitting on the kitchen table, like it somehow showed what a tough guy he was. He was just the kind of moron to leave it loaded too.

Maybe Jordie hid in the maid's room when she heard the door open that night. Maybe she had the gun already. Maybe, when Mac Constantine turned around and saw her, just before he ruined Taylor's rug with his brains, he didn't take her seriously. Maybe he laughed.

It was the Nabs that had tipped me off.

When I saw those orange crumbs on the floor and that half-eaten pack sitting on the kitchen counter, I knew Jordie had been there. It was the only thing she seemed to care about eating much of the time, and Taylor kept boxes of them around. It wasn't like a healthy diet was Jordie Randolph's biggest worry. And it wasn't like Mac Constantine to be munching on Nabs. He was more of a foie gras kind of guy.

After she did it, she probably panicked and retreated to the utility room and then, later, up the ladder in the closet to the tool shed on the roof. One time, the first couple of months Kate and I lived there, she'd disappeared for two days, and that's where they found her, living on Nabs and rainwater.

Next morning, Hanford sent word down, via Jackson, that he wanted a tick-tock piece a.s.a.p., telling everything from the history of the Randolphs to Mac Constantine's demise, which he saw as the final chapter in another fucked-up Southern family's spiral to oblivion. He actually used that phrase, which was pretty poetic for Hanford. I saw it as a major invasion of privacy. And the last straw. I went to the fourth floor and told Hanford this, suggesting also that he commit an act of self-gratification. He seemed happy that he didn't have to fire me. That afternoon I walked over to police headquarters and tried to get Gillespie back walking a beat. They listened politely for a while, then not so politely showed me the door. Jordie Randolph didn't deserve to have it end the way it did, but you don't always get what you deserve. Gillespie sure didn't.

Back home in the Prestwould, I called Kate for the first time since she left.

"What are you going to do?" she asked me after the requisite pregnant pause. She sounded worried. I really don't think she hates me.

"I haven't decided," I told her, as honest as I could be. "I'm not sweating it though. A guy like me, I've got plenty of options."

MR. NOT

BY HERMINE PINSON

Devil's Half Acre

T he Raggedy Ann was almost as tall as Tug, who looked not at the doll but at the hand of the man who had flung it on the couch. The man—Mr. Not, as Tug always referred to him, silently—reached up to pat an imaginary loose strand on his head, then looked around the room, as if to survey his property.

"Where'd you find that?" said Tug's mother Velma. "And what's that smell? Ray Harold, I thought you hated Tug having Marguerite. Now you bring him home *another* doll?"

"Oh, Vee, quit yapping. I got it at a toy shop over on Broad Street. The owner sprays everything to keep it fresh." Ray Harold tore at the plastic bag the doll was wrapped in. When he had liberated the thing, he smiled a small, mean smile and thrust the doll at the boy.

"Go ahead, take it, Harold. I told you if you acted like a sissy, I'd treat you like one. You're nine years old. Stop peeing in your bed and maybe I'll buy you something for big boys." Ray Harold bent down and stared into Tug's eyes. The boy stiffened like a miniature soldier at the sour smell of liquor on Mr. Not's breath, but he picked up Raggedy Ann from the couch.

"Thank you," said Tug.

"Thank you, *Uncle Ray*," corrected Velma. "Where're your manners?"

"Thank you . . . Mr. Vermeer," said Tug.

Ray Harold snorted in disgust. "Vee, pour me a drink. I need to sit down and catch my breath. Regina was at it again tonight, threatening to come over here and break all the windows."

"Why don't that woman take care of her own household and quit trying to interfere in mine?" said Velma while she poured her longtime lover a glass of Johnnie Walker. "Tug, this is grown folks' talk. Take your doll to your room. You can watch that new Batman movie I bought you."

"Yes, ma'am." Tug dragged Raggedy Ann by its stitched foot along the hardwood floor. He propped it in a child-size chair in the farthest corner of his bedroom, then inserted *The Dark Knight* into his DVD player and undressed for bed. He kept the sound low, so he could listen to the voices at the other end of the hall. Whenever Mr. Not came around, it was always the same routine. *Tug, go play. Tug, go to your room. Tug, go downstairs. Tug, go next door.* His mother had wanted him to call his godfather Uncle Ray, but Tug refused to call him anything to his face when he could get away with it, and when he couldn't, he called him Mr. Vermeer. The name sounded to Tug like a cat howling to be let in at night. *Vermeer.* He thought it suited the man whose very presence in the house on East Leigh Street spoke *no* and *not*.

Ordinarily, Tug would become engrossed quickly in a movie, but he couldn't concentrate with Mr. Not there. He never knew what was going to happen. Mr. Not changed the way his mother acted. When she wasn't at work in the dining room office downstairs, she spent time doing things with Tug, playing checkers, playing cards, reading to him, taking him skateboarding. But whenever Mr. Not was in the house, her voice changed from being calm and almost musical to sounding whiny and high-pitched. Sometimes, when Mr. Not was around, she even called Tug "Harold," despite the fact that she'd given him the nickname herself.

"Shhh," Tug said to Marguerite. She was a bisque brown porcelain doll in a gingham dress, and he held her close to his chest and tiptoed to his hiding place behind the window drapery on the second-floor landing, midway down the hall from his bedroom. It was an excellent place to listen to his mother and Mr. Not . . .

Velma went to the refrigerator, removed a can of beer, and sat down at the kitchen table.

"Regina says she wants you and Harold out of this house by the end of the summer," said Ray Harold, already on his third drink.

"I never asked to live here. I never did. I used to think you put me and Tug in this house because you loved me, but I now think it was just cheaper than paying rent on an apartment." Velma popped the can's top for punctuation.

"This house is the property of the Vermeer family. We have owned it—"

"For over fifty years," finished Velma, wiping beer foam from her lip. "I know." She glared at Ray Harold, then she laughed.

"The thing about you, Velma? You don't have any class!"

"No, Ray Harold, I don't. I wasn't born the illegitimate great-great-grandson of a Confederate captain. I didn't graduate from Hampton University. I didn't grow up on Quality Row. And my grandfather didn't work for Charles T. Russell, the famous black architect." Velma sat down and faced him across the table. "I don't have any class, but I do have you, may God have mercy on my soul!" She stood up again. "I'm tired and

I'm going to bed. I want to take Tug skateboarding tomorrow, and later on I have some paperwork to do . . . for you!" She turned off the kitchen light and climbed the stairs to the master bedroom.

"For me," said Ray Harold. "That's right. The cancellation of that bid to renovate the Eggleston. And make sure you do it correctly." He sighed and stared into the bottom of his empty glass.

"Don't you worry about it. I always do," replied Velma from the top of the stairs, dragging out the last three words to register her disgust.

Ray Harold was now climbing the stairs behind her. "Yes, you always do, you always do. But in return I let you live here in luxury. I paid for this house—"

"And now I'm paying for it." Velma moved around her bedroom, finally settling at the vanity to wipe off her makeup.

"Don't start that shit!" barked Ray Harold, stomping into the room.

"Start what? I don't know how you treat Regina. I only know how you treat me. And sometimes it takes me months to recover from your brand of loving." She rubbed her jaw as she checked her reflection in the mirror.

"Then why do you stay?" Strolling over to his mistress, he massaged her neck and shoulders with a gentleness that also declared his ownership.

"Good question."

"Baby, let's not fight. I'm going to go home soon and get this mess straightened out."

"Uh-huh."

Except for the rustle of sheets and some low groans of pleasure, things were quiet now. Tug guessed they had made up, so he tiptoed back to his room. He left the DVD playing and got into bed, holding his hand over Marguerite's mouth to keep her from screaming out, *Go home, Mr. Not!* It took awhile before he fell asleep.

In his sleigh bed, Tug flew in living color. He was Mr. Spock looking down at a huge bright planet from his starship in space, a great wizard scanning a shining magic world below. He swooped down and surveyed blue pinetops and green grass that grew into a thick jungle right before his eyes. Then, as he floated in the quiet of dreamtime, clouds started to gather behind and above him, below him, all around him, and the air took on a strange smell with the sweetness of synthesized flowers. Uh oh! Was that a zig-zag? Was the Sandman near? The phone rang. Tug could see Mr. Not's clown face and smeary smile when he talked. "Regina, I told you to stop calling here. I'll see you when I get home." Then Batman sat on Tug's bed. *I see what I have to become to stop men like him.*

Tug woke to the feeling of a draft on his bottom. The odor of pee and sweat and sleep stuck in his nose. He got up and stripped the sheets from his bed.

When his mother met him coming out of his room, Tug didn't bother telling her how the zig-zags had wrapped around his legs and squeezed his stomach until he had to land, and she didn't ask him why he'd wet the bed again. She took the soggy sheets from him.

"Your breakfast is ready, Tug," she said as she headed to the washing machine in the basement.

"Can we still go to the cemetery?" he called after her, afraid she might not allow him to go skateboarding in the parking lot anymore.

"I don't see why not," she answered, her voice calm and even.

Nearly every weekend in good weather, the two of them, and Marguerite, made the trip to the cemetery parking lot on 15th and Broad. Tug's mother told him it was a sacred space where the ancestors slept below the streets.

"Will they ever wake up?" he'd asked her once.

"Not till Judgment Day, I expect, but they won't hurt us. This place is special, because most all the people buried under here lived way back, during slavery. Gabriel the Blacksmith is buried here, and he led a slave revolt two hundred years ago. They caught him and hung him on the gallows, but he was a hero to the people."

"We're not slaves, Mommy."

"No, Tug, we're free, we've been free for over 140 years now."

"Then why does Mr. Not try to own you?"

His mother opened her mouth, then shut it again. "Your godfather loves us, honey. If he seems a little gruff, that's just his way. I love your . . . him, maybe too much," she finally said.

"Gabriel was a blacksmith? Does that mean he worked in a forge, like the black god you showed me in that big book on Africa?"

"Like Ogun," said Tug's mother, surprised he remembered their conversation about the Yoruba god.

"Yeah, Ogun was a god and a ninja too." Tug thought of the comics he read at night in bed with Marguerite by his side.

According to their usual Saturday routine, Tug helped his mother make the beds, dust, restack magazines, place books back on their shelves. He did it not simply because it meant they would get to the parking lot sooner, but also because he liked being in the house with nice furniture, clean linen. He enjoyed the rhythms of domesticity.

Skateboarding was the only outdoor activity Tug enjoyed. He looked forward to sailing over the concrete, arms out, knees bent, with open space and no cars to dodge, while his mother and Marguerite watched him fly. Somehow knowing that the parking lot was also a cemetery comforted him. His mother once told him that ever since he was three years old, he'd always had a special affinity for graveyards, turning to look and point whenever they passed one in a car. Now he imagined the graves as a city below the ground, with Gabriel Ogun presiding.

As they were finally preparing to leave for the parking lot, Tug heard the front door open and close. Mr. Not was back. He didn't usually come around until nighttime.

"Vee, I have to talk to you. Regina threw my clothes and my good shoes outside this morning, and now she's threatening to come over here and run you out of this house. Harold, go and play while I talk to your mama. And take your sissy doll with you." Mr. Not grabbed Marguerite and flung her at the boy.

"Go on, it's okay," said Tug's mother. "When we finish discussing business, I'll take you to the parking lot. Okay?"

Tug backed out the door with his eyes fixed on Mr. Not.

He went and sat in the swing, humming to Marguerite and rubbing her back the way his mother sometimes affectionately rubbed his.

"Go ahead, Marguerite, you can hum too. I lost you last night when I hit the zig-zags. Next time, hold my hand tight, so the Sandman and the zig-zags won't get us." Tug had brought his skateboard and backpack with him, and now he rolled the board underfoot back and forth.

He continued to hum while he listened to the escalating discussion in the kitchen. Suddenly, his song was interrupted by the Raggedy Ann doll sailing out the back door, head first, landing in a heap on the ground. The doll had lost its green cap and lay there with legs splayed, its smiling face kissing the grass. Tug left the swing and walked past Raggedy Ann to see who had thrown it out. At first, he thought it was Glenda the Good Witch, but when she said his name he realized it had been his mother. With her silk dressing gown streaming behind her, she strode over to Tug and grabbed him by the hand. Tendrils of hair had come loose from her long ponytail.

"I'm going to bring you next door to Mrs. Richardson's house, and you stay there until I come get you."

"But you said you were going to take me skateboarding."

"I am, I will, but just wait there until I come get you."

Mrs. Richardson was accustomed to her friend and neighbor Velma Holloway sometimes arriving unannounced with her son. Tug's mother told him to sit down in the family room, then walked with Mrs. Richardson into the kitchen. When they returned from their brief conference, his mother said, "You mind Mrs. Richardson. I'll be back in a few minutes, then we'll go to the parking lot. Let me go get my business straight. Thanks, Betty."

Tug folded his arms and looked away when she tried to kiss his cheek. After she left, Mrs. Richardson inserted a DVD of Tug's favorite movie, *The Wizard of Oz*. "Call me when it gets to the part with the lollipop kids. That cracks me up," she said. Then she returned to the kitchen to finish chopping vegetables while listening to Smokey Robinson croon, "*Ooo baby, babeee . . . I did you wrong,*" on Power 92, oldies-but-goodies radio.

The witch's feet shriveled up and disappeared under the

house, but Tug wasn't thrilled the way he usually was. "Marguerite, do you think Mr. Not's going to make Mommy cry again?" He looked around for Marguerite, only to realize he'd left her and the skateboard by the swing.

Going out the side door, Tug ran from Mrs. Richardson's yard directly into his own. There was no fence dividing the two row houses. He gently lifted Marguerite and patted her head.

"I didn't mean to leave you. It's just that Mommy was rushing me." As he turned to go back the way he came, Tug heard raised voices from the second floor of his house.

With Marguerite in tow, he ran inside and crept up the carpeted stairs. He walked past the bathroom and glimpsed Mr. Not shaving at the mirror that hung over the sink. Then Tug rounded the corner and saw his mother sitting on her bed, arms crossed, smoking a cigarette. He took a few quiet steps back and watched as Mr. Not turned his head at odd angles, like a bird trying to see behind itself, as he delicately pressed blade to skin to get the last bit of stubble from his lower jaw. Silence had overtaken the bickering couple. Tug thought he heard the faint music of an ice cream truck, but didn't run to his mother. He went and hid with Marguerite behind the long velvet drapes on the second-floor landing, where he could observe. He listened for something he could not know he was listening for, a prelude to a kind of dance. Velma's shaking foot kept time . . .

Ray Harold Vermeer studied himself in the mirror, touched a hand to his temple. The phone rang and Velma got up to see who was calling; when she saw Betty Richardson's number on the caller ID she didn't answer, but let it go to voice mail.

"Vee, I swear, Regina's just bluffing."

Velma placed her cigarette in the ashtray, rose from the

bed, and walked toward the bathroom, as if she had been summoned. "Then why did you come over here this morning? You say this is my house, but when you and Regina argue, she threatens to fly on over here and act a fool, same way she did the time we moved in, calling me a slut in front of my neighbors." Pulling another cigarette and matches out of her robe, Velma lit up with trembling hands.

"Will you forget about her for one minute! Why can't we just spend a little time together like we used to before Harold came into the picture and Regina went on the warpath? Take off that bathrobe. Daddy wants to show you something when he comes out the bathroom."

"Ray Harold, I'm tired of you thinking you can show up here any time you feel like it and disrupt my plans, just so you can get some and then go on about your business."

"Hey, wait a minute. I didn't come here just to bed you, woman. I got good news!" Ray met Velma in the hall and stood there in his undershirt. The phone rang again. Neither made a move to answer, until finally Velma could stand it no longer. She went and picked up the receiver.

"Regina, stop calling my house." She listened. "Well, bring it on, then!" She slammed the phone down. "That's it. We're moving! As soon as I can get my things together, me and my son are leaving this house. I don't care if it's in the historical register, it's never going to be mine!"

"Wait a minute, Vee. Look, I was going to surprise you, but I guess I'll go on and tell you. I think we're close to getting a contract to start work. You remember I told you the mayor knew my daddy and my granddaddy? Well, he put me in touch with some people I need to know. People who matter. I want you to be cool until I get this contract on the old Hippodrome. Vee, we're going to—"

"Ray Harold." She called his name as if it were a command to be quiet. "I'm not interested. When are you going to acknowledge to everyone, including Tug, that he is a Vermeer, that he is your son, your *only* son? And when are you going to stop belittling him? I'm tired of being laughed at by my enemies, pitied by my friends, and scorned by my family, all because I haven't figured out how to leave you." Velma walked past Ray Harold and into the bathroom, shutting the door behind her.

Ray Harold banged on it.

"Velma, come on out so we can talk this over. I don't have much time before—"

"Before what?" said Velma through the closed door. "Before you have to go home to that witch? You know, I used to be impressed with you, how you were a man of position in the community, one of the top black contractors in Richmond and from a good family. I didn't think you wasn't honorable the time one of your schemes to be a major player in the renovation of downtown fell through." Velma opened the door to the bathroom with tears in her eyes. "You remember that night? You buried your head in my lap and cried like a baby. I had a boyfriend who wanted to marry me, but I gave him up for you, and when I had your son, you didn't even claim him until you saw he looked just like you. That's when you moved us into your daddy's house. *Your daddy's house.* This isn't my house *or* yours!"

Ray Harold slapped Velma so hard she stumbled backward into the bathroom. He followed her inside and shut the door.

Why did they go in there? What are they doing? Tug couldn't see them, so he left his position on the landing and lay on his side in the hallway inhaling dust as he peered under the door. Mr. Not's feet flanked the toilet bowl. *His pants aren't falling around his legs like mine do when I'm sitting down so he must not be using it. What's he doing?* A few inches away, his mother's feet faced the toilet bowl.

"You told me I made you feel brand new. You told me you were getting a divorce. You didn't tell me I'd have to share you with your wife, and you won't even tell our son you're his father, acting like you're some kind of white man and I'm your concubine."

Tug bit his underlip till it hurt, then kept biting it.

"You can't leave well enough alone. I brought you from nothing. You and that little faggot live in a fine house, you wear the best clothes money can buy. You use my credit card and it says Vermeer. People know that boy's my son. And you know I'm still trying to work things out with Regina so that things can be divided—"

"You go ahead and divide whatever you want to. I'm taking Tug back to Charles City."

Mr. Not's shoes tapped the floor three times. The second tap made the fine mahogany floorboards ring as the door rattled and bounced in its frame. Startled, Tug rolled back, then returned to the same spot, desperate to see what was happening. It didn't occur to him that the door might fly open at any second. All he knew was that he had to get closer to see as much as he could.

"You're not leaving me or taking my son anywhere!" shouted Mr. Not. Then Tug heard a rattle-bang of flesh against metal. His mother's feet stumbled, and he moved even closer, sticking his nose as far under the door as he could. He saw two knees on the bathroom floor—hers.

"Ray Harold, please! Don't do this!"

What's happening in there? Marguerite, we have to help Mommy! Somebody! Mrs. Richardson! Batman! Gabriel Ogun!

He cried out, "Mommy!" and the door opened suddenly, and sunlight beaming through the stained-glass bathroom window put Mr. Not's face in deep shadow. He stood with his legs wide apart, his face a mask of anger when he looked down and saw Tug on the floor.

"Go play"—he inhaled all the air around him—"son. Your mama and I have to discuss some things."

"You're not my daddy," said Tug. "You're Mr. Not!"

"Go play, Tug. It's all right," said his mother, but she didn't look him in his eyes. Instead, she stared at the back of Mr. Not's head.

Something heavy, a zag, wrapped around Tug's stomach and squeezed and squeezed and wouldn't let go until it released itself down his legs. He was awake and the blue zig-zags were marching across his wide-open eyes.

"Go change your underwear, sissy," said Mr. Not. Then he stepped back into the bathroom and closed the door in Tug's face. When Tug's head cleared, he knew the zig-zags were really drops of blood on the tiled floor. He knew Mr. Not wouldn't disappear under the house like the Wicked Witch. What would Mr. Spock or Batman do? What would Gabriel Ogun do?

Tug grabbed Marguerite and dashed downstairs to the dining room where Mr. Not kept a glass-paned bookcase. Some shelves held books and building models, but on one shelf there was a set of fancy long knives, glinting in their velvet exhibit covers. Tug had always admired them for their beauty. They made the bookcase look royal and mysterious. Tug gazed now at the array of knives, not knowing an East African panga from a Malaysian golok, but he went into the drawer of the antique desk across the room and got the big key and picked a panga from the case.

Holding Marguerite in one hand and the panga in the other, Tug climbed the stairs to the hallway bathroom. Then he set Marguerite on the floor and slowly opened the door. His mother sat with her back pressed against the tub. Mr. Not was kneeling down with his hand wrapped around her silk bathrobe, the one he had given her as a Valentine's Day gift. Her nose was bleeding, and she was staring at the floor.

Tug heard the rhythm of a hammer crashing down on an anvil with the force of a black god. With both hands on the long knife, Tug raised it high above his head and plunged it deep into Mr. Not's back. The man straightened with a sharp intake of breath and looked up at the ceiling. He reached behind him to remove the knife, which had pierced his kidney. Then he turned around to face his attacker and peered into Tug's eyes, but his mouth couldn't register surprise. Mr. Not had only enough strength left to slump down next to Velma, who did not glance up until he was sitting beside her, leaning his head on her shoulder.

Tug jumped back into the hallway, picked up Marguerite, stuffed her in his backpack, continued out to the swing set, grabbed his skateboard, and ran and ran and ran. He didn't know where he was headed as he sprinted down East Leigh with its manicured lawns behind wrought-iron fences. When he got to Broad Street, he stopped and just stood there, looking neither left nor right. A wiry man of average height sidled up to him.

"Look lively, son. Where you headed?"

Tug glanced up at the Tin Man. "To the cemetery. I mean, to the parking lot."

"Well, you're on the wrong side of the street. Cross here and catch the Riverview or the Churchill bus. That'll get you where you want to go. What's your name, son?"

"Harold Holloway. Are you the Tin Man?"

"No, they call me Dumptruck. Be safe, son." The man smiled him on his way.

Tug caught the Riverview and the driver let him ride without paying a fare. He got off the bus when he recognized 12th Street and Broad and walked the rest of the way to the overpass with the historical marker that told of the exploits of Gabriel the Blacksmith, who was hung on the gallows and buried in the Burial Ground for Negroes. Tug followed the cobblestone path that led to the empty parking lot with numbered spaces and overgrown grass in the medians.

After setting his backpack down, he took Marguerite out and leaned her against some tall weeds. "Marguerite," he said, "don't think about it. Don't talk about it. Don't want to." He jumped on his skateboard and rode it as best he could on the expanse of concrete. He glided back and forth over the blacktop for hours.

The lights of the city started winking on. MCV Medical Center glowed on the hill. Tug wanted to go home. He wanted to see his mother, but didn't know if she would be angry with him. He remembered once when Mr. Not had slapped her and Tug tried to come between them, his mother had swatted him firmly on his buttocks and sent him to his room with the warning to stay out of *grown folks' business*. Where could he go? Back to Mrs. Richardson's house?

There were places to hide under the old tracks, but he was afraid to go into the dark wooden enclosures that looked like they'd once kept slaves penned up. Tug wanted to be headed home on the *Starship Enterprise* with Mr. Spock or in the Batmobile with the Dark Knight. He wanted to be in the house on East Leigh Street with his mother, watching Dorothy click her heels. He turned to the stone arch under the freeway. There, the concrete parking lot gave way to dirt. What had his mother told him about those black ancestors who slept below the ground? She had said they wouldn't hurt him. *Gabriel, where are you? Will they hang me on the gallows?* Tug found a place under the freeway. Exhausted, with his back against the wall, he sat Marguerite on his lap to comfort her.

The sun shone brightly down on the parking lot. As Tug flew over it, he watched brawny black men and strong black women holding down the Sandman so he couldn't get away. When Tug drew closer, he saw that it was Mr. Not they all held fast. His face was chalk-white and his lips were smeared in a grotesque smile. *Bury him*, said Gabriel Ogun.

Yes, said the people, *dig a deep hole!*

After explaining to the police how Ray Harold Vermeer came to be sitting lifeless on the bathroom floor, Velma enlisted their aid in finding her son. The police questioned people up and down East Leigh Street. The answers they got led them to Broad Street, where they talked to shopkeepers and bystanders, including a little man named Dumptruck, who confirmed Velma's suspicions. The police drove her out to the Burial Ground for Negroes, where she found Tug under the overpass. With Marguerite sitting beside him, spotless in her gingham gown, the boy was asleep on his knees. In front of him was a hole three feet deep and a foot and a half wide. Tug's fists were filled with red soil. On his lips were the words of the people: "Bury him deep! Bury him deep!"

THE APPRENTICE

BY CLINT MCCOWN

Hollywood Cemetery

Yes, I understand the gravity of my actions. I'm no idiot. I'm something of a historian, in fact, and I know that history itself is more or less a record of our greatest collective depravities: who did what to whom and for how long. And the desecration I've committed—yes, I admit it was a desecration—strikes at the heart of something we in these parts hold dear. This is Richmond, after all, capital of the Confederacy, where history is still a living, breathing animal, with teeth and fangs and a clear sense of identity. And once you start messing with identity, you're treading on dangerous ground. Eddie sure found that out. He's the one who put me up to it, by the way.

It wasn't a political statement, though I'm sure there'll be reporters who try to turn it into that. But nothing could be further from the truth. I treasure my Southern roots. My family used to be one of the most prominent in the city, having once owned the ironworks factory on the James River during the war. Had Grant's army not driven my ancestors into exile when the city fell, I might have been a person of some influence in our community. But sometimes the world spins off-kilter. My inheritance was siphoned off by carpetbaggers. As a consequence, I was never allowed to take my rightful place among the aristocracy, and have instead been forced into a series of menial occupations, the most recent being that of a bulldozer's apprentice. You might think that a family's reversal of fortune shouldn't weigh so heavily on a descendant born a century after the fact. But I assure you, the pain is as acute to me as if I'd suffered the loss only yesterday.

My doctor refuses even to acknowledge my fallen state. He says I've manufactured a personal family history from the intellectual pieces of my former life. That's an intriguing tactic on his part, I have to admit. I suspect he has an article in the works and I'm his guinea pig in what he imagines will be some breakthrough form of therapy. But he's destined for disappointment. I could never disavow my heritage.

My *misstep*, let's call it, was no easy chore. Cemeteries have always given me the creeps. But besides that, the place tends to be crowded. Hollywood Cemetery is like the Disneyworld of final resting places. It's in a beautiful spot, up there on that high bluff overlooking the James River. Young lovers picnic there. Artists set up their easels. Photographers prowl around the statuary. Kids climb on the mausoleums. Historians walk the avenues taking notes. I used to do that myself, actually, when I was researching my dissertation. I was writing about the military and political history of the United States in the nineteenth century, so Hollywood Cemetery was the ideal field trip for me. President Monroe is buried there, and President Tyler too. Tyler was the father-in-law of Jefferson Davis, by the way. And there's General George Pickett, of the infamous Pickett's charge at Gettysburg. He's buried at the north end of the cemetery, along with eighteen thousand regular Confederate soldiers. J.E.B. Stuart is in Hollywood, and General Fitzhugh Lee, nephew of Robert E. Lee. Twenty-five Confederate generals in all. General Longstreet isn't there, but three of his children are, killed by the scarlet fever epidemic of 1862. Seven governors of Virginia. And, of course, the proverbial jewel in the crown, President Jefferson Davis himself.

I wish the place weren't named Hollywood, though. That makes it sound too phony, fake, like it's a hangout for dead movie stars. But Hollywood Cemetery was a landmark in Richmond long before the first silent films ever came out of that other Hollywood. Maybe that Hollywood was named for this one. In any case, our Hollywood is the greatest Confederate cemetery in the country. Maybe even in the whole world.

As you can probably tell, I'm highly educated. I might have been a renowned scholar but for my accident. Apparently—and I say apparently because I have no memory of the event—I was struck by a car while riding my motor scooter without a helmet. Why a scholar would be on a motor scooter, I haven't a clue. Motor scooters are undignified—scholars should drive used Volvos. In any case, they say I suffered significant head trauma—something I believe because I do get terrible headaches almost daily.

There was another side effect of the accident that's been a slight problem. When I came out of the coma, I developed a compulsion to keep talking, even when no one is around, like those people I've heard about on the subway trains in New York City. It's like the accident turned on a faucet in my head and words just keep pouring out all the time, except when I'm on medication. I can't explain it. As soon as I get a thought, it comes right out of my mouth. So they give me pills to stop the leak. Of course, the bad thing is that whenever I stop taking the pills they find out right away because I can't keep myself from telling everybody about it. That's one reason the police know every detail of what I did in the cemetery. I might as well have given them documentary footage.

So, anyway, I know there was an accident, and I know there were consequences.

Much of what they tell me about my condition, however, is untrue. They say I'm given to violent outbursts, but that's all a matter of perspective. They say I've lost certain social skills, that I no longer comprehend the subtleties of human interaction. Yet who among us comprehends our neighbor? They say I don't make logical connections the way normal people do.

By *they*, of course, I mean my therapist, Dr. Myles, and sometimes my Uncle Morty. Uncle Morty is a good man, but he's been duped by Dr. Myles. He believes everything the doctor tells him about me, almost as if he were the doctor's apprentice. Though Uncle Morty isn't an apprentice, he's a general contractor.

I know about apprentices because that's one field in which I have truly excelled. When I first came to work for my Uncle Morty two years ago—no, wait, it's been longer than that. Let me think. Seventeen. Yes, that's it, seventeen years. And in the seventeen years I've worked for my Uncle Morty, I've been every kind of apprentice you can think of. It was Uncle Morty and Aunt Eileen who took me in after I lost my fellowship at the university. They say they're my parents, and that's sweet of them, but I don't feel comfortable enough to allow them that level of intimacy. Still, Uncle Morty figured out the perfect job for me. He said I could be the company apprentice. It's almost the same thing as being a student, except you don't have to write papers or study for tests.

"All you have to do is watch," he told me. "Watch and learn." I think we both thought it would help me regain my focus. And we were right.

I started off as a janitor's apprentice and I stayed at the

main building all day. Uncle Morty owns a big construction company, and he has a sheet-metal warehouse where he keeps his heavy equipment. As you might imagine, floors have to be kept clean in a place like that, and my job was to watch Arby the janitor keep everything in order. Just watch and stay out of the way—that was my entire job description, and it came straight from Uncle Morty. I did that job pretty well, and after a while I got promoted to groundskeeper's apprentice. In that job, I had to watch Miguel ride the lawn tractor and patch the driveway and fertilize the grounds. That's what we called the yard around the building—the grounds. I don't know why we didn't call it a yard, because it sure looked like one. I thought about asking Miguel about it once, but I didn't. Asking questions wasn't part of my job.

I was an excellent groundskeeper's apprentice. I stared at Miguel all day long, even on our breaks, which probably made him feel important. Pretty soon Miguel talked to Uncle Morty and the next thing I knew, I was promoted to plumber's apprentice, watching Big Dan. I watched him like a hawk, or like an owl, maybe, until he went to Uncle Morty and got me another promotion, this time to carpenter's apprentice with Wilber. I liked working with Wilber because he had the same name as the guy on *Mr. Ed*, which was a TV show about a talking horse. I liked that show a lot. It proved that anything was possible.

After Wilber I became an electrician's apprentice for Gus, which I also liked because Gus sounded like a proper name for an electrician. Then I was a mason's apprentice for a guy whose name I can never remember because I keep thinking his name ought to be Mason, which it isn't. Then I began to move through my apprenticeships on all the pieces of heavy equipment—the forklift, the backhoe, the grader, and finally, all the way to the top of the apprenticeship mountain, the bulldozer. Basically, they're all excavators. My favorite is the Cat 312CL because it has an enclosed cab and a mechanical thumb. The enclosed cab makes it less noisy, plus you can keep away from bad weather. But the best part is the mechanical thumb, which is what separates it from an ordinary backhoe. A normal backhoe claws and scoops, but an excavator with a mechanical thumb can actually grab things. The dredger bucket clamps tight around whatever you're trying to pull up. I don't know why they call the extra part a thumb, though. To me it's more like the bottom half of a set of jaws, like on a giant dinosaur. There's true power in an excavator with jaws like that. It's a dangerous piece of machinery.

But just because I got shifted around through so many positions in the company, don't think I couldn't hold a job. The job was pretty much the same whatever it was, because whatever it was, I was still the apprentice. I watched and I learned, and I stayed out of the way. But at the same time, I was moving up through the ranks. I think Uncle Morty was trying to familiarize me with the whole operation—you know, grooming me to take over the business when he retires. I could do it too. After so many years of apprenticing there, I know how everything works.

Eddie knew how everything worked too. He was site foreman on the cemetery project. I know that was a tough job because I used to be a foreman's apprentice and I've seen how busy things can get.

Uncle Morty was real happy when he first got the cemetery contract, but it turned out to be a nightmare. That's what I heard him say, that the cemetery project had been a nightmare. One nightmare after another, he said, starting with the retaining wall and ending with Eddie and Aunt Eileen. I don't know what Aunt Eileen had to do with any of it. She's not really on the payroll. But she was sure there a lot. She used to come out to watch us on the days Uncle Morty had to be away at other projects, I guess to report back to him on what kind of progress we were making. She and Eddie would eat lunch together behind the chapel, I guess so he could fill her in. It's not the best spot in the cemetery, as far as getting a good view is concerned. It's way too overgrown with bushes. I prefer the spot just across from President Tyler. That's where you get the most picturesque view, and when I look out at the broad stretch of the James below—where it's too rocky and shallow for boats to navigate—I can almost forget I'm in a cemetery surrounded by skeletons and who knows what other bad things.

The problem with the cemetery was that parts of it were starting to fall away into the river. Erosion. And, of course, a lot of the most important bodies were planted near the edge of the bluff, where big chunks were already starting to crumble away. I don't know why so many of the famous people got buried near the edge, but that's how it is. Maybe folks thought they deserved a nice view. Jefferson Davis was a good twenty paces from the edge, which afforded him a few more years of security, in terms of natural processes. But Presidents Monroe and Tyler were in more imminent danger. Tyler was buried barely eight steps from the precipice. One good mudslide and he'd be floating down the James and out to sea, with Monroe only about five steps behind him.

So the city hired Uncle Morty to erect a retaining wall along the bank to keep every body in place. It's hard to build a wall on the face of so steep a bluff. And even if you get the wall in place, it'll block the drainage, which increases the weight and makes the problem worse than it was before. What you have to do is drill drainage holes under the graves to allow the excess water a way to escape. And I can tell you, from my time as a driller's apprentice, that's one tricky feat of engineering.

It's risky work too. I almost went over the edge myself one day when I sat on a stack of twenty-foot PVC piping. The stack gave way and about half the pipes rolled over the cliff. Eddie tried to blame me for it, but Uncle Morty said it was Eddie's own fault for putting the pipes too near the edge and for not keeping an eye on me like he was supposed to. I sided with Uncle Morty in that argument. So it was Eddie's fault we lost half a day's work getting the pipes back up to the work site.

The time I didn't side with Uncle Morty was when he tried to fire Eddie. I know Uncle Morty was under a lot of emotional strain, because Aunt Eileen had just told him she was leaving him for somebody else. That came as a big surprise to me. Things had been peaceful at home, with nobody ever saying anything to anybody, so I'm not sure why Aunt Eileen was so unhappy. In any case, it was understandable that Uncle Morty might have been a little on edge. But Eddie hadn't done anything wrong all day, everything was going just as smooth as could be, when Uncle Morty drove up in his Cadillac and got out, already mad as I'd ever seen him. He told Eddie he was fired and good luck supporting his new girlfriend without a paycheck. Eddie said he'd file a union grievance and bring the whole project to a standstill. That stopped Uncle Morty on the spot. He paced around for a minute like he was about to explode, and then he said, "Fine, then you're not fired. But you're not the foreman anymore." Then he pointed a finger straight at me. "You work for *him* now," he said, and Eddie looked at me with his eyes squinted and his forehead wrinkled.

"What's that supposed to mean?" Eddie asked him.

Uncle Morty got a satisfied look on his face. "From here on out, you're his apprentice."

Eddie seemed baffled, and maybe a little angry too. "That moron don't do shit around here," he said.

Uncle Morty smiled, but not like he was happy. "You're free to quit if you don't like the job," he said.

That was a proud moment in my life. After years of being everybody else's apprentice, I finally had an apprentice of my own.

Eddie wasn't happy about it, though. I still had Ted, the bulldozer operator, to watch, and a bulldozer is a pretty interesting piece of equipment. But all Eddie had to look at was me, and I can tell you I'm not that interesting. I tend not to move much, because watching something closely takes a lot of concentration. That's what makes me a good apprentice. So Eddie had a pretty dull time of it. At first he complained a lot. He said nobody could treat him like that and get away with it. But after a few days he calmed down, and took on a whole new attitude. He told me dirty jokes and offered me chewing gum and sometimes he'd put his arm around my shoulder like we were golfing buddies. He asked me a lot of questions about my accident—which is not a proper thing for an apprentice to do, but I didn't correct him. It was kind of nice having somebody take an interest in me. In just a week's time, I had more conversation with Eddie than I'd had with anybody else in all the years I could remember. And Eddie listened to everything I said, almost like Dr. Myles. Sometimes he even took notes like Dr. Myles, which was certainly flattering. Eddie said he disagreed with most of Dr. Myles's diagnosis. He didn't think I was paranoid at all. And he thought it was unfair that Uncle Morty wouldn't let me run any of the heavy machinery, especially since I'd studied how to operate every type of excavator we had.

One day we took a walk around the old part of the cemetery on a break—sometimes you just need to stretch your legs—and we walked by the black wrought-iron dog near the top of the first hill inside the main entryway. I told him that dog had been made in my family's ironworks factory before the war. It's a cute dog, life-sized, and it stands watch over the grave of a little child. Sometimes people leave toys there at the dog's feet, which is sweet I guess, though not very practical. Anyway, that got me talking about my family's history. One thing led to another, and pretty soon I was telling Eddie about the loss of my family's fortune after the war. I thought he'd just tell me to get over it, like everybody else, but he didn't. He took a genuine interest in my pain, and promised to look into the matter for me. I didn't know at first what he meant by that. But the next day, which was Sunday, he called me up and told me to meet him right away out at the cemetery. He said he'd be waiting at the Jefferson Davis gravesite. He said he had the answers I was looking for.

It took me awhile to get there because I had to take the bus, and then I still had to walk a good ways after that. By the time I got there, Eddie had already put up construction tape across the car paths at that end of the cemetery. I asked him what the tape was for, and he said we needed privacy to sort everything out.

"Sort what out?" I asked him, and he explained it all. He said he'd got on the Internet and found out that Jefferson Davis had spent all the years after his presidency collecting evidence that certain prominent families of Virginia had been swindled out of their fortunes by carpetbaggers, and that my family was among them. He said that President Grant had been obsessed with preventing the Davis papers from ever coming to light.

"The Grant administration was the most corrupt in history," I told him.

"Well, there you go," he said, obviously pleased that I'd know such a thing.

The problem, Eddie explained, was that all the incriminating documents had disappeared when Davis died. But if somebody could find those documents, the government would have to pay restitution to the victims' families.

"And here's the interesting thing," Eddie said, smiling. "Jefferson Davis died in New Orleans, and that's where they had his funeral."

"But he's right here," I told him, and I pointed to the life-sized stone likeness of the president of the Confederacy standing atop the gravesite.

"That's what they want you to think," Eddie said.

"But they shipped his body here and reburied it," I said.

Eddie shook his head. "Not his body. A coffin. And nobody every looked inside."

Then he laid it all out for me, and it made perfect sense. The government had used President Davis's death as a cover to hide all the evidence that would have brought down so many of those who had prospered illegally after the war. All the papers that would restore my family's fortune were stashed away inside the president's casket—the last place anyone would ever think to look.

"And here's the clincher," Eddie told me. He put his arm around my shoulder again and led me over to the Davis grave. I looked down at the broad, flat stone that claimed to be covering the remains of President Davis and his wife, Varina Howell Davis. Then Eddie pointed to an adjoining plot directly in front of the stone statue of the former president. Not ten steps from the foot of the Davis grave, a more modest tombstone rested on a well-trimmed patch of ground, and it had a single word carved into its face: *GRANT.*

I was dumbfounded. There's no way the president of the Confederacy would be placed in a spot where his statue had to stare forever at the name of the man who brought about his ruin, the man responsible for the fall of Richmond itself, the man who forced Lee's surrender a few weeks later at Appomattox Courthouse. I felt a chill run up my spine.

"But what can I do?" I asked Eddie. He frowned and scratched his chin like he was thinking, but I figure maybe he had his answer ready all along.

"If it was me," he said, "I reckon I'd dig up those papers and set everything right again." He took a slow breath and shook his head. "'Course, that would take a mighty big piece of equipment."

I'd never been more excited in my life. "I can run the bulldozer," I told him. "It'll scrape these marble slabs right out of the way. The statue too."

"Say, that's a smart idea," he said, and he patted my shoulder.

"You wait here," I said.

"Oh, don't worry," he answered. "I wouldn't miss this for the world."

I hustled back to the chapel area where we stored the heavy equipment and climbed onto the bulldozer. I'd never really run the machine before, but that didn't matter. The point of being a good apprentice is to be ready when the time comes, and so I'd always watched carefully when Ted operated the controls. I knew exactly what to do.

It took me a minute to get the hang of steering. I don't

even have a driver's license—the state of Virginia won't issue me one, I think because of my headaches. And I do feel bad about all the gravestones I knocked over on my way back to the Davis family plot. Collateral damage, I think it's called.

When I got there, I wasted no time. First, I positioned the bulldozer in front of the memorial, raised the blade, and plowed ahead into the stone base of the statue. It cracked loudly, and the statue broke off at the ankles, toppling backward onto the ground. Then I backed up a bit, lowered the blade to scraping level, shifted the bulldozer into a more powerful setting, and rammed into the covering of the so-called graves. The bulldozer barely slowed as it scooped the shattering marble away, shoving the ragged pieces onto the broken remains of the fallen statue.

I backed away again and shut off the engine. Eddie walked up beside me as I climbed down from the seat and we both stepped to the edge of the grave to see what I'd uncovered.

Nothing. Just the next layer of ground.

"You'll need the backhoe," Eddie said. "You've got to dig deeper."

I could see he was right. So I trotted back to the chapel and climbed onto the excavator I liked the best, the Cat 312CL, the one with the mechanical thumb. It was easier to drive than the bulldozer, and in a matter of minutes I was back at the Davis gravesite, lowering the opened jaw into the soft earth. I was careful to keep to the left side of the pair of graves, because I didn't want to disturb Mrs. Davis, since she might really be down there. The sky was starting to spit rain now, and Eddie stepped away to the protection of the nearby doorway of the tomb of General Fitzhugh Lee. Rain didn't bother me, of course, because I was safe inside the Plexiglas walls of the cab.

268 // R_{ICHMOND} N_{OIR}

After about fifteen minutes, I pulled up a few splintered board fragments, and I knew I was almost there. I dipped the jaws back into the hole and bit off another chunk of ground. I had hoped to fish up a strongbox, watertight and ready to have its lock broken.

But of course that isn't what came up at all.

There, dangling like a hanged criminal from the end of the Cat 312CL, was the great man himself. Or, rather, the remnants of the great man, for he was now just a decomposed corpse draped in dark rags. His bright finger bones hung from the ragged sleeves, and I could see parts of his rib cage through the disintegrated jacket and shirt. I couldn't see the face, because the skull was clamped tight inside the jaws of the excavator. In a panic, I swung the arm away from the hole, which was a mistake, because that popped off the skull and flung the remains of the former president onto the macadam pathway. I looked over at Eddie in horror, and this time he was talking on his cell phone. He smiled and gave me a thumbs-up.

So there were no documents about the Confederacy. There never had been, I realized. The only thing in that hole was the long-dead leader of my long-dead country. And I had defiled his remains.

The rain was coming down harder now, and the wind shifted so the Fitzhugh tomb wasn't keeping Eddie dry anymore. He trotted over to one of the broad, stately trees by the opened grave and sheltered himself against the trunk. I just sat there in the cab of the Cat 312CL, watching rain slide down the Plexiglas.

"I can't wait to read about this in the papers," Eddie shouted.

I opened the cab door so I wouldn't have to raise my voice. "You lied to me," I said.

My calm demeanor may have misled him.

"Blame your Uncle Morty. I told him, nobody treats me like he did and gets away with it."

Sirens started up in the distance.

"You hear that, moron? That's the cops." He held up his cell phone and grinned. It was as evil a grin as I ever hope to see.

At that point there was only one thing I could do. I stepped down from the Cat 312CL and climbed back onto the bull-dozer. Eddie just stood there with his arms crossed, gloating, while I cranked up the engine. I guess he figured I was going to try to move Uncle Morty's equipment back to the chapel before the police arrived. But that wasn't what I was thinking at all. In fact, because of my peculiar medical syndrome—the one that makes me talk too much—I said right out loud what I was about to do. But I guess he didn't hear me over the racket of the bulldozer. If he had, he wouldn't have just stood there looking so smug.

I raised the blade a couple of feet, swung the bulldozer around toward him, and hit the throttle. He barely had time to stop smiling. I think he hollered something, because his mouth flew open and his eyes got very wide. But I rammed him anyway. The concave blade covered up his torso completely, so that when it pinned him against the trunk, his head popped off just like Jefferson Davis's. One of his legs got pinched off too. Naturally, those were the details they played up in the newspaper—which I found annoying, if you want to know the truth. It cast me in a ghoulish light, as if the dismemberment had been intentional. But I swear on the Holy Bible, I only meant to kill him.

I feel bad for the trouble I've caused Uncle Morty. He's family, and I see now that I should have been more concerned with protecting him than with connecting myself to relatives I never even met. It's good to respect one's ancestors. But the living deserve some consideration too. That's a new perspective for me. I imagine Dr. Myles will be pleased with my progress.

I'm not especially worried about going to jail. Since everything I did was justified, I can't see myself as guilty. So even if they do lock me up, I wouldn't really be a criminal. I'd be more like a prisoner of war. Not a full-fledged prisoner of war, of course, because the war ended a long time ago. I guess I'd be more like an apprentice.

Yeah, that's it: a prisoner's apprentice. The best they've ever seen.

Editors' Acknowledgments

Believe it or not, the following volumes were consulted during the research and conceptualization of this book: *Poe's Richmond* by Agnes Meredith Bondurant; *Richmond: The Story of a City* by Virginius Dabney; *The River Where America Began: A Journey Along the James* by Bob Deans; *The American Scene* by Henry James; *True Richmond Stories: Historic Tales from Virginia's Capital* by Harry Kollatz Jr.; *James Branch Cabell and Richmond-in-Virginia* by Edgar MacDonald; *The Air-Conditioned Nightmare* by Henry Miller; *The Book of Numbers* by Robert Deane Pharr; *Love and Hate in Jamestown: John Smith, Pocahontas, and the Heart of a New Nation* by David A. Price; and the 2008 edition of the *Richmond Magazine Complete Source Book*.

Thanks are owed to the following for their help and advice: Ray Bonis and the staff of Special Collections and Archives at the James Branch Cabell Library at Virginia Commonwealth University; Katherine Wilkins and the staff of the Virginia Historical Society; and the staff of the Edgar Allan Poe Museum.

For support, patience, and brainstorming, we are grateful to Rachel Albright, Liz Canfield, Crystal Castleberry, Santa De Haven, Mandy Dunn, Steve Dunn, Jamie Fueglein, Jonathan Heinen, Jeff Lodge, Cynthia Lotze, Lauren Maas, Ryan McLennan, Ann McMillan, Peter Orner, Faye Prichard, Patty Smith, Ward Tefft, Kelsey Trom, Adam Wayland, and the good people at the Virginia Commonwealth University Department of English.

We'd especially like to thank Johnny Temple and the staff of Akashic Books for their enthusiasm about the project, and for their support during some extremely rough patches.

We owe special thanks to Tom Robbins, whose praises we shall sing until time eternal.

Lastly, we are greatly indebted to David L. Robbins, whose wonderful story "Homework" can be found in this collection. David was the first writer who signed on to the book, and he has been its tireless promoter ever since. Without his efforts, *Richmond Noir* would not exist.

ABOUT THE CONTRIBUTORS

X.C. ATKINS was born in Zeist, Netherlands. He holds a BA in English from Virginia Commonwealth University. He recently moved from Richmond, Virginia to Philadelphia, Pennsylvania, the City of Brotherly Love.

MINA BEVERLY is a Richmond, Virginia native. She holds a BA in English from Spelman College and an MFA in Fiction from Virginia Commonwealth University. She currently resides in Atlanta, Georgia and works as an English teacher.

ANDREW BLOSSOM is the founding editor of the literary journal *Makeout Creek*. He lives in Richmond, Virginia.

Eric Dobbs

LAURA BROWDER'S most recent book is *Her Best Shot: Women and Guns in America*. She is currently collaborating with photographer Sascha Pflaeging on a book based on their gallery exhibition *When Janey Comes Marching Home: Portraits of Women Combat Veterans*. She teaches at Virginia Commonwealth University.

Crystal Castleberry

BRIAN CASTLEBERRY has worked as a cook, a dishwasher, a teacher, a carnie, a shoe salesman, a receptionist, and a writer. He lives in Virginia with his wife and their two dogs.

Chris Smith

CLAY MCLEOD CHAPMAN is the creator of the rigorous storytelling session *The Pumpkin Pie Show*. He is the author of *rest area*, a collection of short stories, and *miss corpus*, a novel, both published by Hyperion Books. He teaches writing at the Actors Studio MFA Program at Pace University.

Sarah Weisiger

DENNIS DANVERS has published seven novels, including *New York Times* Notables *Circuit of Heaven* and *The Watch*, and the near-future mystery *The Bright Spot* (writing as Robert Sydney). Recent short fiction of his appears in *Strange Horizons, Intergalactic Medicine Show, Realms of Fantasy, Lady Churchill's Rosebud Wristlet*, and *Space and Time*.

TOM DE HAVEN is the author of seventeen books, including *Freaks' Amour, Sunburn Lake, It's Superman!*, and the Derby Dugan trilogy of novels (*Funny Papers, Derby Dugan's Depression Funnies*, and *Dugan Under Ground*). *Our Hero*, a book-length essay about the history and cultural impact of Superman, is forthcoming from Yale University Press's Icons of America series. Since 1990 he has taught in the graduate creative writing program at Virginia Commonwealth University in Richmond, Virginia.

Andy Smith

DEAN KING is the author of nine books, including the national best seller *Skeletons on the Zahara* and, most recently, *Unbound: A True Story of War, Love, and Survival* about the women of Mao's Long March. A former contributing editor to *Men's Journal*, King has written for *Esquire, Outside,* and the *New York Times*. He is a cofounder of Richmond's award-winning James River Writers organization and serves on the Library of Virginia Foundation board.

Dawn Cooper

CLINT MCCOWN'S six books include the novels *The Member-Guest, War Memorials,* and *The Weatherman.* He teaches in the MFA programs at Virginia Commonwealth University and the Vermont College of Fine Arts.

Jane Nardone

HOWARD OWEN is the author of eight novels. He and his wife Karen live in Fredericksburg, Virginia, where both are editors at the *Free Lance-Star*. Owen's first novel, *Littlejohn*, was nominated for the Abbey Award (American Booksellers Association) and a Barnes & Noble Discover Great New Writers Award. His novels *Turn Signal* and *Rock of Ages* were Book Sense selections. Owen, who lived in Richmond for twenty-nine years, has just finished his ninth novel.

CONRAD ASHLEY PERSONS was born in Savannah, Georgia. He attended the University of Virginia before living in New York, London, and Tokyo. He currently resides with his wife in Brooklyn, where he is finishing his first novel, *A Honeymoon*.

Lynda Koolish

HERMINE PINSON has published three poetry collections: *Ashe, Mama Yetta and Other Poems*, and *Dolores Is Blue/Dolorez Is Blues*. She also released a CD, *Changing the Changes in Poetry & Song*, in special collaboration with Yusef Komunyakaa and Estella Conwill Majozo. She teaches creative writing, as well as American and African American literature, at the College of William & Mary.

Adam Ewing

DAVID L. ROBBINS was born in Richmond and received his undergraduate and Juris Doctorate degrees from the College of William & Mary, where he recently taught as writer-in-residence. He has published nine novels, the most recent of which, *Broken Jewel*, is set in the Philippines during World War II. Robbins is the founder of the James River Writers nonprofit literary group. This is his first published short story.

Alexa Robbins

TOM ROBBINS is the best-selling author of ten books of fiction and numerous articles for national magazines. His novels have been published in twenty-two languages and several have been optioned by Hollywood. An honors graduate of Virginia Commonwealth University and a former copy editor for the *Richmond Times-Dispatch*, Robbins has resided for many years in the Seattle area. His latest work, *B Is for Beer*, is a children's book.

PIR ROTHENBERG wrote and taught in Richmond, Virginia from 2003 to 2008. He currently resides in Buffalo, New York. His work has appeared in *Harpur Palate*.

MEAGAN J. SAUNDERS grew up in a family of five. She spent the first years of her life on Richmond's Southside before moving to Beaverdam, Virginia, a rural community on the outskirts of Hanover County. She received her B.A. in English and History from the College of William & Mary.

ANNE THOMAS SOFFEE is the author of *Snake Hips: Belly Dancing and How I Found True Love* and *Nerd Girl Rocks Paradise City*. She currently writes for *Richmond Magazine* and lives in Southside Richmond with her family, just up the pike from Rudd's Trailer Park.

Also available from the Akashic Books Noir Series

D.C. NOIR
edited by George Pelecanos
316 pages, trade paperback original, $15.95

Brand-new stories by: George Pelecanos, Laura Lippman, David Slater, James Grady, Kenji Jasper, Jim Beane, Ruben Castaneda, Robert Wisdom, James Patton, Norman Kelley, Jennifer Howard, Jim Fusilli, Richard Currey, Robert Andrews, Quintin Peterson, and Lester Irby.

"[T]he tome offers a startling glimpse into the cityscape's darkest corners . . . fans of the genre will find solid writing, palpable tension, and surprise endings."
—*Washington Post*

D.C. NOIR 2: THE CLASSICS
edited by George Pelecanos
330 pages, trade paperback, $15.95

Classic stories from: Edward P. Jones, Langston Hughes, Marita Golden, Paul Laurence Dunbar, Julian Mayfield, Elizabeth Hand, Richard Wright, James Grady, Ward Just, George Pelecanos, Jean Toomer, Rhozier "Roach" Brown, Ross Thomas, Julian Mazor, Larry Neal, and Benjamin M. Schutz.

"Rather than traveling the same mean streets as the first *D.C. Noir*, this new anthology of sixteen works draws on more than a century of published writings . . . Dark as many of these stories are, there's light in them yet, and it's the layering of the two that helps the collection to dazzle."
—*Washington Post*

BALTIMORE NOIR
edited by Laura Lippman
252 pages, a trade paperback original, $14.95

Brand-new stories by: David Simon, Laura Lippman, Tim Cockey, Rob Hiaasen, Robert Ward, Sujata Massey, Jack Bludis, Rafael Alvarez, Marcia Talley, Joseph Wallace, Lisa Respers France, Charlie Stella, Sarah Weinman, Dan Fesperman, Jim Fusilli, and Ben Neihart.

"Mystery fans should relish this taste of Baltimore's seamier side, the eighth volume in Akashic's series showcasing dark tales of crime and place. Editor Lippman offers both a fine introduction and the lead story, which is one of the anthology's best . . . Baltimore is a diverse city, and the stories reflect everything from its old row houses and suburban mansions to its beloved Orioles and harbor areas."

BOSTON NOIR
edited by Dennis Lehane
240 pages, trade paperback original, $15.95

Brand-new stories by: Dennis Lehane, Stewart O'Nan, Patricia Powell, John Dufresne, Lynne Heitman, Don Lee, Russ Aborn, Itabari Njeri, Jim Fusilli, Brendan DuBois, and Dana Cameron.

"In the best of the eleven stories in this outstanding entry in Akashic's noir series, characters, plot, and setting feed off each other like flames and an arsonist's accelerant . . . [T]his anthology shows that noir can thrive where Raymond Chandler has never set foot."
—*Publishers Weekly* (starred review)

BROOKLYN NOIR
edited by Tim McLoughlin
350 pages, trade paperback original, $15.95
*Winner of Shamus Award, Anthony Award, Robert L. Fish Memorial Award; finalist for Edgar Award, Pushcart Prize.

Brand-new stories by: Pete Hamill, Arthur Nersesian, Ellen Miller, Nelson George, Nicole Blackman, Sidney Offit, Ken Bruen, and others.

"*Brooklyn Noir* is such a stunningly perfect combination that you can't believe you haven't read an anthology like this before. But trust me—you haven't . . . The writing is flat-out superb, filled with lines that will sing in your head for a long time to come."
—Laura Lippman, winner of the Edgar, Agatha, and Shamus awards

NEW ORLEANS NOIR
edited by Julie Smith
300 pages, trade paperback original, $15.95

Brand-new stories by: Ace Atkins, Laura Lippman, Patty Friedmann, Barbara Hambly, Tim McLoughlin, Olympia Vernon, Jervey Tervalon, Christine Wiltz, Greg Herren, Julie Smith, and others.

"The excellent twelfth entry in Akashic's city-specific noir series illustrates the diversity of the chosen locale with eighteen previously unpublished short stories from authors both well known and emerging." —*Publishers Weekly*

These books are available at local bookstores.
They can also be purchased online through www.akashicbooks.com.
To order by mail send a check or money order to:

AKASHIC BOOKS
PO Box 1456, New York, NY 10009
www.akashicbooks.com, info@akashicbooks.com

(Prices include shipping. Outside the U.S., add $12 to each book ordered.)